New Atlantis

Kingdom of Youth

by R.W. Garrett

Eloquent Books

Eloquent Books
An imprint of Strategic Book Group
P.O. Box 333
Durham CT 06422
www.StrategicBookGroup.com

ISBN: 978-1-60911-401-5

Cover Illustration: Kalpart Team

For Ethan and Annie

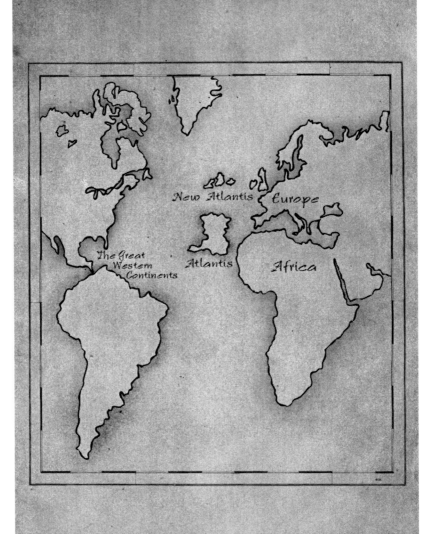

New Atlantis

Atlantis

NEW ATLANTIS: SOCIETAL STRUCTURE

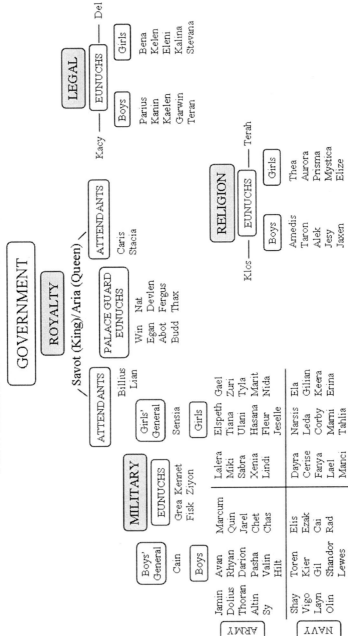

SERVICE

MEDICAL
Boys	Girls
Calum	Phaedra
Denit	Livia
Emery	Beryl
Peri	Risa
Aldo	Zea

ARCHITECTS
Boys	Girls
Medo	Fara
Travus	Kezi

CIVIL ENGINEERS
Boys	Girls
Artur	Joesy
Jeth	Percia
Darien	Kyla

CONSTRUCTION

EUNUCHS

EUNUCHS	
Gunter	Jok
Yogic	Phip
Dain	Emery
Plat	Camlo

Boys		Girls	
Jaran	Corwin	Boylee	Nasha
Davin	Florian	Quatra	Reni
Gabe	Tiril	Sari	Belicia
Zane	Hamlin	Trissa	Chiana
Oren	Ashur	Leola	Malori
Ethin	Kimbon	Jamy	Viola
	Brennan		Hadiya
			Taryn

SUPPLIERS

CARPENTERS
Dack — EUNUCHS — Flyn

Boys	Girls
Adom	Vida
Arin	Taci
Gustin	Bree
Zinon	Calla
Yancy	Melcia
Carlin	Tori

FISHERS
Dace — EUNUCHS — Bern

Boys	Girls
Pendil	Sunni
Balin	Trella
Kristo	Farida
Ulan	Hayley
Coty	Milana
Tad	Liris
Cadeo	Thalia

MERCHANTS
Howy — EUNUCHS — Rik   Rance

Boys		Girls	
Durrill	Von	Brina	Vanya
Barton	Anson	Lissa	Shira
Chal		Kori	

SMITHS
Rance — EUNUCHS — Tak   Vito

Boys	Girls
Aramis	Lavena
Beldin	Maya
Kit	Ferni
Checy	Ceil

MILLERS
Vito — EUNUCHS — Ansel

Boys	Girls
Arden	Meli
Blane	Lexia
Kory	Maura
Vidor	Ani

FARMERS
Aubry — EUNUCHS — Damon

Boys		Girls		
Reef	Averil	Drake	Brisa	Nicola	Kym
Gowan	Basil	Coby	Cali	Keelia	Cameo
Ristan	Zhovan	Flavion	Lia	Joya	Larry
Antony			Meril		

MINERS
Bur — EUNUCHS — Ami

Boys	Girls
Ambros	Quint	Lusi	Lilis
Birk	Collan	Jiana	Fala
Teman	Hunt	Elsy	Jade

Pronunciation Guide
for New Atlantis

Savot: să-vŭt (the 'o' as the 'u' in 'up')

Aria: är-ē-ŭ (the first 'a' as in 'father'; the second 'a' as the 'u' in 'up')

Jorash: jôr-ăsh (the 'o' as in 'order')

Sophea: sō-fē-ŭ (the 'a' as the 'u' in 'up')

Galen: gā-lĕn

Lian: lē-ŭn (the 'a' as the 'u' in 'up')

Jamin: jā-mĭn

Toren: tô-rĕn (the 'o' as in 'order')

Dolius: dō-lē-ŭs

Caris: kăr-ĭs

Stacia: stā·shŭ (the second 'a' as the 'u' in 'up')

Leander: lē-ăn-dĕr

Dayra: dā-rŭ (the 'a' as the 'u' in 'up')

Sensia: sĕn-sē-ŭ (the 'a' as the 'u' in 'up')

Lalera: lă-lĕ-rŭ (the second 'a' as the 'u' in 'up')

orichalcum: ôr-ĭ-kăl-kŭm

Zhovan: zhō-văn (the "zh" as the 's' in 'leisure')

Choridan: kôr-ĭ-dăn

Amedis: ă-mĕ-dĭs

Phaedra: fā-drŭ (the second 'a' as the 'u' in 'up')

Medo: mē-dō

Table of Contents

Chapter 1

Casting Lots for the King

It was a clear, spring morning in the practice yard. *CRASH—RING!* Two flashing swords met harshly in mid-air. Savot's shiny black hair flew from side to side as he dueled with his toughest opponent—Cain.

Cain was larger and stronger, but Savot was quicker. The two boys were among five fourteen-year-old candidates for king of the soon-to-be nation, New Atlantis. The other three candidates—Jamin, Toren, and Shay—also practiced their swordsmanship in the courtyard. Each of the other three fought a fourteen-year-old eunuch champion but Cain had insisted on dueling with Savot this fateful day. Although the contests were spirited, the eunuchs were no match for their three opponents. But Savot and Cain seemed quite equally matched.

Sword fighting was a daily task on Savot's agenda and had been for the past two years of his training. Dueling seemed almost second nature to him now. Sometimes he even fought an opponent in his dreams. But today's duel was different.

As he sparred with Cain, an even more vigorous battle churned inside Savot's gut. His thoughts tossed him from self-doubt to self-confidence, and then back again. Today the decision would be made. Which of the five of them would be selected as king of New Atlantis?

Could it possibly be me? Savot wondered. If so, could he actually succeed in reigning over his 267 fourteen-year-old peers?

The year was 498 B.C. and Savot's mother continent, Atlantis, was at its zenith of power.

The lot to be cast today in the Temple would determine the entire direction of Savot's future. He couldn't believe the day was finally here. Before nightfall either Cain, Toren, Shay, Jamin . . . or Savot himself would be king over the islands of Atlantis' daughter nation.

"All right, whichever of us wins this match is going to be king," Cain taunted, acting the prophet. The lot's outcome was obviously foremost in his mind as well.

The two boys pressed their swords together in a frozen struggle. The weight of Savot's sword slowly bent Cain's arm outward away from his body. Cain's handsome face turned red from strain. Then swiftly he turned, jumped backwards, and postured himself to begin again.

"You wish!" Savot laughed. "But the lot will decide who's king, not this duel. Besides, just how many times is it now that you've actually beaten me?" Both boys knew it was only a few.

Instead of answering, Cain charged Savot. *Crash! Clang! Shuffle! Sweep!* An impish grin widened Cain's already broad mouth, exposing his nearly perfect teeth. Sweat trickled from the tips of his straw-colored hair.

"If the lot chooses you, I'm your general over all the military—right?" Cain asked through grunts of the conflict.

"Yeah, we already agreed on that. And I'm yours if it chooses you," Savot answered. He tried an unusual move on Cain now, his sword slicing briskly through the air at the level of Cain's knees. Cain jumped up swiftly to miss it.

Savot didn't know quite how to feel about the other four candidates today. He just knew he was extremely nervous about the lot.

"Ha! You *are* the best swordsman of the five of us," an impressed Cain retorted, taking a step away from Savot. Then he quickly added, "Except for me, of course." Both boys chuckled uneasily.

At this Cain charged Savot again with his best cross slicing. Savot defended each stroke skillfully. Then their swords locked in another battle of wills, the fabric of their colorful tunics quivering from the combined strength of their muscular arms.

"Draw!" barked their referee. Savot and Cain sheathed their swords and bowed to each other. Just at that moment King Jorash's first minister, Galen, entered the outdoor arena. He was a short, jovial man with the beginnings of wrinkles on his face. Galen was Savot's favorite adult other than his own parents. At the first minister's appearance, the other three practice duels ended too.

"Well, my boys!" the first minister addressed the five candidates. "The ceremony begins in one hour," announced Galen, rubbing his hands together briskly and rocking back and forth from heels to toes. "This is your big day, gentlemen! Time to clean up and prepare yourselves." At these words, tense glances flew among the five royal candidates.

This is so strange, Savot thought. He and the other four had become close friends over the past two years in the candidate school. Yet the competitive environment of their training ground—the palace of King Jorash, ruler of Atlantis—had often required them to behave like worst enemies. On occasion the five had contended bitterly; at other times they'd seemed willing to die defending one another. Savot didn't feel either close friendship or animosity toward the others today—just a sort of numbness. All he could think about was the lot.

The five candidates—Savot, Cain, Jamin, Shay, and Toren—gathered up their gear and filed stiffly out of the arena. The three fourteen-year-old eunuchs who had been sparring with Jamin, Shay, and Toren followed. For a change no one spoke and there was none of the usual horseplay. Despite the spring morning's buoyant sunshine, the sober reality of the hour loomed over the royal contestants like the shadow of a dragon.

***

Inside the palace, Princess Aria sat on a white satin hassock, her golden eyes fixed blankly on the gilded mirror in front of her. Caris and Stacia, Aria's attendants and best friends, twittered about her. They decorated her slender fingers with rings, her delicate feet with silver slippers, and fussed over placing gem-pins perfectly in her curly, honey-colored hair.

The elaborate purple, knee-length dress Aria wore over embroidered pants sparkled with rubies, emeralds, and silver threads. The princess had admired this outfit for almost a year as it had hung in her closet. But she had never been allowed to wear it until today.

The excitement swirling about the room didn't faze the princess. Aria sat motionless, quiet, and vacant. One would have thought the princess of Atlantis was in a trance until she finally motioned for Stacia to hand her some powder. She patted her nose and cheeks with the powder brush, covering up the light freckles that everyone knew she hated.

"These stupid freckles make me look like such a baby," Aria spoke at last, still with no real expression on her face.

"Aria! What is the matter with you?" scolded Stacia. "We've been looking forward to this day *all our lives*! Why are you acting like this?" Not answering, Aria kept staring at the mirror and sweeping powder onto her nose.

Caris whispered to Foven, Aria's governess, "This isn't at all what I thought she'd be like today."

"This is a big day for her, Caris," Foven answered out of Aria's earshot. "Finding out who her husband's going to be!" It had been determined at her birth that Aria would marry the young man chosen as New Atlantis' king. "Caris, you must remember, you've always known you'd be marrying Billius." At the mention of Billius' name, Caris scrunched up her shoulders and grinned.

"But that's exactly the point," Stacia debated. "That's why she should be excited. I mean, she can't lose any way the lot falls. All five of them are so handsome!"

"Yeah, but we know which one she wants," snickered Caris. Foven sent a modest grin back to Caris. Both smiles faded, though, as all eyes turned to Aria. She seemed not to have heard the comment; her face remained as somber as ever.

***

In the middle of the Temple's Great Hall stood a sturdy and elaborately carved oak table. Only one object rested on its surface; a golden box with a jeweled star on the lid. Promptly at noon government officials, the royal family, and the five candidates for king of New Atlantis filed into the hall and gathered around the lot table. Everyone assembled in the Great Hall wore formal garments, brightly colored and ornate. Hushed murmurs echoed in the large, domed room.

Then King Jorash entered. The king's dark, commanding presence shifted the crowd's mood from tension to awe. The tall, distinguished monarch of Atlantis took his place next to Leander, the high priest.

Besides King Jorash, Leander was the most esteemed person on the continent. All Atlanteans knew that the high priest had to be present to verify any appearance The Ghost might make to a king. But The Ghost, the messenger of the Unknown God, had not appeared to King Jorash in fifteen years.

"Silence!" commanded King Jorash. There was silence.

The five boys who could be king stood at the end of the table with Savot in the middle. Because he was the shortest of the five, Savot had always felt a bit inferior to the other four. Keenly aware of the height difference now, Savot dared not look at the other candidates. Instead he fixed his large, lavender eyes on the sparkling container that held his future.

Princess Aria stood beside her beautiful and stately mother, Queen Sophea. The princess held her breath, staring intently at the lot box.

"Let the lot be cast," Jorash ordered. The sound of the king's authoritative voice bounced off the chamber walls and lingered in everyone's ears.

Leander shook the box several times and then opened the lid. With a swift motion, the priest cast the lots onto the table. Small, black onyx cubes tumbled in every direction. The only cube stamped with a golden star rolled directly toward and stopped only inches from where Savot stood. No debate was possible. The lot had chosen Savot to be king of New Atlantis.

King Jorash's mouth opened as if to speak. But within seconds, a controlled and regal smile crossed the king's face as his eyes met Savot's. The new young king felt the room spinning around him. *This just has to be a dream*, he thought.

When he had steadied himself, the newly chosen king warily eyed the other candidates. He looked toward Jamin first. His best friend was beaming. But neither Toren nor Shay would look at Savot. Their heads were lowered in undisguisable disappointment.

And then there stood Cain. He was glaring at Savot with narrowed, lizard-green eyes. His face was crimson, making his wiry, blond hair look even lighter. He bit his lip as tiny wet beads grew on his forehead. What other reaction could Savot have expected from the competitive and hot-tempered Cain?

Savot's next thought was of Aria. He looked up to catch her reaction, but she was gone. "Congratulations Savot," King Jorash said, striding to Savot's side. "At last. My counterpart for New Atlantis is revealed." As he shook Savot's hand, the king's eyes swept the small gathering, giving permission for the others to respond.

The applause began with Jamin. Cain clapped reluctantly when he realized he was the last to join in the congratulatory gesture. As the company cheered for Savot, King Jorash eyed Cain for only a split second. Then Cain advanced toward Savot, extending his hand.

"Congratulations, Savot," he forced the words out. They clasped each other's right hands awkwardly. Then Cain asked, "I'm your second-in-command, right?"

"Yes, of course." Savot could feel something threatening bubbling inside himself as he shook his rival's hand. Cain then hastily broke the sweaty grip and left the Temple. Shay and Toren shook Savot's hand with similar discomfort. But then Jamin rushed to the new king and gave him a big guy-hug.

"YES!" Jamin proclaimed. "I knew it would be you!" Jamin's support was real. And it was a huge morale-booster for Savot at this point. *Still*, he mused, *this just can't be happening!*

Before he could give much more thought to anything, King Jorash slapped his hands together twice and two officers stood on either side of Savot to escort him out of the Temple.

***

The celebration feast that night drew citizens from all regions of the sprawling continent of Atlantis. Around the banqueting area on the vast palace lawn, 100 Atlantean flags rippled in the cool evening breeze.

Each of the large, round flags held three inset circles of color—the outermost blue, the next green, and the innermost yellow. The presence of 100 Atlantean flags always signaled a significant national event.

All 268 Chosen Children who would make up the population of New Atlantis were present at the feast, enjoying profuse attention from their countrymen. Each of the Children was a celebrity tonight.

The attire for the evening was extravagant. While all Atlantean clothing was brightly colored; the dress code tonight required that only the finest of the world's fabrics be worn. The boys and men sported silken pants, shirts, and festive tunics with elaborate belts and boots.

The women and girls donned floor-length split skirts over same-colored satin or linen pants in brilliant blues, purples, reds, oranges, golds, and greens. The feasting area looked much like an ever-moving rainbow.

Aria didn't leave her mother's side the whole evening. She politely received greetings and compliments from hundreds of citizens. But the heavy melancholy that had pressed down upon the princess earlier in the day now seemed to have doubled itself in invisible weight.

"This is so unlike her, Foven," Queen Sophea whispered to Aria's plump, apple-cheeked nanny. "She'll hardly even speak. She denies that anything's bothering her. But . . . just look at her."

"Your Majesty, she's only a child," Foven comforted in her motherly voice. "This is just too much for her to take in all at once. Don't worry yourself, My Lady. Just give her time."

The queen continued as though she hadn't heard Foven. "She's been so quiet lately. And she's usually so fun-loving and full of laughter. And, you know . . . loud!" Foven snickered at the truth of the last word, but stopped herself as Sophea continued expressing her distress.

"I know she respects Savot. And they have always been good friends. I thought she'd be pleased . . ." The queen's voice trailed off as her eyes caught a glimpse of Savot approaching. This would be the critical first encounter between the future king and queen.

Savot, looking quite princely in a cobalt-blue outfit, tentatively approached the tent under which his future wife sat.

"Good evening, Your Majesty," Savot addressed Queen Sophea, bowing.

"Good evening, Savot," the queen greeted. "And congratulations!" She nodded at Savot graciously and then took Foven by the arm and began leading her away from the area. "You'll excuse us?" she asked the question that was not really a question, and the two left Savot and Aria alone. Only now could Savot attempt to discover Aria's thoughts about marrying him.

"Aria?" he ventured. The princess had her head slightly bowed and didn't answer or raise her eyes to meet his. *How awkward*, Savot thought. "I take it you're disappointed with the choice of the lot," he stated, instead of questioned.

"No, My Lord," Aria replied in a determined, formal tone. "The Unknown God has chosen you." She finally looked up at him and forced a slight smile. "You are to be my husband. And we're going to rule New Atlantis together. It's decided." The smile remained on Aria's mouth but there was no sign of it in her eyes.

"Did you call me 'My Lord'?" Savot blurted out before he could think.

"Well, you're going to be king. It's what I should call you," Aria declared flatly.

What in the world is wrong with her? Savot tried to reason with his future bride. "Come on, Aria. We're practically best friends. Don't call me that. I mean, please." Aria lowered her eyes again, not answering him.

Savot went back to his original concern. "Anyway, you sure don't seem happy that I was the one chosen," Savot faltered. Then he asked in a lowered tone, "Could we talk in private?"

Aria hesitated, then rose and walked with him into the palace garden. Queen Sophea and Foven, standing at a distance, watched closely as the young couple strode together out of their sight.

"Aria?" Savot asked, searching his princess' face, trying to recognize his old friend. "What is it? Did you think the lot would choose somebody else?" He bit his bottom lip lightly. "Were you *hoping* it would be somebody else?"

"Well, actually," the princess began, stiffening her posture even more, "I did think it would be one of the others."

Savot's heart pounded hard in his chest as he silently choked back his disappointment. *Who did she think it was going to be?* He took a stab at the answer.

It took Aria a moment to respond. "Actually, yes," she admitted. "I did think it would be Cain."

"And you wanted it to be him?" Silence followed as Savot waited patiently for this important answer.

"Mmm . . . not necessarily. I just always thought it would be. Look, Savot, I don't want to talk about this now." Aria seemed determined not to gaze into Savot's dazzling eyes, which were the color of amethysts and lined with thick, black lashes. "Just give me some time. I need time. Do you understand?" She sounded irritated.

"All right, Aria. I understand," Savot lied. But he just couldn't let the conversation end there. "It's just that, I want to know how you *feel* about this, Aria," he persisted.

The princess faced him squarely. She was definitely perturbed. "I feel fine about it, Savot! I told you. I just need to adjust. Can't you give me some time to adjust?" At this she whirled around and stationed herself firmly with her back to her fiancé.

Savot answered at half Aria's volume. "All right. But there's one thing you need to know."

He stepped around in front of Aria and motioned an invitation for her to sit on a nearby bench. She complied, but uncomfortably. Once the two sat side by side, the lavender eyes locked onto the golden ones. Savot took a deep breath. Finally he could tell her.

"Ever since I was selected as a candidate two years ago, I've prayed every day that I would be chosen king." Savot felt his hands shaking, so he sat on them. Aria's eyes didn't leave his now. She fidgeted but he continued.

"Not because I wanted to beat out the other guys. I just thought—and I hope this doesn't sound conceited—but I thought I could do a good job as king."

Aria responded quickly, though somewhat mechanically, "And you will. You'll be a wonderful king."

"Well, that's not the only reason I wanted the position," Savot almost whispered, and then he took another deep breath. "I wanted to be king because I knew whoever got the title also got . . ." the word stuck in his throat, but he finally pushed it out, "you".

Savot wasn't sure, but he thought Aria startled slightly when she realized what he was saying. Then she broke his gaze, lowered her eyes, and stared at the ground.

"Say something. Please," he entreated. Then he saw it. A crystal drop fell from Aria's cheek onto the lap of her purple satin gown, staining it. Savot, before he knew what he was doing, reached up and stroked away the next tears from his fiancée's cheeks before they had a chance to fall again to her satin.

The last time he could remember touching her was when they had arm-wrestled two years earlier, before he was a candidate. She had almost beaten him (because he'd pretended to be weak), and she had never let him forget it. *What a different Aria she is now*, Savot thought. *She would never tease with me like that now.*

At first, he hoped her tears were those of joy. But then an awful thought entered his mind and instantly his happiness fell to a sense of crushing defeat.

"You hate me." His greatest fear just popped right out of his mouth. "That's it, isn't it?" At this, Aria stood up quickly and, turning her back on Savot again, walked a few paces away. She motioned for him not to follow her. The princess was shaking and her hands alternately moved to her face and back again to her sides. Savot couldn't think of a single word to say. Then Aria's shoulders raised and lowered slowly. When she finally turned back around, her eyes were pink and her face blotched. Freckles displayed themselves vividly on her cheeks. *Those freckles are so cute,* Savot thought, momentarily forgetting the gravity of this conversation.

"Of course I don't hate you," Aria spoke in a controlled, steady tone. "It will be a privilege for me to be your queen."

Somehow Savot didn't feel relieved.

"Then why are you crying?" he questioned.

At this Aria became irritated again. "Savot, I'm just very tired. Could we talk about this some other time?" She turned and started back toward the feasting area.

Savot wanted to stop her. He wanted to know why her demeanor didn't match her words. A dozen potential sentences rushed through his brain. But before he could decide which one to use, Aria turned back briefly and spoke.

"Goodbye for now, My Lord," she said, resuming her formal tone. She turned again to leave.

'My Lord'—she said it again! But he stopped himself from correcting her this time and kept quiet.

Then, looking back over her shoulder again, Aria added, "Savot, I've always thought you'd make the best king." She gave him a negligible but more genuine smile this time. The new young king wandered back to the feasting area well behind Aria, mumbling to himself in utter exasperation, "Girls! I'll *never* figure them out!"

Chapter 2

Seeds of Insurrection

When Savot returned from his mystifying talk with Aria, the celebration festivities were just reaching their peak with dancing in the middle area, and a hearty obstaball game underway on the concourse. He wandered over to the sidelines and took a seat. Though Savot loved obstaball, he only half-mindedly watched this particular game. He couldn't stop wondering what was going on with Aria.

The players on the two teams of eleven were all boys from the Chosen Children, and most who had decided to play were the eunuchs. Only three of the other 115 boys who were not eunuchs played. The rest mingled with the girls because it was their last chance to do so for the next month. After that night the gender groups would have to be separated for four weeks.

The adults and other children paid more attention to the obstaball game than any of the Chosen Children. This game was an exciting one. The two teams contended with gusto on the huge square field. The large blue, ball traveled around the arena rapidly as the contestants whacked it with their sticks and kicked it unmercifully, bouncing it off the obstacles and off each other. The players seemed charged with electricity tonight. Savot thought maybe the players were releasing the pent-up tension they had all felt over the choosing of the king. Or perhaps they were behaving like wind-up toys all set to begin the long-anticipated New Atlantis Project the next day. They'd been preparing for this their entire lives.

***

The festivities lasted long into the evening. But three attendees left the party before anyone else. Aria left first, then her father, then Cain. King Jorash had asked to meet with the two young people at midnight in his personal chamber.

The three had been meeting in secret for the previous two years. And this would be the most critical of the covert meetings yet. Cain reached the king's palace chamber soon after Jorash, but before Aria. He found King Jorash pacing back and forth on his elegant oriental carpet. The king stopped momentarily to acknowledge Cain's presence, and then instructed the boy to sit down.

"There's not much time now," Jorash spoke briskly as he resumed his pacing. "I know we've been over the alternate plan many times. But now that it's the one you'll have to use, I need to make sure you both completely understand it . . . *and* agree to it." Then lowering his voice, the king confided, "We must make certain that Aria will still cooperate."

"Your Majesty," Cain answered assertively, "I'm sure Aria will be loyal to our ultimate goal. It *will* be more difficult for her now—as it will for all of us—but I know she can do it. You have a strong daughter, Sir."

Just at that moment a weak knock came at the door. Cain jumped up and rushed to let Aria in.

"Ah, my almost-bride," he greeted playfully, bowing and beckoning the princess into her father's chamber. "Don't worry, Aria, we'll still end up together." Aria grinned nervously as she passed Cain.

King Jorash wasted no time in getting down to business. "Well, my daughter, things don't always turn out as we plan, do they?" Aria shrugged, answering her father with only a modest smile.

Jorash went on speaking, now in a most optimistic tone. "We can still make New Atlantis work the way we've designed it," he assured his daughter. "It'll just take a little more effort."

"Absolutely! We *can* still do it, Sir," Cain boomed, nodding to Aria for her to agree. She gave him one nod as an answer.

Then Jorash lowered his head and shook it. "I felt certain you'd be the one chosen, Cain. But we knew there was only a one in five chance of that. The lot is one thing I can't control."

"So," Cain broke in self-assuredly, "as we've discussed all along, we'll just use our other plan." He looked to Aria for agreement.

"Yes," Aria stated in a strong voice now. "We know that's what you want, Father. So that's what we're going to do." The apathy that had engulfed the princess all day seemed to have disappeared now. Instead, a solid resolve exuded from her face.

"You *do* remember the timeline for the back-up plan, don't you, Aria?" the king queried his daughter.

"Yes, Father." She then rehearsed the sequence of events as they should play out on New Atlantis according to the alternate plan the three of them had devised. When she finished her recitation, King Jorash beamed at Aria and walked to where she stood with his hands clutched behind his back.

"Aria, for a daughter, you are the best a father could ask for. Your loyalty has always made me proud." King Jorash spoke as tenderly to Aria now as ever he had. She was his only child and, though he had always denied it, Aria knew her father had been disappointed that his only heir had not been born a male.

"I know you take the future of this new kingdom very seriously," Jorash told the princess.

Aria beamed warmly at her father. But instead of giving her the hug that seemed appropriate, the king stayed at a distance—untouchable.

***

Dayra, the girls' Navy captain, had returned earlier than the other girls to the large sleeping chamber they had all shared for the past two years. Dayra was intent on setting up a prank for the other 114 Chosen girls who were soon to join her. After she got the joke ready, she pretended to be asleep in her bunk as the others trickled in and prepared for bed.

The first to discover the trick was Sensia, the general of all the girls' military. Sensia plopped her bushy head of brown hair down on her pillow, exhausted from dancing. Then she felt something wet and sticky on her cheek.

"What in the world?" she barked. Examining her pillow, Sensia found half a dozen overripe figs inside the pillowcase, smushing through the fabric. She yelled as if her lungs would burst. "DAY—RA!"

An explosion of laughter sounded from across the room.

"I'm going to kill you this time, Dayra! I mean it," the gooey-faced general bellowed. The tallest and strongest of the girls, Sensia dashed across the room and bludgeoned Dayra with her dripping pillow.

Dayra, now curled tightly into a ball, howled even louder. Within a few seconds, Sensia's angry shouts dissolved in to uncontrollable giggles as Dayra fought back with her own unblemished pillow.

When both girls had worn their arms out and caught their breath, Dayra convinced Sensia to join in the ruse. Each successive girl who entered found the others supposedly asleep only to discover that she, too, had been had. All the girls were excited that Aria had decided to spend this night with them instead of in the palace. And now the victims couldn't wait to see the princess' reaction when she also got slimed.

Aria was the last to come in for the night. When she discovered the trick, she went absolutely hysterical with good-natured revenge. What followed was the biggest, messiest pillow fight ever.

After the blizzard of feathers settled and all the girls were exhausted from the battle, Aria straightened herself and announced in a commanding voice, "All right, everybody. We've got to get some sleep. We have a long ride tomorrow."

"Aria, it's so good to see you acting yourself again," Caris whispered, standing beside the princess. "You were so depressed all day." Dayra heard her.

"Yeah, what was that all about, Aria? Good grief, you get to marry Savot! He's so good-looking!" Dayra added.

"Definitely! Savot is the best of the five. *You are so lucky!* I wish he'd be left for me," added Lalera. This beautiful redhead had never concealed her hope of being paired with Savot had he not been chosen king. But now her fiancé was Jamin (which was the case only because Jamin had begged the Court for it to be so).

Lalera now joked with the princess playfully, "And you'd better watch out, Aria. I think Savot likes me back." Narsis threw a pillow at Lalera, hitting her squarely in the face and knocking her backward off her bunk.

This started the laughter all over again until someone said, "Well, I think we should just break the Marriage Rules once we get to New Atlantis and let us choose who we want as husbands." It was Narsis who had made the bold proposal. Several girls agreed heartily and some whispered names to each other.

Narsis continued, "And I think Aria might just choose 'someone else' if she could."

Giggles echoed throughout the room of fourteen-year-old girls. "So what do you think, Aria? You could arrange for us to pick who we want, couldn't you?" someone else asked.

A queenly expression suddenly settled over Aria's face, and a hush descended on her audience. While the girls all knew Aria had a wide streak of zaniness, they also knew that she took her royal responsibilities seriously. "All the rules of our mother continent Atlantis will remain intact once we're on New Atlantis," she declared.

No one responded but some of the girls frowned.

The princess continued, "And besides, you're just saying that because . . ." Aria hesitated, inconspicuously grabbing two pillows; then, like lightening, a mischievous look crossed her face. She then shouted, "ALL of you want my fiancé!" Aria wrinkled her nose at Lalera for a split second before swinging the pillows in all directions, whacking several girls at a time. Laughter even louder than before filled the room, and it was three in the morning before the girls' quarters finally became quiet.

***

By the time Savot got to the boys' bunkroom, several of his peers were already in bed exhausted from the obstaball game. Some were still washing up and climbing into their bunks.

Marcum sat on the floor removing splinters from his knee that were jammed there after running dead on into one of the obstacles during the obstaball game. But Marcum was probably the toughest boy of the whole bunch. He plucked the jagged fragments of wood out of his skin without wincing.

"Hail to the King!" Cain boomed—not even sarcastically—when he noticed Savot had entered the room. This awakened all the boys who had fallen asleep, and a lively group discussion started about how Savot planned to rule New Atlantis.

Almost all of the boys had requests, questions, and suggestions. Most wanted Savot to change something about the design of the government or the Atlantean laws. But Savot, a firm rule-follower, practically quoted from the guidebook that he and the other candidates had studied for the previous two years. He insisted they follow the Atlantean laws just as they stood, and that the government be structured just as Atlantis' had always been.

Throughout their debate, Cain agreed heartily with everything Savot said. This was quite out of character for the Cain who Savot knew, especially after the angry reaction his competitor had displayed earlier that day. To Savot's surprise, most of the other boys seemed allegiant as well.

Savot had expected loyalty from his best friends—Jamin, Billius, and Lian . . . *where was Lian, by the way?* But he hadn't expected compliance from his well-known contenders, Cain having always been the fiercest. Now, however, Cain went on and on about what an extraordinary king Savot was going to make.

Cain's sudden devotion made Savot uncomfortable. And there were four others Savot had expected opposition from. Toren, Shay, Marcum, and Dolius—his strongest competitors on the obstaball field—had never liked him, and Savot knew that well. Yet now, all four remained silent and stoic, never once entering into the discussion. Suspicion nudged the new monarch.

As the political dialogue wound down, Lian finally made his entrance.

"Where've you been?" Billius reprimanded.

"Talking to Stacia. You got a problem with that?" Lian retorted impishly. Then, once he had everyone's attention, he turned his back to the room of boys. Yanking his pants down to his knees, Lian bent over, flashing his bare backside to the group.

This signature greeting of Lian's invoked yowls of laughter. The boys had long ago become accustomed to Lian's ill-mannered antics and now enjoyed them immensely. And with Lian's gesture, any thoughts of continuing a serious discussion were ended. After some light horseplay, the tired boys settled into their beds. Laughter died down to yawns, sighs, and a few lingering snickers.

But before he could sleep, Savot just had to ask Cain a question. He whispered to his new general, whose bed was closest to his, "All right, Cain. I've just got to know. Why are you all of a sudden on my side? I saw how mad you were when the lot fell to me."

Cain responded promptly, "Savot, you're one of my best friends. But you know my temper." He raised his eyebrows as if expecting a response but then continued, "And you know how bad I wanted to be king. It just took me a little while to accept the fact that, hey, you're the one. Not me. That's all. I really think you'll do a great job."

"Thanks," Savot replied tentatively.

"And I get to be your 'number two' guy. That's the next best thing," Cain said. "We'll make New Atlantis great together, you and me," he concluded enthusiastically.

Savot, who always tried to think the best of people, lay back satisfied for the moment. And besides, he was so worn out from his extraordinary day that he couldn't keep his eyes open any longer. He said goodnight and quickly settled into a deep sleep.

***

Excitement filled the morning hours as the Chosen Children finished packing to leave for their Year of Preparation. Soldiers loaded construction materials, food, and other supplies into dozens of horse-drawn wagons.

The Children would travel today to a remote peninsula on the western side of the continent. There, for the following year, they would 'practice' building their new civilization under the instruction of 100 masters from all fields of Atlantean society—the Mentors, they were called.

King Jorash had planned a quick departure for The Chosen that morning. He knew that most of them had already been weeping for days over this year-long separation from their parents and siblings. Then, after the Year of Preparation, the youngsters would be allowed only a brief reunion with their families before sailing to the three islands far to the north of the continent that the Unknown God had designated as New Atlantis. And who knew when—or even if—they'd ever see their families again?

Savot's parents waited to bid him farewell at the king's palace. His father, battling tears, embraced Savot proudly. At the same time his mother held her arms tightly around her special son, not even attempting to restrain her sorrow. Savot was their only child.

Savot hadn't expected to cry at leaving his parents. But he did. Having lived away from home for two years while at the candidate school, Savot thought he'd grown accustomed to life without his family.

But now he felt like a little boy again, and all he could think of was how much he wished he could just go home with his mother and father. Just forget the whole New Atlantis Project and live out his life as every other Atlantean had before him.

"We'll go to the Temple every day and pray for your safety and success, Son," his father reassured with a quivering voice. "We're so very proud of you."

"Remember all we've taught you about the Unknown God," his mother admonished. "He will reward you if you honor him."

Finally, though his goodbyes had taken longer than he had expected, Savot broke away from his parents and returned to the bunkhouse to gather the last of his belongings. The thought that this wasn't absolutely the last time he'd ever see his family comforted him a little.

"The king orders your departure in one hour, My Lord," a guard informed Savot upon his return to the boys' quarters. Savot wasn't sure he liked this 'My Lord' stuff. He had not anticipated all that went along with kingship.

***

On the road to the peninsula, Savot traveled in a horse-drawn carriage decorated with heavy, purple curtains. His coach was second in luxury only to the one in front of it, King Jorash's. A brilliant tri-colored Atlantean flag flew at the front of Jorash's lead carriage.

Behind Savot's coach, twenty more carriages transported the 100 Mentors. Following that, the rest of the Chosen Children rode in sixty-six more carriages. A multitude of other vehicles transported luggage, foodstuffs, and building materials for the Peninsula Project.

Savot's two favorite eunuchs, Win and Nat, were the young king's riding companions. These twin brothers had scraggly, light brown hair and were uncommonly bulky for eunuchs. Nat and Win's father was an unusually tall, muscular man, which explained the twins' size. And for that reason, the twins had been chosen as Savot's bodyguards for this trip.

Savot tried to sleep but his companions' noisy chatter wouldn't allow him to.

"Can you believe we're actually doing this?" Nat blasted with zeal.

"I'm so excited, I'm about to pee in my pants!" squealed Win. Win could be crude at times. Almost as bad as Lian.

"This is it! We're going to be all on our own. Well, almost. At least *getting ready* to be on our own." Nat's voice grew louder as his eagerness built.

"Guys, I'm trying to sleep here," Savot interrupted.

"Oh, come on, Savot . . ." Win started, "I mean, Your Highness, uh . . . Your Lordship. Your Majesty?" Win looked confused. "What're we supposed to call you any-way?"

"Savot's fine when it's just us," Savot answered through a yawn.

"How could you possibly sleep right now?" Nat inquired. "I mean—Savot—you're the KING!"

Win added, "Yeah, and am I ever glad it was you, not Cain. He'd really have been a tyrant."

"That's for sure! He's one harsh guy," agreed Nat.

Savot defended Cain, but the eunuchs insisted Cain was nothing but an arrogant bully.

"Well, he *would* have been a tyrant! You're the man for the job, Savot. And we're gonna be there for you," Win bubbled, wiggling in his seat.

"We're gonna be your most loyal men," Nat added bravely. "We'll protect you from anything. You're safe with us, Savot."

"Don't you worry, Your Majesty!" said Win, emphasizing the 'Your Majesty'.

"I appreciate that, guys. But listen, I had a late night, so let me get some sleep. All right?" Savot settled his head against the tufted side of the carriage.

"Not a problem, we'll whisper." They tried, they really did. But the longer they talked, the louder they got again. Savot was so sleepy that he drifted off anyway, catching only parts of their conversation. Besides, he'd heard the story they were starting to tell a hundred times before. Nat began imitating the famous Atlantean storyteller, Choridan with his voice quaking.

"It was a dark and stormy night when The Ghost first appeared to King Jorash. After years of silence from the Unknown God, The Ghost had been sent with a most important message for the king.'" Win picked up on the narrative, doing an even better Choridan impression.

""King Jorash of Atlantis, your kingdom has become the greatest among all the peoples of the earth; the strongest and wealthiest of all lands. Therefore, I have been sent with a command for you."'" At this, Nat interrupted, copying King Jorash's deep, booming voice.

"'"Speak, O Messenger of the Unknown God, and your servant Jorash will obey."'" Savot, half asleep, roused for an instant thinking it was really Jorash. When he realized it was only Nat, he closed his eyes again.

Nat's voice changed back to simulate Choridan's. "'"You shall appoint each child born during the next year as one of a group you shall call 'The Chosen Children'. They shall be set apart from their birth and educated in all the traditions of your great land.

"'"Their number shall be two-hundred and sixty-eight, and they shall be raised as princes and princesses of Atlantis. When they reach the age of sixteen years, you shall resettle my Chosen Children on the triple islands to your north. And thus you shall expand the great glory of Atlantis."'"

At this Win broke in, using his own voice. "And now it's happening! How many times have we heard about this? And now it's actually happening. Oh, I'm really about to pee in my pants now, no kidding. You think we're going to stop anytime soon?"

"Oh, just hold it, Win. You're such a GIRL!" Nat teased. But this was not the kind of thing to say to Win—ever.

"No more of a girl than you, *Missie*," Win snarled. Then his head dropped, and he said no more.

Rolling his eyes, Nat apologized. "Okay. I know it really bothers you. I'm sorry."

"What I can't figure out is—why doesn't it bother *you*?" Win whimpered.

"I don't know. It happened when we were so little. I don't even remember it. Plus . . ." Nat added, checking to insure Savot was asleep. "I don't really see the disadvantage. I mean, look how much trouble all the regular guys are having with their future wives." He spat out the window. "I'm glad I won't have to put up with a *woman*."

Win's mute pouting told Nat that he didn't agree.

This was the first time in a while the twins had spoken seriously about their castration at age two. It wasn't exactly a comfortable subject. There had been more boys born than girls the year the Unknown God had designated for the Chosen Children to be born. It was not unusual for males to outnumber females on Atlantis in general. So King Jorash had decided it would serve the new nation well to make the extra 38 boys into eunuchs. The other 115 boys would be marriage partners for the 115 girls born that year.

Most of the boys who had been castrated resented the fact. But today, as they stood on the cusp of their pre-determined destinies, the importance of the roles they would play on New Atlantis seemed to weigh heavily on both of these brothers. Savot slept deeply the rest of the trip as Nat and Win stared wordlessly at the passing landscape.

Chapter 3

The Year of Preparation Begins

The sun was dissolving into the vast Atlantic Ocean just as the Chosen Children and their entourage reached the peninsula at the western end of the continent. The first object the Children saw on their arrival was a giant blue, green, and yellow Atlantean flag flying high above the field where the experimental palace was to be built.

Temporary but sturdy houses had already been constructed for the Children and their Mentors to live in during the Year of Preparation. Similar homes would be awaiting them when they arrived on New Atlantis a year later. King Jorash had already sent construction crews to the islands to clear land and begin building.

Everything on the peninsula had been designed to exactly prefigure the Children's coming life on the islands, except for one important element. While the plan was for their Mentors to accompany them to New Atlantis and supervise their beginnings there, after the first six months the Mentors would leave them. Most of the Children had not given much thought to that portion of their project, even Savot. But now with the responsibility for the entire new society on his shoulders, being on New Atlantis alone with no adults was definitley in the forefront of the new king's mind.

* * *

Since Princess Aria had napped most of the trip, she awoke refreshed when her carriage stopped. In a lighter mood now, Aria hopped to the ground and fluffed her skirt. She looked around the site, clearly brimming with excitement over her new adventure on the peninsula.

Aria's roommates on the peninsula had been decided months earlier. She had requested—and it made sense— for her roommates to be her attendants and best friends,

Caris and Stacia. King Jorash had seen no danger of these girls dissuading Aria from her secret mission, so he had granted permission.

"Caris," Aria called in her strong, sing-songy voice, "please make sure the eunuchs don't drop my smaller trunk. It has my figurine in it."

"All right, Aria," Caris caught herself. "I mean . . . yes, Your Highness."

Aria laughed. "You don't have to call me, 'Your Highness'! I mean, why now? You never have before."

Caris explained, "Well, because you're going to be the *queen* now! Queen is . . . well, bigger than princess. We'll need to call you 'Your Highness' when you're queen. So I figure, now's a good time to get into the habit."

Aria chuckled slightly and wrinkled her nose in response, then bounded off toward her house, her long, blond braid swinging side to side behind her. Once inside, she studied the layout of her new home.

"Hmm . . . I need a safe place to display my figurine," she said to herself as Caris and Stacia followed her into the house. A eunuch brought in the smallest of her trunks first and Aria took it from him.

Removing a small mahogany box from the trunk and opening it, she picked up her cherished figurine. It was a delicate crystalline form of a girl with a crown on her head. The princess' father had given it to her as a keepsake.

"I must have a special cabinet made for it. That's the only way to keep it safe," Aria finally decided. She ordered Caris to have the carpenters begin work on the cabinet immediately.

The rest of the 114 girls began settling into their houses, just as enthused as Aria about finally starting their year on the peninsula. Most of the boys and eunuchs didn't take time to unpack. Instead they spent the last hour of twilight exploring the grounds.

In almost every one of the girls' houses, remarks could be heard about how badly those boys needed wives, and how they would be stumbling around in their houses later in the dark, trying to find things. The girls glanced out of their windows occasionally, half amused at and half pitying the boys who had totally engaged themselves in charging through the woods and along the seashore that encompassed the nineteen-mile-wide area of land. It seemed as if they were, by tramping over every square inch of the ground, claiming the territory in the name of New Atlantis. Thoughts of the families they had left behind in Atlantis City seemed absent from the Children's minds—both boys and girls—for the time being.

The 100 Mentors also unpacked their belongings for the year in their quarters. As they worked most of them discussed, in one form or another, their need to begin regarding the Children as adults this year. After all, these youngsters would have to function fully as grown-ups once left alone on New Atlantis—only nineteen months from the present day.

While the other boys explored the peninsula that evening, Savot took the adult civil engineers with him and, by lantern light they surveyed key plots of land. The young ruler asked dozens of questions about where different centers of enterprise would be located. By midnight the future king had it well fixed in his mind exactly where everything was to be constructed in the mock city.

***

Savot had only three other boys living with him, whereas most of the Children lived in houses of six. Jamin, Lian, and Billius, his three best friends, had been Savot's choices as roommates. Lian and Billius, trained as soldiers, were to serve as Savot's attendants and bodyguards. Nat and Win, Savot's bodyguards for the journey, had been appointed to head the Palace Guard. All the eunuchs were trained as military personnel and most of them would serve as 'barriers' between the boys' and girls' sides of the peninsula. Savot's closest confidant was Jamin. He was captain of the boys' Army, serving directly under General Cain.

Billius had begun regarding Savot as his best friend five years earlier when Savot stood up to some bullies making fun of him over his speech impediment. Even now, Billius hadn't completely overcome his difficulty with pronouncing 'r's'. He still called his fiancée "Cawis" and was still ridiculed.

All four roommates' fathers had been military commanders. Often away on missions for King Jorash, the fathers had missed most of their sons' childhoods. The four boys had practically grown up together, their houses close together in Atlantis City. Even before they were moved from their homes at age twelve to live with the other Chosen Children, Savot regarded Jamin, Billius, and Lian almost as though they were his brothers.

***

The first morning on the peninsula, Savot awoke before any of the other boys and before most of the Mentors. His roommates were still sleeping soundly as the new king quietly closed the front door of his house behind him. He was surprised to find Galen approaching him just at that moment.

"Good morning, King Savot," Galen greeted him brightly, squinting in the new sunlight. Galen had served as King Jorash's first minister for several years but now had been temporarily reassigned as Overseer of the entire nineteen-month Preparation Project. Well-known for his wisdom and leadership abilities, Galen had been the logical choice. Savot liked him a lot. As well as being Overseer of the project, Galen was also to serve as Savot's Mentor during the three weeks out of each month that King Jorash was absent from the peninsula.

"Well," began Galen, "are you ready to be king, my boy?" He placed his strong hand on Savot's shoulder as they walked together.

"I guess I'd better be ready, right?" Savot's chuckling answer was a nervous one. "Mr. Galen, do you really think everybody will accept me as their king?"

"I certainly hope so! For their sakes as well as for yours. If they don't, they may have to be left behind, you know,"

Galen reminded Savot. Then he added as an aside, "You can just call me Galen now, Your Highness."

Savot had almost forgotten the Elimination Rule Galen was referring to. The Chosen Children knew that if they showed any disloyalty toward the chosen king, they would risk being left on Atlantis and thus eliminated from the New Atlantis Project. And that would be most humiliating. This relieved Savot of his momentary anxiety. It assured him that everything didn't depend on his ability to win each of his peers' loyalty. And maybe that's why the boys had shown him so much allegiance the night before. Savot decided he would put that matter aside for the moment and allow his mind to follow his stomach.

"Finally, breakfast. I'm starved!" Savot told Galen as the two approached the mess hall. Galen followed his protégé's lead into the building from which the delicious aroma of roasting ham wafted.

"After your meeting with the High Council, all of the Chosen Children will gather for your first official speech!" Galen told Savot excitedly as he grabbed a plate from the table and stabbed a chunk of meat. "Oh, and Antony. He's going to be your secretary."

Savot gave a quiet laugh and shook his head. "Antony! I'm not surprised he was picked for that job. He's always made sure he knew all my business."

"And everyone else's!" added Galen with a chortle.

Savot tried to ignore what felt like birds' wings flapping inside his chest as he thought of delivering his first speech. But then he turned his attention to breakfast which was fairly easy since the Children hadn't had much supper the night before. The young king ended up eating four big slices of ham and about ten griddlecakes.

***

Three hours later the first national meeting of New Atlantis was beginning. Savot could sense a collective tingle running through the group of 267 boys and girls gathered in the assembly hall as they began the very first day of their predetermined lives together.

The short but sturdy Overseer Galen was to speak first. He strode to the podium as a row of Atlantean flags flapped in the breeze on the platform behind him. The audience hushed. In his calming, paternal tone Galen started out by acknowledging the importance of this day and of the New Atlantis Project. Then, in more practical terms, he outlined for the Children what their standard Work Day schedules would be for the year. The Children listened in wide-eyed anticipation.

The likeable Overseer informed his audience that each seventh day would be a Rest Day, and that their reward for each month of hard work would be a day-long Monthly Feast. The Chosen Children cheered at this report.

After Galen finished, King Jorash, already seated on the platform, stood to speak. A rigid quiet blanketed the assembly of fourteen-year-olds. Their lifelong monarch began his address majestically. Savot could easily perceive the Children's deep reverence for Jorash. *Will they ever respect me that much?* he wondered.

King Jorash reiterated much of what Galen had said but in more flowery language. He proclaimed the magnificent nature of the Children's mission and its immense importance in the ongoing history of the world-renowned kingdom of Atlantis. Savot's peers listened in awe as the king praised their future achievements.

After the long speech, Jorash announced that he had a surprise for the Children. With a commanding motion of the king's hand, the Mentors distributed to each Child a small gift wrapped in green silk.

The young people wasted no time opening their presents. Inside each package they found a wristband woven of gold, silver, and another precious metal—orichalcum. This hard, shiny, bluish substance was mined exclusively on Atlantis and was world-renowned for its beauty and high trading value.

"Let these wristbands be worn by each citizen of New Atlantis from this day forward," King Jorash commanded. "And be sure to understand the symbolism of these bracelets." He cleared his throat loudly to make sure the Children paid close attention to his explanation. Most of them took their eyes off their impressive wristbands and looked back up at King Jorash. "The gold represents the great worth with which we regard each of you, our Chosen Children. The silver symbolizes the brightness of your future as an independent nation. And the orichalcum is to remind you never to forget your homeland and your people."

At this King Jorash thrust his right arm out toward his audience, revealing an identical bracelet on his own wrist. "I had one made for myself as well. To always remind me of you," the king announced affectionately and at full volume.

Some of the Children blinked tears out of their eyes as they placed the shimmering gifts on their right wrists, following their ruler's example. At the height of this poignant moment, King Jorash introduced Savot. Applause began immediately and grew louder and louder. As Savot ascended to the platform, he felt every ounce of confidence he'd ever possessed drain from his body. *How in the world will I ever get through this speech?* he asked himself silently. He took a deep breath and steadied himself. Then he just opened his mouth and started.

"New Atlanteans, the hour has arrived for us to begin the monumental mission we were all born for." He stumbled slightly over the tongue-twisting triple-'m' phrase he was reading. Holding his hands behind his back so no one could see them trembling, Savot stood as tall as he could and forced himself to keep speaking.

"Our elders have equipped us well for this day and for every other day that will follow. We *will* succeed in our assignment to expand the great and glorious empire of Atlantis."

At this Jorash began to clap and the Children followed suit.

The fledgling king forced a pseudo-confident smile, and then continued reciting every word of the speech King Jorash had written for him. He felt awkward with the formal language. It was so different from his normal conversation.

Savot faltered several more times during the speech. But as he spoke, a curious dynamic seemed to develop between himself and his subjects. Though their faces didn't quite radiate the same way they had at King Jorash's address, the Children seemed to welcome Savot's every word.

That's good enough, Savot told himself. And strangely, he somehow felt now as if he were addressing a group of much younger children. His hands fell to his sides. With his confidence slowly growing, Savot restated the instructions that Galen had outlined earlier for life and work on the peninsula.

"Today we must begin building the prototypes for our future homes and centers of industry, agriculture, education, religion, and government. Yes, *today!*" Savot tried to speak more loudly and firmly now as Jorash had instructed him to at this part in the speech. He was surprised that his subjects were responding to him with nods, smiles, and even cheers—acknowledging him as truly being their leader. He was amazed!

But now it was time for Savot to present the most objectionable subject within his speech—the Rules of Separation. Galen had purposely not addressed this difficult subject when he had spoken. He had told Savot he wanted to see the Children's reaction when they heard something unpleasant from their new king. Savot's hands started trembling again so he held them behind his back. But he swallowed hard and began.

"The girls' houses will be built on the opposite side of the peninsula from the boys', with the Mentors and eunuchs living in between." The groans and grumblings that had been expected rose from the crowd of New Atlanteans, but Savot tried to ignore them and hurry on so he could get to the good part.

"This design is purposeful. For the next two years, this Year of Preparation on the peninsula and our first year on New Atlantis, boys and girls are to be separated. Eunuch guards will be posted continuously day and night to ensure the two groups do not intermingle."

Sideways glances and murmurs of protest spread throughout the crowd as Savot explained the Rules of Separation more specifically. Resentment hardened the faces of some Children. Savot's eyes fell on Cain who was stationed in front of him below the stage. His general stood loyally staunch and unflinching.

Savot now had to clutch his hands hard behind his back to hold them steady. *What am I worried about?* he thought. *If anyone objects, there are plenty of adults around to control the protest—even King Jorash himself.*

The Chosen Children had always known about the Rules of Separation to come. But they despised them above all the other Rules. As Savot continued outlining every detail of the Separation Rules, the Children looked serious and sad, especially those who Savot knew were pleased with their chosen fiancés.

All marriages within this special group of age-mates had been prearranged during the Children's infancy; boys and girls having been paired according to the common occupations of their parents. Only the five royal candidates' marriages had not been decided since those matched had depended on how the lot fell. Princess Aria was to marry the chosen king and four other girls had been selected as wives for the unchosen candidates: Sensia, Narsis, Dayra, and Lalera.

As Savot surveyed the crowd, he realized how clever King Jorash had been in the design of this speech. Now was exactly the right time to remind his subjects about the 'good news' part of this unsavory arrangement.

"But let's not forget," Savot's voice brightened, "we get to have a day-long feast—*all together*—once a month to celebrate our accomplishments!" His wording here departed a bit from the exact words of his script.

When the Children were reminded of the monthly reunion feasts, mild grunts of satisfaction rose from the boys and sighs of relief from the girls. But Savot could tell from their still smileless faces that the Children really dreaded being segregated beginning today and continuing for the next month. The Mentors, most of them standing beside the stage facing the Children, eyed them all with calculated warning.

During the entire speech, Aria sat dutifully behind Savot on the stage, attending to his every word and not drawing attention to herself. Cain's eyes scanned the audience, his hand on his sword the whole time, vigilant against any disorder. Sensia, Cain's female military counterpart and now his official fiancée, stood at attention beside the general.

Savot's speech ended with more praise for the Chosen Children. That seemed to rekindle some of the loyalty he'd sensed from his peers earlier. With this, Savot again thought about the shrewdness with which King Jorash had constructed this speech. The elder monarch obviously had anticipated tension during the part about the Separation Rules. Therefore, deliberate words of flattery at the end lifted the audience's spirits. *Will I ever be smart enough to write speeches like this?* The question passed briefly through Savot's mind, making him pause in his speech. Then he went on with more compliments for the Children, building the volume of his voice louder and louder as he had been taught.

When the young king finished on the highest note of all, the audience gave Savot a standing ovation—clapping, whistling, and cheering like he had never expected. Savot had to control himself not to let his eyes bug out and his mouth hang open. King Jorash rose and walked to Savot's side, placing his arm around Savot's shoulder.

"New Atlanteans," Jorash announced robustly, "your king has proven himself worthy of his position by his wise words this morning." *My wise words? You mean, your wise words*, Savot thought. He still felt vastly incompetent despite his manufactured success with the speech.

After King Jorash's short concluding remarks, the Chosen Children hoisted their right arms into the air and chanted the Atlantean slogan of allegiance that traditionally ended a king's speech:

"Hail to the king! Hail to Atlantis!"

"Hail to *New* Atlantis!" King Jorash added, and the Children quickly echoed the new addition to the slogan.

The shining new bracelets sparkled on the raised wrists. Savot exhaled, his nervousness easing a bit. King Jorash dismissed the gathering, commanding the Chosen Children to follow their Mentors and begin their training.

***

Queen Sophea and King Jorash stayed on the peninsula for the rest of that first week. The king met daily with Savot, instructing him in the responsibilities of royalty. But each night, Jorash also met secretly with Cain and Aria.

Galen attended the daily meetings between Jorash and Savot. Antony tagged along everywhere they went taking notes. Savot regarded Antony as such a bother. He talked overabundantly, even in the presence of King Jorash.

Queen Sophea was her daughter's Mentor. She spent each day educating Aria about different aspects of being a queen. The last day of that first week, mother and daughter walked together along the beach. This time they discussed men and married life.

"Mother," Aria asked, "what if you're not really in love with the man you marry?"

"So. It's true. You're not in love with Savot," her mother concluded.

Aria said nothing. She just lowered her gaze to the sand.

"Well, you have to think about more than just yourself, dear." Sophea, a gentle and loving woman, was accustomed to playing the compliant wife. "You have to consider that your husband is the king. He has great responsibilities. And he needs you, above all others, to be loyal to him."

Aria listened carefully but silently.

"And you must remember at all times that all the other girls will be watching you," Sophea stated strongly. "You,

Aria, will be the model for every young wife on New Atlantis."

Aria walked on pensively beside her dignified mother, whose hair was the same glowing gold as her daughter's.

"You have to show them, not necessarily that you're madly in love with your husband, but that you're . . . well, content. And especially that you support him. That you believe in him and trust him. Then they'll trust him, too. Do you understand?"

"Yes, mother. I do understand. I'll be content," Aria replied, but with sadness in her voice.

Chapter 4

What Are Rules For
(If Not to Be Broken)?

The Rules of Separation applied to Aria and Savot as much as to any of the Children. The future king and queen didn't see each other for the entire first month. Savot and Aria received instruction from their respective Mentors about how to perform their duties as monarchs. King Jorash allowed Queen Sophea to stay with Aria the first month whereas he returned to Atlantis City after the first week. Galen, as planned, had taken over as Savot's Mentor in Jorash's absence. Each of the Chosen Children, likewise, spent every day of Month One learning from their adult counterparts.

Atlantean Army and Navy commanders trained Cain, Toren, Shay, Jamin, and the twenty-seven other military boys. On the girls' side of the peninsula, the thirty military girls—including Sensia, Dayra, Narsis, and Lalera—also studied warfare under military Mentors who were, of course, men.

"I'm not so sure I like this," grumbled Narsis after a hard day of hand-to-hand combat training. "They expect us to fight like guys."

General Sensia retorted quickly, "You've always known this was going to be our job on New Atlantis. So what's the problem now?" Sensia had always made it well known that she was 'as tough as any boy'.

"Women haven't ever had to fight before on Atlantis. I just don't like all the gore. I mean, I don't want to die some gruesome death," Narsis whined.

"Hey, you keep talking like that and I'll replace you in a second with someone else as head of the girls' Navy," Sensia threatened. After that Narsis complained only to select confidants.

"I can't risk losing this position," she told Keera, one of the girls under her naval command. "It gives me at least some control over my future."

***

Queen Sophea's handmaidens trained Aria's attendants, Caris and Stacia. Lian and Billius, Savot's attendants, received instruction from King Jorash's personal valets. Since Lian and Billius had also been trained as soldiers, they doubled as Savot's bodyguards. The eunuchs Win and Nat, sharing the headship of the Palace Guard, also became Aria's personal bodyguards.

The ten Children designated as priests and priestesses in the Temple of the Unknown God learned their duties from Leander, the Atlantean high priest. Leander had been high priest all the Children's lives, preceded by Evran who had died mysteriously the year before they were born.

That first month the apprentice priests began the rigorous mental work of memorizing word for word every message that The Ghost had ever delivered to the kings of Atlantis over the previous millennium since Atlantis had been founded. Knowing these writings inside out was the most important duty of the religious leaders so that they could teach the Laws of the Unknown God to their people.

Young architects studied how to draw building plans under seasoned Atlantean designers. The Children designated as civil engineers learned from their engineering Mentors how to build roads and bridges. Atlantean construction experts trained both male and female construction workers. During the Year of Preparation these protégés would learn—by erecting mock buildings—how to later assemble every structure on the real New Atlantis.

And so it went in every field of the emerging civilization. Adult merchants, carpenters, smiths, doctors, millers, fishermen, lawyers, miners, and farmers trained the girls and boys who had been assigned to each of their specialized areas.

King Jorash's Palace Guard soldiers instructed the 38 eunuchs. A group of eight would guard the palace and the royal family. The other 30 eunuchs were educated to oversee all other stations. In most cases at least two supervised each area of development—one for the girls' group and one for the boys'. Of all the eunuchs' duties, though, the most important for the present and near future was to ensure that the boys and girls stayed separated.

"It's just not fair," Win complained again to his brother one Work Day as they sauntered past the obstaball field. "The reason we were made eunuchs in the first place was to make sure the boys don't mix with the girls for the first two years, right?"

"Yeah, so?" Nat answered.

"The High Council was worried that if the boys and girls were together, they'd be too distracted to concentrate on their missions," Win recited the reason he'd been told.

"Exactly. And you know that's what would be happening right now if it weren't for us," defended Nat.

"But then, think about it—after these two years—our whole purpose in life is pretty much over. *They're* all going to get married," Win sulked. "Then they won't need us to keep them apart anymore. They'll all have partners to share the rest of their lives with, and we'll be stuck—men living all alone. Because we aren't even really *men!*"

Nat had been over this complaint numerous times with his brother, but yet indulged him once more now. It was abundantly clear that Win deeply resented what had been done to him.

"Yeah, but you know we're going to be used in the military after that," Nat tried to encourage. "We've been trained to fight. And we're just as good as the other guys at fighting."

Win just wouldn't give up. "Okay. So we're military guys who can't ever get married. Who can't ever have children." He kicked a stone and sent it flying across the obstaball field. "Ouch," he grumbled at the unexpected pain in his big toe.

"I'm telling you, Win. You ought to be thankful. Women are nothing but trouble," Nat countered.

"Well, I kind of like girls. So there." And that was the end of the argument—for that day anyway.

***

Since King Jorash had left the peninsula after the first week, Savot was expected to begin practicing his rulership of the New Atlanteans. Galen offered Savot much wise counsel about every issue imaginable. Antony still followed Savot everywhere he went. The secretary constantly jabbered about some piece of gossip he'd picked up. Sometimes Savot just wanted to gag him.

By the third week, the Children had settled into their new routines and their Overseer Galen seemed pleased at how well things were going.

However, with the taste of independence that life on the peninsula brought, some of the Chosen had already found ways to break the Separation Rules. Several Children who were displeased with their assigned fiancés pursued others they were attracted to—in secret, of course.

Shay was a tall, strong boy with red hair and piercing gray eyes. As the boys' Navy captain, Shay was engaged to marry his military counterpart, Dayra. But Dayra was in love with Jamin. Jamin, however, was engaged to the girl he loved, Lalera. But Lalera had always had a huge crush on Savot. Shay, though engaged to Dayra, had always flirted with Narsis, another Navy girl. Narsis liked Shay in return, but she was engaged to Toren. Many such 'love polygons' existed among the Chosen Children.

There were some couples, though, who were completely pleased with their matches. Amedis and Thea, the head priest and priestess, were intensely enthralled with each other. The lawyers Kanin and Kelen let everyone know of their shared affection. Caris was delighted with her engagement to Billius and the feeling was mutual.

Billius and Caris couldn't stand the thought of only seeing each other one day a month. So they soon arranged to leave messages under a designated stone. When the boys and girls traded shifts at their training site, each found a new message from the other. And before long the pair established a secret meeting place in the middle of the night. Similarly, Shay and Narsis invented a means to see each other at least once a week in secret. The two agreed to lead their intended spouses to believe they were wholeheartedly in favor of their arranged marriages. They did this in hopes that they could somehow convince Savot to change the Marriage Rules once they reached New Atlantis.

Several other couples found clandestine ways to meet as well.

***

Lian and his fiancée Stacia were yet another story. Having known all their lives they were intended for each other, Lian and Stacia had always seemed happily matched. Stacia thought Lian's outrageous pranks were cute . . . most of them, anyway. But Savot had always felt that the dynamics of Lian and Stacia's relationship were complicated. And fascinating. And fragile.

Since Stacia was a strict adherent to rules, Lian tried his hardest to follow all the rules as well. But that was totally against his nature. He was crazy about Stacia and everyone knew he always had been. Because he knew how tender Stacia's conscience was, Lian never even discussed the idea of meeting secretly.

Late one night Lian woke Savot up for a conversation about Stacia. He hardly ever talked about girl-related things so this was a rare occasion.

"Savot, I need to talk to you," Lian whispered in his husky voice, shaking his sleeping friend who was particularly tired that night. Savot reluctantly opened his eyes, dragged himself out of bed, and followed Lian out of the house. Quietly, against the backdrop of a cricket symphony, Savot heard Lian's dilemma.

"It's Stacia. I'm such an idiot, Savot!" Lian vented.

"What happened with Stacia now?" Savot asked, shuffling over to a nearby log to sit down.

"I thought I was getting better. Man! I really tried. But she's mad at me again."

"You haven't even talked to her in three weeks. Why's it just now bothering you?" Savot wondered.

"Oh, it's *been* bothering me. I've been trying to forget it but I just can't. It's really getting to me. I can't even sleep, Savot," Lian confided, sitting down now on the log beside Savot.

"What'd you do *this* time?"

"Okay. The last time we were together—you know, before the separation here on the peninsula—she wanted to talk about children," Lian said, and then puffed and kicked at the dust under his feet. "Children! Can you believe it?"

Savot could believe it. Children usually became an issue once a couple got married. But he knew Lian well. There were two distinct sides to his friend. While in some circumstances Lian could amaze Savot with his maturity, at other times he acted pretty much like an oversized toddler. He could tell Lian was in the latter mode now. But still Savot accommodated Lian's question.

"Yeah, I can understand that. Girls like to plan ahead."

"Well, I thought it was ridiculous to be thinking about children already. So I just said, 'Yeah, sure. Let's have a dozen right away!' I know that was sarcastic, and I probably shouldn't have said it, but guess what she did?" Lian's voice was getting louder, well beyond a whisper.

"What'd she do?" Savot humored.

"She slapped me!" Lian retorted. "I was just kidding. Good grief, why does she have to take everything so seriously?"

This was typical of Lian's history with Stacia. Lian had always admired Stacia's upright character. He actually looked up to her—in a spiritual sense. The slender, black-eyed, olive-skinned Stacia was irresistibly attractive to Lian, and he let everyone know it. And Stacia had strong feelings for him—most of the time positive feelings, sometimes negative—but always strong.

It was hard for anyone not to love Lian, deep down. His amiable personality enchanted all who'd ever met him. Dimpled and cute as any boy could be, Lian had straight, brown hair that he kept short but unkempt—usually sticking out in all directions. And his smile could charm a cobra, the girls all agreed.

But Lian was, at the same time, about as rough around the edges as they come. Showing his behind to a group of friends was just one of his coarse clown acts. Another was to spit a big glob of snot on the ground at the feet of just about anybody, barely missing their shoes—just for a joke. Body noises were also a specialty of Lian's. He often challenged the other boys to belching or farting contests . . . and always won. And since the boys had recently started growing extra hair on their bodies, Lian loved to pull out one of the other boys' chest hairs when he could see one.

Lian often offended his friends by calling them insulting names. His favorite was 'moron'. But then, the next moment, he'd be tackling and tickling the same boy he'd slighted. No one could stay mad at Lian very long. Savot just hoped that someday his friend would actually grow up.

Lian was, by far, the most affectionate of all the Children. He reminded Savot of a lumbering, large-breed puppy dog. When he was tired, he'd cuddle up to one of his friends—a rare act among Atlantean boys. But everyone knew he meant the snuggling innocently, as he did his physical expressions of love toward Stacia. It didn't take Savot long to surmise that Lian's latest mistake with Stacia was just more of his same old pattern of—like a puppy—blundering all over himself. He had advice for Lian.

"All right. Here's an idea. At the feast," Savot instructed, "just apologize for being insensitive . . . again." After some argument, Lian finally agreed that he would apologize. He seemed to have blown off all the steam he needed to for now, so he let Savot go back to bed. *I wonder if she'll ever be able to put up with him?* Savot wondered before dropping off to sleep.

***

Aria was the first authority to hear about the secret rendez-vous. Stacia told her about Narsis and Shay. After calling Narsis privately to her quarters, the princess threatened to report the couple to Galen if the illegitimate meetings didn't stop immediately. But after hearing how intense Narsis' heartache was over not being able to marry Shay, Aria agreed to keep quiet about the couple's concealed get-togethers.

Savot found out about this and other couples' secret meetings—not surprisingly—from Antony. Having awak-ened on one occasion in the middle of the night, Antony had gone for a walk and had spotted Caris and Billius strolling hand in hand in the forest. When he confronted them, Caris also told him about Narsis and Shay. When Savot heard the report the next morning, he instructed Antony to keep the information to himself.

For three days Savot struggled over how to handle the situation. He even prayed about it to the Unknown God. This was the first truly hard situation he'd had to face as New Atlantis' king.

And he had feared something like this would happen, knowing how intensely his buddy Billius loved Caris.

What should I do? Savot pondered. *If I don't order pun-ishment for these first violations, how will I ever enforce any laws on New Atlantis?* He didn't feel quite as badly about punishing Shay, *but why does Billius have to be one of the ones I have to punish first?* he asked himself. Before he decided what to do, Antony had told Galen.

***

The Overseer immediately called for a meeting of all the Chosen Children. It was still four days before the boys and girls were to be reunited at the First Feast, but Galen and Savot agreed that a meeting of the entire group was necessary.

Once all were assembled, Savot reminded the Chil-dren that any infraction of the Rules of Separation re-quired strict punishment. And that the penalty was to be doubled if the two caught together were 'unintendeds'. Then Savot announced the discovery of the two law-breaking couples, though almost everyone had already heard about both violations.

Toren, Narsis' fiancé, hadn't heard. He promptly stormed out of the assembly, infuriated that Narsis had betrayed him. And with Shay! He and Shay had always been best friends . . . until now. When the Mentors finally brought Toren back to the assembly, his eyes were gleaming like a snake about to strike and his face shone scarlet.

Galen had insisted that Savot decide what the culprits' punishments would be. And so Savot ruled that Billius and Caris' sentence would be to spend a week working fourteen hours a day digging moats around the city. And they were to spend the nights in prison. In anticipation of such a need, both a girls' and a boys' prison had been constructed.

Shay and Narsis were sentenced to do the backbreaking shovel work and live in prison also, but for twice as long since they were engaged to others. This meant, of course, that the four of them also had to miss the First Feast.

Before the day was over, Savot also dismissed Antony from his job as secretary. He replaced him with a lawyer named Teran. Savot had Antony reassigned to the farming sector where his fiancée Meril already worked.

Even after the Children had witnessed the two couples' sentencing for violating the Separation Rules, most of the secret rendezvous continued anyway—just more covertly than ever. The night guard eunuchs often fell asleep on duty, to the end that only seven couples were ever indicted for illegal contact during the entire Year of Preparation.

Before the end of the year, Shay and Narsis would be caught and punished four times.

Meanwhile, Savot's love life was nonexistent. He distracted himself during the days with the business of New Atlantis, but at night—when he lay in bed—his thoughts always floated back to Aria.

Jamin slept in the bed closest to Savot's. One night, after listening to Savot tossing and sighing for almost an hour, Jamin had a suggestion for his royal friend.

"Hey, Savot. You awake?" Jamin asked the needless question.

"Yeah," moaned Savot.

"What are you thinking about?"

Savot groaned.

"So you think she hates you, huh?"

"What else am I supposed to think?"

"I can really understand how you feel," sighed Jamin. "My whole life I've wanted to end up with Lalera. After the lot, when I found out I'd been paired with her—man! I was so happy!"

"Yeah, I remember," Savot reflected. "But what do you mean you know how *I* feel?" Savot asked.

"You're pretty sure Aria hates you. Well, Lalera hates me, too," groaned Jamin. "And it's killing me. I love her so much, she just melts me."

"What? Jamin, of course she doesn't hate you."

At this Jamin sat up in bed and crossed his legs. "For a guy who's so smart, Savot, you amaze me how clueless you are sometimes!" Jamin almost shouted in exasperation.

Jamin's disrespect didn't bother his friend, the king, but the comment definitely aroused his interest. Billius, whose bed was on the other side of the room and who could sleep through a hurricane, didn't budge at Jamin's outburst. Lian grunted and turned over but didn't fully awaken.

"What am I clueless about?" Savot whispered, sitting up in his bed.

"Savot, are you totally blind?" Then Jamin spoke slowly and plainly as if to a child. "Lalera is in love with *you*."

"Jamin. That's ridiculous! Lalera?"

"Oh, good grief, Savot! Haven't you ever noticed how she looks at you? How she tries to be wherever you are? How she giggles at any joke you tell, even if it's not funny . . . no offense, but you know you're not the best comedian."

"No. Lalera has never given me any special attention," argued Savot.

"Uh!" Jamin puffed. "Like I said, clueless! Listen, every time I try to catch her eye when you're around, it's impossible. She's always looking at you." At this Jamin dropped his voice and his head. "I just don't stand a chance with her."

Jamin was a good-looking boy. With almost white-blond hair, stunning blue eyes, and a square jaw, he looked like what Savot had always imagined one of the legendary Athenian gods might have looked like. And he was by far the kindest of all the Chosen boys. *How could Lalera not love him?*

Neither Savot nor Jamin spoke for a while. Then Savot broke the silence.

"What're we gonna do, Jamin? If what you're saying is true—man, I feel terrible," sympathized Savot.

"It's not your fault," Jamin assured his friend. Then he brightened and sat up straighter. "All right, I've been thinking about this a lot. Here's the plan. The way I figure it, things couldn't get any worse between me and Lalera. And you're feeling the same about you and Aria, right?" Savot nodded.

"So, here's what we can do. At the feast next week, you just ignore Aria and I'll ignore Lalera," Jamin proposed.

Savot was puzzled. "And what's that supposed to do?"

"I'm not finished. I ignore Lalera, but you don't," Jamin proposed with a sly smile.

"You mean you want me to flirt with your girl?" Savot blurted.

"Yeah. Flirt all you want. I mean, that's what she wants anyway. Just make sure Aria sees you," Jamin said, then raised his eyebrows and winked at Savot.

Savot's mouth dropped open in disbelief. "You are such a rat, Jamin!" But then he reconsidered. "But maybe, just maybe, it *would* make Aria jealous." In a low tone he added, "Oh, I doubt it."

Then he continued, "Anyway, you're telling me to just *use* Lalera? I thought you cared about her. Now you're wanting me to set her up to be hurt?"

"Well," reasoned Jamin, "I figure it this way—and this is the part you might not like—if you keep flirting with her all year, then dump her when we move to New Atlantis . . ." He flung both arms out to his sides, "guess who will be just waiting to comfort her?" Jamin wiggled his eyebrows up and down. "And in the meantime Aria may realize she does like you after all."

Savot was speechless, staring wide-eyed at Jamin. Then he shook his head, changing his mind about even considering Jamin's proposal.

When he finally spoke, he said, "Jamin, I just can't believe you! Not only do you want me to use Lalera but you also want me to trick Aria? I thought you were made of better stuff than that."

Jamin suddenly looked ashamed. After a few sulking moments he conceded, "You're right. It's all twisted. I'm just so desperate. It's all I could think of to do." Jamin flung himself back down on his bed and covered up. "Just forget I ever said anything."

Savot lay back down too. After both boys had tossed and sighed quite a bit more, they finally fell asleep. But Savot had a dream that night about Lalera.

Chapter 5

The Obstaball Contest

After what seemed like forever to Savot, the day of the First Feast arrived. It was nearly noon by the time the girls had primped enough to travel to the location appointed for the feast. Anticipation coursed through the air as the boys and girls ambled into the feasting area from their respective sides of the peninsula. The two gender groups moved tentatively toward one another in roughly parallel lines, like one unprepared Army facing another.

Some of the boys seemed much older already, the girls agreed as they whispered to each other. Among the boys, elbow punches, quiet comments, and muffled snickers spread as they surveyed the girls. Finally Parius and Kelen, twin brother and sister, broke the awkwardness as they ran to embrace each other. Some of the intended couples then started up conversations. Before long, lively flirtations flourished throughout the reunited group of Children.

The food spread out on the tables for the feast seemed to be a lower priority, even to the boys. The eunuchs though, who had been around both groups all month, ran to the tables and gorged themselves on the fresh breads and cheeses. King Jorash had returned from Atlantis City for the feast. The bubbly interaction among the Children amused the adults.

"They really do enjoy one another's company, don't they?" Queen Sophea asked Galen. With a hearty chortle, his own mouth full of bread, Galen agreed with a nod.

At last the Children sat down at the long feasting tables and their Mentors served them their meals. Almost without exception the fiancés sat together. Savot felt extremely tense sitting beside Aria. He only nibbled at his meal as he attempted to make conversation with her. But the princess would only give short answers to his questions. She chatted cheerfully with the other girls near her though. Aria's coldness toward Savot had not changed since they had last spoken a month earlier.

***

After the feasting ended, it was time for an obstaball game. The construction workers had made sure that the playing field was ready for use by the Month One Feast, complete with seating for spectators.

Normally obstaball was of utmost importance to the boys. And the boys who had their eyes on girls other than their fiancées stuck to that mindset and joined eagerly in the game. As a result, circles of pouting girls dotted the feasting grounds for the rest of the day.

Most of the boys who were pleased with their fiancées —and the feelings were mutual—wanted to spend time with them rather than play obstaball. Then there were some boys who liked the girls they had been paired with but the girls didn't like them. Some of those opted for obstaball and some spent the evening trying to connect with their fiancées.

Although Savot loved to play obstaball, he declined playing today. He wanted even more than ever to engage Aria in conversation. He still had Jamin's plan in the back of his mind—as a last resort—but first he wanted to have a real talk with Aria if she seemed at all willing.

Savot strolled over to the stands and sat down at King Jorash's left. The queen was already seated beside the king to his right. Shortly Aria came over and sat on the other side of Queen Sophea.

This is definitely awkward! Savot thought. *How am I ever going to talk to her with her mother and father sitting in between us?*

In most obstaball games, a mixture of boys and eunuchs comprised each of the two eleven-man teams. This time they'd decided it would be a boys' team versus a eunuchs' team.

"KICKOFF!" bellowed the referee. Toren let the blue obstaball drop and slammed it forcefully with the top of his foot. It soared along a wide arc in the air toward the eunuch team.

Nat caught the ball, the force of it almost knocking him down. Once he steadied himself he was off with all speed toward the eunuchs' goal line. Boys rushed him from every direction. Cornered, Nat passed the ball under the arm of Calum (on the boy's team) to Win. Known for his uneunuch-like strength, Win hurled the ball to his teammate Phip who was waiting twenty paces away.

Jamin shot like an arrow toward Phip and, before anyone could stop him, tackled the ball-carrying eunuch. Whenever a successful tackle was made, as the rules dictated, advantage was given to the tackling team. The eunuch players had to kneel on one knee for a split second as Jamin began his sprint toward the boys' goal.

After barely touching their knees to the ground, the eunuchs sprang up and darted after Jamin. By pushing, shoving, and elbowing—which was all allowed—the defense held most of the eunuchs back. Toren grabbed Nat by his shirt, swung him around, and rammed his head into one of the obstacles. This one was a short, oaken stump. The horn blasted out a foul. Jamin stopped in his tracks and stuck the obstaball he'd been carrying under his arm.

"PENALTY!" shouted the referree. Toren was banned from the game for the next two scores. Elis replaced him. All players, frozen by the sound of the horn, waited for the horn to activate play again.

"Good thing that wasn't one of the stone obstacles," a girl near Savot commented. "Nat could have really been hurt." As it was Nat just rubbed his forehead and moved his neck around in a circle as he got up. He didn't acknowledge the gash on the top of his head even though blood dripped slowly from his hair. Wiping sweat and blood from his face and shooting an angry glare at Toren, Nat took his position again.

Savot realized that his peers were again using this vigorous game to release their tensions. If they'd been feeling even half as much pressure to perform as he had this past month, he was glad they had this game as an outlet. *I really should be out there playing*, he told himself. *I could really use some stress relief myself about now.*

The same voices of self-doubt he'd been hearing in his head for weeks now flooded his mind again. Would he and his peers succeed with this huge project? Would their Mentors think they could handle this enormous challenge? Would their families miss them after they left?

Honnnk! The horn startled Savot out of his short daze.

Jamin clutched the obstaball tightly and bolted from his position. He tore through the blocking group of eunuchs only to face an obstacle he hadn't been able to see behind his opponents. This one was a boulder.

Agile as a deer, Jamin swerved around it but, as he did, the rough stone ripped most of the top layer of skin from the side of his lower right leg. Apparently mindless of his bad injury, Jamin careened toward the boys' goal. Even the fastest eunuch couldn't catch him as he sped across the goal line with no opposition.

Score for the boys' team! The spectators clapped and cheered. Jamin glanced at Savot as if for praise. Savot shot both arms up into the air, forefingers pointed at the sky, as he beamed congratulations toward his friend. Only then did Jamin notice the wide abrasion on his leg. He took off his shoe and slung a cupful of blood out of it. His captain ordered him to sit out for bandaging.

As the next round began, Win got to be the kicker. He walloped the ball with his shoe and sent it straight along the ground, but at an unexpected angle. The boys' team was ready though. Amedis got to the ball first, picked it up, and ran. He passed it off to Dolius who threw it to Lian who pushed it to Cain with the side of his foot.

Savot watched Aria when Cain got possession of the ball. She wasn't cheering for him. Cramming the ball under his arm, Cain barreled toward the boys' goal. As several eunuchs converged on him, Cain threw the ball almost straight up in the air. *What in the world is he doing?* Savot wondered.

With the eunuchs' eyes on the bright blue ball and not on him, Cain rushed around them to where the ball was now descending. He pushed both eunuchs and boys out of his way and caught the obstaball. Only a few inches from the goal now, Cain did a silly little dance as he hopped over the line. Still Aria didn't seem impressed.

"Show-off!" laughed Marcum who sat on the field in front of Savot. Marcum couldn't play tonight, having broken his arm in a military exercise.

The eunuchs were mad now. Not only the eunuchs playing, but the others on the sidelines as well. Savot understood that they had something to prove. They'd had something to prove for as long as they could remember. But this was the first real situation where the face-off was clear. This was a definite contest between eunuchs and boys.

Nat and Win called a huddle before the next kickoff. All the spectators could hear from the eunuch cluster were fierce grunts. But it was clear that the underdog team was devising a hard-hitting strategy.

The scorekeeper signaled the drums to sound, ordering the players into place.

"KICKOFF!" This time Win kicked the ball along the ground toward the eunuchs' goal. Zhovan, another eunuch, quickly came up beside Win and took possession of the ball with his foot before anyone on the boys' team could reach it. But he changed the direction of the ball—he was moving it toward the boys' goal.

Savot could tell the boys' team was confused. Eunuchs bunched together close to the boys' goal. A new and unusual eunuch strategy was in play.

Zhovan kicked the obstaball to Elis, a member of the opposite team! A puzzled look crossed Elis' face for a second but then he picked the obstaball up and threw it to Calum. Surprisingly, none of the eunuchs charged the possessor of the ball. Cain then motioned for Calum to hand the ball off to him. Calum complied and tossed the ball to Cain but shook his head and rolled his eyes.

Then, like a charging bull, Cain ducked his head and hurled himself further toward his team's goal. All eleven eunuch players locked arms in front of him. When Cain tried to run around them the whole line rapidly shifted to block him.

Jamin and several other boys, however, were able to slip around behind the line of eunuchs, all waving their arms for Cain to throw the ball over the eunuchs' heads. Cain ignored his teammates. Determined to break through the line, he flung himself with all his might at the barricade of eunuchs.

Ramming himself into the pretzel made by Rance and Phip's arms, Cain struggled to break through the gridlock. Straining until his red face looked sick, and growling like a barbarian, he finally succeeded. But he was met by six eunuchs who had broken loose from each side of the blockade and barreled through Jamin's group of boys behind the line. They pounced on Cain, burying him on the ground.

Somewhere in the scramble, the obstaball bounced out of the mountain of eunuchs. Nat scooped it up and charged in the opposite direction. The boys' team chased and almost tackled him, but he managed to throw the ball an impressively long distance to Win who stood waiting about a foot from the eunuchs' goal line.

Win was always determined not to be outdone by Cain in either showmanship or masculinity. Before he stepped over the goal line, Win eyed the charging boys' team, snarled and spit as far as he could toward them. Then, re-alizing he still had time, he trampled the ground under his feet, kicking up a cloud of dust. As the boys neared him, Win twirled around, displaying the blue ball over his head, and made a graceful dance leap over the goal line.

The whole stadium laughed and stood to their feet cheering. Even those who had been rooting for the boys' team applauded the clever strategy of the eunuchs and especially Win's performance.

Next, two injuries on the boys' side allowed the eu-nuchs to score three times in a row. The eunuchs were elated. Savot overheard Win's comment during a brief time-out.

"So what if we don't have 'everything' they do," the bulky eunuch growled. "We can still beat their pants off!"

And so the fierce competition continued with the score running close the entire first half of the game. Players running into the obstacles caused more injuries than

Savot had ever seen in any obstaball game. But the competitors seemed to disregard all pain tonight. There was more at stake than just the immediate contest.

Jamin played more aggressively than usual during this game, but he stepped up his efforts even more after the eunuchs began leading. Lalera, as usual, paid no attention to Jamin's outstanding moves even when other girls raved over them . . . and over him.

Calum also played his heart out trying to ignore the fact that his 'true love' Livia was pretending to enjoy her fiancé Denit's company on the sidelines. Savot interpreted Calum's illegal kicks into the shins of his opponents as acts of sheer frustration. This, along with Calum's frequent glances toward Livia, made Savot suspect what was the truth about the two. Calum and Livia—an illegitimate couple—had been meeting in secret during the previous month as well as the two other couples who were now sitting miserably in prison. They just hadn't been caught.

Denit, knowing full well that Livia was just putting on a show for the Mentors, kept slipping away from her. But, to keep up her farce, Livia kept finding him and latching on to his arm. Denit had a disgusted look on his face for most of the Feast Day.

Savot tried to watch the game as well as keep an eye on Aria. But he couldn't help noticing—for the first time—that Lalera was always within his sight. Maybe Jamin was right. A weird mixture of feelings began to rise inside him. Flattered that this pretty redhead might really be interested in him, Savot was also perturbed at her for hurting his best friend.

Every time Savot looked in her direction, Lalera smiled warmly at him. That definitely reinforced Jamin's theory. Savot felt his naturally pink cheeks getting even more flushed. *I never noticed how pretty Lalera really is*, Savot thought.

Then, toward the end of the game, Lalera did the most brazen thing. She walked right up to Savot with a goblet of fruit juice, extended the chalice toward him, and asked, "Would you like something to drink, My Lord?" King Jorash, Queen Sophea, and Aria all stared at her indignantly.

Stammering a word of thanks, Savot took the drink from Lalera's hand. His face felt even warmer now, first from embarrassment and then from anger. A short time-out had just been called in the game. Savot shot a glance toward Jamin. Jamin caught his friend's eye with an 'I told you so' look.

Then, without really thinking what he was doing, Savot found himself standing and offering Lalera his hand. "Would you like to sit down?"

"Oh, how kind of you, Your Highness. Yes, I'd love to sit here and watch Jamin play," she answered loudly enough for the royal family to hear. Lalera sat on the bench as close to Savot as she could without actually touching him. Aria bent forward and hurled a hot glare at Lalera, and then sat back again.

As the contest on the field resumed, Lalera commented on each play, interacting with Savot as much as possible. She tugged at his shirtsleeve and giggled each time a player made a blunder.

All right, Savot told himself silently, *if she thinks no more of Jamin's feelings than this, I'll play this game with her.* At least Jamin would know that he was pretending.

In the middle of the game, the referee called for a break. People rose from their seats and began moving about.

"Have you tried the pies yet?" Savot asked Lalera.

"No," she replied, "are they good?"

"Delicious. The fig is my favorite." He wavered but then decided he'd go ahead fully with Jamin's plot.

"I wouldn't mind having another piece. Would you like one?" Savot asked, offering his hand to Lalera, as a gentleman of course. The two rose from the stands and passed right behind Aria and her parents. The princess, sitting stiff-backed, did not even turn around.

As the two walked toward the dessert table, and after he knew Aria was determined not to look at him, Savot let go of Lalera's hand.

Lalera cut some pie for the two of them. Savot stole another quick glance at Aria just in time to catch her watching him. *Good!* He sat down with Lalera and made light conversation as they ate their dessert, all the while sneaking glimpses at the princess. But after he had caught her watching once, she never looked back. The game resumed but, before long, Aria got up from the stands and strode to the opposite side of the concourse out of Savot's sight.

As Lalera and Savot sat conversing after eating their pie, the Project Overseer approached them with a stern countenance. Galen had noticed what had happened on the stands and thereafter between the two.

"Could I speak with you privately, Your Highness?" Galen asked in a calm, steady tone. "Please excuse us, Lalera."

Once off to the side where no one else could hear, Galen rebuked Savot sternly.

"What do you think you're doing, Savot? Don't you know all your subjects are watching you?"

"I was just getting a piece of pie," Savot defended weakly.

"With Jamin's fiancée?"

"We were just being friends. The way all of us have always been." Savot knew the words coming out of his mouth were not helping him.

"Well, things can no longer be the way they've always been, Savot," scolded Galen. "If you pair off with a girl who isn't your intended wife, that signals to the other boys that it's acceptable for them to do the same. And— heaven knows—we've been having enough trouble with that already."

Is everyone really taking their cues from me? Savot wondered. Suddenly he felt horrible for having followed Jamin's scheme. It felt like someone had splashed him in the face with cold water. The young king hung his head, owning his guilt.

"You're right. Of course you're right. I'm sorry, Galen," Savot apologized. Galen snorted and nodded emphatically. Then Savot asked his Mentor, "After the feast tonight could I talk to you some more? I think I need your advice on this guy-girl thing."

"Certainly, Savot," his Mentor answered, softening. Galen's fondness for Savot was once again obvious. "Let's have a late tea together in my quarters."

Savot returned to Lalera and quickly excused himself. Then he went back to the stands and took his seat beside King Jorash at the obstaball game which was just about to end. Aria never returned to her seat.

"Twenty-one to twenty-one, a tie," the scorekeeper announced. The spectators stood in anticipation of the next play. A score of twenty-two won the game, so the tie now had to be broken. The eunuchs had the ball.

Sweaty, young players battled like savages—now by torchlight—to gain control of the obstaball. Savot didn't follow how it happened exactly but before he knew it, Nat had passed the goal line with the ball.

The eunuchs had prevailed over the boys! It was a momentous victory that went down thereafter in eunuch history. The other 27 eunuchs who had not played in this game hoisted the eleven players up on their shoulders, all bellowing victory chants. One would have thought they had won a war. They celebrated long into the night while the exhausted players from the boys' team went to bed.

Dancing and other activities went on that evening, but Savot took little notice of them and never considered participating. He tried to approach Aria several times, but she continually evaded him.

***

As soon as the feast was declared officially over, Savot made his way to Galen's quarters. Fortunately the two were able to speak in private because Galen's Mentor-roommates had not yet returned.

"So, you want to talk about girls, Savot?" Galen grinned and handed him the cup of tea he had prepared, beckoning Savot to sit.

"Is that a condescending smile?" Savot asked, a bit offended. He took the tea, but immediately set it down.

"Oh, no. It's just amusing to me. I mean . . . *you.* You're by far the most discerning of all the boys. But even you are baffled by the mysteries of women!"

"Mysteries. That's the perfect word for them!" Savot bolted out of his seat as he said this, then he slapped the palm of his hand against his forehead and turned sideways to Galen. "I can't believe I was actually trying to make Aria jealous today. It just kind of happened, Galen. What's wrong with me?"

"Oh, my dear boy," Galen started, rising from his seat and placing a reassuring hand on Savot's shoulder. "I know you don't think she has any feelings for you. But I've watched her closely. She looks at you sometimes when she knows you won't be able to see her."

Savot whirled around. "She does? Are you sure?"

"Oh, she's clever. Yes, indeed. Very clever. And very guarded about it, but . . ."

"But what?"

"I think . . . well, I could be wrong." Galen hesitated.

"No, go ahead. Please," begged Savot.

"I'm not all-wise, Savot," Galen started, not knowing that Savot was thinking his Mentor was incomparably wise. "But I do believe she just might have some feelings for you. Somewhere deep down."

"Well then, why in the world does she hide them from me? It would be all right, you know. I *am* her fiancé." Savot slumped back down into his chair.

Galen seemed very much like a father to Savot now. And he obviously wanted to give his young protégé every thread of hope that he could.

"Even after all my years of marriage, Savot, I must admit I still don't fully understand women. But you're right. I would think she'd be responding differently to you. I've talked with her about it myself, you know."

"Yes, you've told me. She tells you all the same things she tells me. That I'm the best one to be king. That she respects me. That it'll be a privilege to be my queen . . . blah, blah, blah," Savot droned.

"But even while she's telling me all those things," Galen interjected, "there's—I don't know—some kind of sadness in her eyes when she speaks of you." Galen paused pensively. He shook his head with a furrowed brow.

"Well, yeah," said Savot. "She's sad that she has to marry me."

"No. It's not like that," the Mentor countered. "And if I was only judging from the way she treats you most of the time, I'd certainly have to conclude that she truly doesn't care for you. But those glances she gives you sometimes. And that strange sadness that comes over her when your name is mentioned. Those are the only hints I get from her that there may yet be hope."

"Hints! Is that all I'm ever going to get from her?" Savot threw his head down on his folded arms at the table. "What's going to happen when we get to New Atlantis? When the Year of Merger comes? Galen, I don't want to just *make* her marry me."

Galen got up from his chair and walked in a slow circle around the room, scratching his chin. "Maybe you need to be doing more to win her heart, Savot. I mean, you have been terribly busy with the affairs of the Peninsula Project." He stopped, then twirled on his heel to face Savot.

"How about giving her flowers? That might help. My wife always used to warm up to me when I brought her a bouquet of flowers." Galen's wife had died the year before from a fever.

"Of course!" Savot's face lit up. "I could send her flowers! She'd like that. All girls love flowers. Why didn't I think of that before?"

And so Savot's 'flower campaign' began.

Chapter 6

What's a Princess to Do?

The second month seemed to fly by. The Children were used to their training schedules now, and the construction work moved along more quickly than it had during the first month.

Savot had his attendants pick a bouquet of tropical flowers once a week and take them to Aria for him. But at the Month Two Feast, Savot found that his flower crusade seemed to have backfired.

"Thanks for the flowers, Savot," Aria said with definite sarcasm. "But are you sure you didn't intend them for Lalera?"

Savot was stunned. *So, seeing him with Lalera at the last feast had bothered her.* And she was still mad about it. The princess didn't speak to him the rest of the day. So during the whole Month Two Feast, Savot took every measure to avoid Lalera.

After the feast, as the Children began the third month of their training, Savot continued to send Aria flowers every week with notes saying things like, "These are for YOU!" He even wrote poems with her name in them to assure her that his affections were only toward her. But the princess never gave him a response beyond an obligatory 'thank you' through the eunuch who delivered the flowers.

Toward the end of the third month, Savot's exasperation over Aria came to a peak. One day over a private lunch Galen proposed a new courtship strategy for Savot to try.

"Savot," Galen began, "what if it was decided that you and Aria needed to meet to discuss 'affairs of state'—say, once a week? That would allow you to give her the flowers in person. And also give you two a chance to talk more."

"Well, I've got to try *something* else." Then Savot wondered, "Do you think the High Council would approve of us breaking the rules to meet with each other? Would King Jorash approve?"

Galen pushed his chair away from the table, as full of confidence as he was from his meal. "Don't worry about them. I think I can persuade both the king and the Council that it has become a necessity. I mean, you and Aria will need to talk a lot about the government once on New Atlantis. You should start collaborating now! This is official business, after all," Galen said with a wink.

***

And so it was. Galen arranged for Savot to go to the girls' side of the peninsula to meet weekly with Aria at her house for 'government business'. Each time he took her a beautiful bouquet . . . and he also added some kind of gift just for good measure.

At their first meeting Aria took the extravagant bunch of multi-colored flowers from Savot's hand and carelessly crammed them into a nearby vase. Then Savot gave her the gift he'd brought her, a delicate gold bracelet. Savot could tell she liked it but Aria quickly laid it on a nearby side table and responded very officially, "Thank you, Savot. Now, what issues do we need to discuss?"

For the next three weeks when they met, the future king and queen repeated a similar ritual. Aria's formal manner never wavered toward her future husband. And after the Month Three Feast, Savot discovered something that further discouraged him. Still he held it in as long as he could.

At their first weekly meeting during Month Four, the two discussed 'affairs of state' as usual. But Savot was about to burst; finally he broke the protocol Aria had wordlessly set and started by asking his princess,

"Are you still mad at me about Lalera?"

Aria glanced at Win and Nat, the usual chaperones for this meeting. Savot ordered the twin eunuchs to leave the room. The brothers argued with him a little (because they were supposed to), but at last they left Savot alone with Aria. As soon as the eunuchs were gone, Aria answered Savot's question with a question of her own.

"Why were you spending time with her?"

Completely frustrated, Savot spouted, "What does it matter to you, Aria?" Then he made himself calm down so he could carefully construct his next sentence. "You don't need to lie anymore." He leaned closer to her and whispered, "I saw you and Cain together in the grove the other night."

"What?! What are you talking about?" Aria looked terrified.

Savot continued in a whisper. "It's all right. No one else saw. And I won't tell anybody." He paused and then hesitantly disclosed, "I saw him kissing you."

Aria shot out of her seat and began pacing around the room.

"You don't have to explain. I understand, Aria," said Savot miserably.

Aria then faced Savot squarely, her gold, teary eyes blazing. "No! You don't understand!" Then she flipped her long, yellow curls behind her, turned and rushed out the door. Savot followed her to the doorway.

He stood gazing after the frazzled princess as she scrambled into her carriage and ordered Win to drive away. Win, taken off guard, clambered into the driver's seat with a bewildered expression and obeyed.

What had just happened? Savot couldn't seem to get his breath for a minute. She said he didn't understand. *What in the world was there not to understand?* Nat stood beside him at Aria's front door.

"I don't envy you a bit," said Nat. "I'm glad I'll never have a problem like that."

"Thanks for the sympathy, buddy," Savot replied facetiously. He went inside and wilted hopelessly into a hard chair. Knowing Aria wouldn't want him there when she returned from . . . wherever she had gone, Savot left after a few sulking minutes.

***

King Jorash, on his monthly week-long visits to the peninsula, continued his midnight meetings with Cain and Aria. Details for Savot's overthrow on New Atlantis became firmer. But during their meeting at the end of Month Four, Aria had to tell Cain and her father what Savot had discovered.

"Savot knows about Cain and me meeting at night," Aria reported.

"How did he find out?" questioned Cain angrily.

"He saw us. If he tells Galen . . ."

"If he tells Galen," Jorash calmly stated, "you'll both deny it." The shrewd schemer had obviously thought through the pitfalls of the couple's rendezvous before he had agreed to let Cain initiate them with Aria during Month Two. "All the Children know there's interest between you two," King Jorash continued, "and that Savot's jealous. No one will believe him if both of you deny it."

Then Aria added, "And he promised me he wouldn't tell." She bit her nails as she paced.

"Then nothing's lost," concluded Cain. "We're safe if he keeps it to himself. And we're safe anyway if he tells." And that was the end of that discussion.

***

Aria kept completely quiet about both sets of her secret meetings—those with the mutiny team and those between herself and Cain. Just before the Month Four Feast, Cain drew Toren into the insurrection plan by order of King Jorash. Cain had promised Toren his own general's position after Cain became king so Toren was well motivated to keep the secret.

Jorash had also been instructing both Cain and Aria all along to build loyalties among the leaders in each area of New Atlantean society. If they secured the favor of the Area Heads, there should be no opposition when Cain assumed control after Savot's 'kidnapping'.

What Aria didn't know was that after each of her secret meetings with Cain and her father, Cain returned for an even more secret meeting alone with Jorash.

Cain had always wanted to be king of New Atlantis. All the five candidates had wanted that. But King Jorash had decided that he wanted Cain to be king.

***

Jorash had his own design for New Atlantis. And his plan was dramatically different from the one The Ghost had commanded upon his last appearance to the king—fifteen years earlier.

Of the five royal candidates, Jorash had concluded that Cain was the only one capable of executing his goals for the offshoot nation. Cain possessed many of the same qualities as Jorash himself: a love of luxury, an overly strong estimation of his own value, and a capacity for deceit—even cruelty—if necessary.

The choice of Cain gave Jorash his best hope that New Atlantis would be furnished just as lavishly as the continent Jorash ruled. Anything less than absolute magnificence on New Atlantis, the king concluded, would bring shame to the legacy of 'Jorash the Great'.

And, even more importantly, Jorash wanted New Atlantis to retain the reputation of superiority over other lands that he had gained for its mother kingdom should the prophecy of Atlantis' annihilation that he had received ever actually come true.

Halfway into the candidates' two-year training program in his palace, Jorash had carefully approached Cain with his blueprint for New Atlantis. At first Cain had cringed at the violent strategy, being only thirteen then. But his hunger to be king soon overruled his conscience. Cain agreed if Jorash could ensure him the throne, that he would execute the insurrection, and then replicate Jorash's international policies on New Atlantis.

Once Cain had vowed his allegiance to Jorash's proposal, the king educated his new protégé in the covert (and forbidden) military strategies that he himself had employed for many years. The more the king revealed about his history of raiding—instead of trading honestly with—the Mediterranean lands, the more Cain's excitement seemed to grow.

Jorash's full plan required that Princess Aria be included. At first, Cain had been doubtful about Aria's willingness to cooperate with the two of them.

"Leave that to me, Cain," Jorash had assured. "I know how to handle my daughter. She'll be convinced it's best for New Atlantis." But Jorash made it extremely clear to Cain that Aria should only know part of their plan. Queen Sophea, after all, had never known anything of her husband's surreptitious activities. And neither should Aria. King Jorash, during that same conversation, instructed Cain to begin courting Aria.

One month before the lot was to be drawn, Aria had been won over by her persuasive father. Jorash convinced the princess to join in the plot to overthrow any candidate who might be selected by the lot unless it was Cain. The king had approached his daughter one sunny afternoon as she practiced her fencing in the palace courtyard.

"Aria, may I have a word with you?"

"Of course, Father." The nimble young princess quickly sheathed her sword and then took off her belt.

"I have something for you. But first we must talk," King Jorash began. Father and daughter walked casually along the lane behind their elegant palace.

"Whoever is chosen king of New Atlantis will be your husband, as you know. But I've been increasingly concerned about a few of the candidates' competency. I've been watching each of them train over the past two years."

"But Father, from what I've seen they've all performed very well," Aria started. "I mean, Cain has said the same thing but . . ." she abruptly stopped speaking because she had been ordered not to spend time alone with any of the candidates.

King Jorash ignored her slip of the tongue. And he had prepared for his daughter's every question and objection.

"Oh, Aria, of course! They're all putting forth their best performances when you're around. But I've studied them many times when they didn't know anyone was watching them."

"Really?" Aria asked, looking worried. "Please tell me more."

So Jorash told her more. Most of it wasn't true. But, as usual, her father spoke with great authority and used sophisticated and compelling words. The king told of numerous displays of cowardice and indecisiveness he had observed in Jamin, Shay, Toren, and Savot. He also exaggerated examples of Cain's leadership abilities and inflated stories of his valor.

Finally he declared, "Aria, I've come to the conclusion that Cain is really the only qualified candidate." Aria seemed bewildered.

"But Father, what if the Unknown God chooses one of the others?"

"Oh, Daughter," chuckled Aria's father, "I've known many priests in my time. You can't always be sure it's the Unknown God who fixes lots around here."

"You mean you don't trust the priests, Father?"

"Don't misunderstand, my child. I'm sure they mean well. They just overestimate their own wisdom sometimes," Jorash explained. "I've caught them on more than one occasion—shall we say—'adapting' things to make the Unknown God say what they think he should." This was a lie. The Atlantean priests of the day were known to be men of supreme integrity, with the exception of the high priest Leander, the king's puppet.

The increased concern on Aria's face now prompted Jorash to continue quickly. "But don't worry, Daughter, the will of the Unknown God shall be carried out. After all, I'm the only person now living on Atlantis who has actually had a face-to-face encounter with The Ghost. I think I understand the will of the Unknown God for New Atlantis and who will be best as its king."

Jorash insisted that, 'for his peace of mind', they should devise a plan to insure that Cain ended up ruling New Atlantis in case one of the other candidates was chosen by the lot.

"If Cain isn't chosen by the lot, I'll appoint him head of all the military. That will set him up to be second-in-command." Aria looked skeptically at her father through squinted eyes but Jorash kept talking.

"You'll be safe with Cain as your husband . . . and as the king. I would really worry about you if you married one of the others. Believe me, I know what it takes to rule a kingdom."

Feigning concern for Aria, Jorash then wrinkled his forehead. "As much as I hate that it's the case, I honestly believe that none of the five—except Cain—has enough backbone and good judgment to reign on New Atlantis."

The pair had stopped at a bench in the rose garden. Jorash motioned for Aria to sit and they both did. While the princess still struggled to absorb all her father had just told her, Jorash removed a small mahogany box from his cloak and ceremoniously handed it to his daughter.

"Now for your gift," he stated regally. He handed Aria the box, and she slowly opened the velvet-laden container to reveal a dazzling crystal figurine of a slender young woman wearing a bluish-silver crown.

Speaking majestically now, Jorash declared, "This is you, Aria. You are my flesh and bone. You are my heir, and New Atlantis is my prized legacy."

"Oh, it's truly exquisite, Father!" Aria exclaimed, mesmerized.

"It is up to you—as my sole descendant—to preserve the majesty of Atlantis in your new land," Jorash charged Aria. "If the lot doesn't choose Cain, we'll make sure he ends up reigning anyway."

"Aria, I repeat, there is no doubt in my mind that Cain is the only candidate who can help you build New Atlantis by my designs. None of the others even come close to complementing *your* royal stature. Your strength. Your nobility."

As he spoke these words, the king looked adoringly at his daughter. In fact, he had never looked at her quite that way before in her entire life. Aria smiled warmly at her father's unfamiliar tenderness and the lavish words of praise that he had carefully enfolded within his sales pitch.

But then her smile faded and her brow furrowed. "Father, what if the lot *does* choose one of the others? What will happen to the chosen one?"

"I have a plan for that too, my dear. Don't worry. I've thought of everything to take care of you," her father spoke with an unfamiliar nurturance. He rose and bid Aria to continue their walk. She carefully placed the figurine back in its box, tucked the box gently into the crook of her arm, and strolled with Jorash again.

"You trust your father more than any priest, don't you?" he queried.

"If what you say about the priests is true, then yes," Aria replied, but she still looked confused.

"The one who is chosen, if it's not Cain, won't be hurt," Jorash assured her. Before the Year of Merger, he—whichever one he is—will surely have concluded that the job of king is too much for him anyway. I've planned a way to depose him without humiliating him. You'd have to be part of that plan, too." Aria strode along silently.

Jorash went on, "You and Cain will explain to him, once he's been abducted, supposedly by pirates . . ." At this point Aria gasped. "Don't worry!" the king continued. "There won't really be any pirates. You'll explain the whole thing to him. You'll tell him that it was my desire that he serve as New Atlantis' ambassador to Athens instead of being New Atlantis' king. You and Cain will present this idea to him, and he will go along with the 'pirate' story because, believe me, by then that news will be a relief to him. He'll be taken to Athens and welcomed by its king who knows me and trusts me implicitly." This statement may well have been the biggest falsehood Jorash had yet told his daughter.

Aria strained in concentration, trying to take in all of the implications of what her father was proposing. She seemed to be thinking too hard to even respond so Jorash explained more.

"You see, this way he'd be saved from the embarrassment of having to admit to the other Children that he's just not fit for the job."

"But, Father, what if he doesn't prove incompetent?"

At this Jorash laughed aloud. He then proceeded to fabricate even more elaborate lies about Savot, Shay, Toren, and Jamin. Each report appeared to convince Aria a little more about the lack of kingly ability in the four.

"Oh, they're all smart boys," King Jorash added tactfully. "They were each able to display enough of a façade to fool the elder statesmen who chose them. But I'm the one who has to entrust my only child's future to one of them. And I trust only Cain."

When her father had finished speaking this time, Aria stopped their walk and declared,

"Father, I had no idea! Thank you for looking out for me and for all the Children." She resumed walking with the king but pensively. Just as she started to speak again—before she could ask any more questions—Jorash summarized the plan in order to tie up any loose ends that might have been dangling in his daughter's mind.

"Again, Aria, if Cain isn't chosen king, then we'll arrange for the young man who is chosen—after he's proved his incompetence—to be 'kidnapped by pirates' (he grinned as he spoke those words in a different tone). He'll be taken to live among our friends the Athenians as an esteemed dignitary from New Atlantis. You see, that would be a much more honorable and comfortable life for him.

Aria appeared to be in a daze and said nothing else so Jorash wasted no time in ending the conversation.

"Very well. Then it's settled," he concluded. "But promise me this: that you will always treasure this figurine to remind you of the trust I'm placing in you today."

Aria gazed at her father and nodded.

And thus the princess was tied into the plot.

***

King Jorash reported the entire conversation to Cain later that day. He believed he had convinced Aria that Cain was the only worthy candidate, at which news Cain seemed relieved. But Jorash was not satisfied with this. In order for Aria's place in the plot to be fully secured, Cain needed to increase his intensity in courting her.

"The rest depends on you, Cain," the king told his apprentice. Jorash fixed his eyes intently on Cain. "Are you sure you've won Aria's affections fully?"

"Oh, I have. Definitely," Cain claimed. "She's crazy about me, Sir."

Jorash probed more deeply. "When, exactly, do you think she started favoring you over Savot?"

"Well, I think she's always liked me," replied the arrogant Cain. Then, noticing the unease on Jorash's face, he thought harder.

"But I guess it was about six months ago. Yeah, I had told her before that I had feelings for her—you know, right after you told me to start courting her? But it took her a while to come around. She kept talking about what if I wasn't chosen and all that. But I think when I first kissed her that she liked it. It was her first kiss, you know. And after that she started acting differently toward me."

Jorash looked pensive.

"What's your concern, Your Majesty?"

"I need to make sure she's really in love with you. That's the only way she'll stay completely loyal to you. If there was any chance she had feelings for any of the other four, our whole design for New Atlantis would be in grave danger."

"Oh, don't worry about that, Sir," Cain laughed. "She can't stand the other four now. After all the bad stuff I've told her about them, she thinks they are all weak fools."

"Good. I told her my opinion of them as well. Let's make sure she keeps hearing those unfavorable reports. And increase your physical involvement with her. That should help also." The king sighed and stroked his chin. "Women are peculiar creatures, Cain. They must be handled skillfully if we want them on our side."

***

And so, to take every precaution, Cain had begun having secret rendezvous with Aria during Month Two on the peninsula. Of course, they had to be more careful than any of the other couples who met at night. But both he and Jorash thought it was worth the risk. Cain had studied the behavior of the most 'romantic' boys to learn what girls like to hear, how to gently touch their faces and gaze into their eyes, give them gifts, and other such tactics. He also followed Jorash's advice and let his touches turn into caresses and their kisses became longer and more passionate each time he and Aria were alone together.

And after all, Cain was quite handsome with his broad shoulders, blond hair, and bright green eyes. Most of the girls had been known to have had crushes on him at one time or another simply because of his good looks. Now he courted Aria as brilliantly as anyone could.

And his lies (now focused on Savot since his election as king) kept coming. He related a new false report about Savot to the princess each time they met. By the Month Three Feast, Cain told Jorash he was sure he owned Aria's heart completely.

***

During the week before each Feast, Jorash traveled from Atlantis City and resided on the peninsula. Supposedly there to Mentor Savot. His real purpose was to further polish the details of the conspiracy in his secret midnight meetings with Aria, Cain, and now Toren also.

After each of these meetings, the princess returned quietly to her quarters and slept restlessly. Noticing a rather depressed mood in Aria on mornings after such meetings, Stacia and Caris would question her. She always told her roommates that she was just tired; that she hadn't slept well.

So Aria's roommates speculated that her gloom was over seeing Cain at the feasts and knowing he wouldn't be her husband after all. Or perhaps it was only the melancholy that all the Children felt from time to time, because each feast reminded them that they would soon be leaving Atlantis and their families forever. Aria was a hard one for anybody to figure out, even her best friends. She kept so much inside.

Chapter 7

To Function as Adults

One morning during Month Four Savot, awoke late. Jamin, Billius, and Lian had already left the house for breakfast. The sleepy, young king commanded his tired body to get up, but his eyes remained closed. Then he startled when he heard a loud, foreign noise.

"Aaaaaaaaauk!"

Savot's ears directed his eyes toward an open window. He had to blink several times to make sure of what he was seeing.

"Aaaaaaaaauk!" screeched a large blue and red bird perched on the windowsill. Savot sat up and studied the creature, afraid to move lest he scare it away. He had heard stories of colorful talking birds but had never seen one.

"Hello there," Savot ventured.

"Hello, hello . . . hello," answered the bird.

"You can talk?" Savot asked the bird.

"Hello," said the bird again.

"What's your name?" Savot asked. He didn't quite know how to carry on a conversation with a bird. Though there were other tropical birds on Atlantis, he'd never seen one as large and colorful as this one. And he'd surely never met one who talked.

"Set sail, you mangy, drunken scavengers!" ordered the bird.

"What? You must be a pirate bird!" Savot guessed.

The bird went back to saying, "Hello, hello." Then it turned its head sideways and looked away.

"Guess he's not so smart," Savot mumbled to himself.

"Not so smart. Not so smart," said the bird, turning back to look Savot in the eye.

Savot laughed louder than he meant to, which scared the bird. It flew away. Dashing out his front door, Savot tried to follow the creature but could only catch sight of a blue streak disappearing into a clump of trees.

At breakfast he told Galen and his roommates about the fascinating bird.

"Oh, yeah, right!" Lian scoffed. "C'mon, Savot, you must have been dreaming!"

"No, there are some biwds that can talk, Lian!" Billius added.

"'Biwds'? Billius! When are you going to start saying your 'r's' right?" Lian criticized.

Galen broke the tension by interjecting, "Actually, I've heard stories . . ."

"About talking birds?" Lian asked sarcastically. But knowing Galen as a reliable source on every other subject, Savot wanted to know,

"What stories?"

"Some tales about pirates. They're known to have talking birds," Galen answered.

Savot exclaimed, "That's just what I thought!"

"A lot of the birds are bred in Egypt . . . in Memphis mostly, I think," Galen said. "Anyway, they are very intelligent birds. They can be taught to say anything they hear."

"Piwates?!" Billius exclaimed, forgetting that he had again mispronounced his 'r'. "Has anyone ever actually seen a piwate?"

"Well," Galen lowered his voice to a whisper and all four boys leaned in closer to him. "Our Navy has encountered many groups of people who King Jorash doesn't want mentioned. For fear of unnecessarily scaring the citizens, you understand. Pirates are one of those groups."

The boys' eyes all got big and they leaned in even closer to Galen.

"Tell us more about the pirates," Lian begged now.

"You've never seen them," whispered Galen, "because our coast has always been so well-guarded. But, boys, they do exist."

This statement infuriated Jamin. "When were we going to find out about this? *Pirates*?" Jamin almost shouted. His outburst got the attention of several boys finishing their breakfast. Galen motioned for Jamin to lower his voice.

"Sure, they might not attack Atlantis," Jamin went on, with control now, "but what about New Atlantis? I mean, we're good fighters, but there just aren't as many of us to fight off pirates as you have on Atlantis. And I'm in charge of the Navy! I need to know these things, Mr. Galen!" Jamin told the Overseer respectfully but firmly.

"That was going to be included later in your military training. Your Mentors just wanted you to master your basic military tactics before they taught you specialties. Pirates are a different breed. They don't follow any established military protocol. All they want is to steal fortunes by any means possible."

"So how do we fight them?" Billius asked, looking worried.

"Actually, they're not usually much of a problem, Billius," Galen assured. "They travel in small bands and stay drunk most of the time. Pirates shouldn't pose any real danger to a well-equipped military force, even a small one."

All the boys debated this point with Galen. Except Savot. He just listened pensively.

Wrapping up the discussion, the Overseer added, "So that bird was most likely one who made its way here somehow after our Navy sunk a pirate ship." This drew Savot's thoughts back to the bird.

"But, Galen, how come the bird speaks our language?"

Galen scratched his chin and thought. "It could be that one of our Navy ships acquired it on one of their missions. I don't really know, Savot."

Lian didn't seem to be listening now. "Wow! A pirate bird!" he exclaimed. "I hope it comes back."

Savot agreed. "So do I. I think it liked me."

***

Every day of every week on the peninsula was the same for the Chosen Children, except for weekly Rest Days and monthly Feast Days. From sunup to nightfall, every

Work Day the Children performed their duties under the supervision of their Mentors.

Area Heads in each occupation, one boy and one girl, led teams of Children. These two Area Heads in each field were engaged to each other.

Every Work Day, six days a week, from right after breakfast until early afternoon, the girls worked in the city or out in the fields. The boys stayed on their side of the peninsula, tending their gardens and having classroom lessons with their Mentors.

Then, after lunch, the boys and girls traded shifts. Eunuchs made sure all the girls had left the city, or field, before the boys came to work there for the rest of the day. Then supper. Then bedtime.

Little leisure time was allotted for the Children on Work Days. At night they played a few games in their quarters by candlelight but no energies went to obstaball or dancing. Most of the Children practiced their instruments during the evening hours. All Atlanteans had been trained since early childhood to play several musical instruments. Lutes were the most popular, followed by a bagpipe-sort of instrument, then other wind- and stringed-instruments. A person was considered more intelligent the more instruments he or she played. So the Children all played at least three each.

And then there was always storytelling. Atlantean fairy tales about mermaids and sea monsters were recited by firesides before bedtime. The girls could often be heard giggling and squealing in artificial fear over the sea-dwelling dinosaur that swallowed the Atlantean ship in one gulp.

But the oral legend of The Ghost appearing to King Jorash, commissioning the Chosen Children for the New Atlantis Project was by far the favorite story. Like most legends, it had changed a little over time.

The boys made a competition of who could do the best impersonation of the old Atlantean storyteller Choridan. Each consecutive retelling of The Ghost's visit made the Children sound more magnificent than the telling before.

King Jorash himself had written the original account of The Ghost's appearance fifteen—now nearly sixteen—years earlier, soon after the sacred encounter. Evran, the high priest, had attended the king as Atlantean law required. But Evran mysteriously died before he could report what The Ghost had said to Jorash. No one had ever investigated the priest's death; King Jorash had described Evran as having suffered a heart attack while they were still in the Temple. And no citizen had ever questioned the credibility of the king's account.

Of all the Children, only the young priests and priestesses had been required to memorize The Ghost's words exactly as Jorash had written them. And their Mentors had warned the priestly protégés sternly about the dire consequences of misquoting The Ghost. Whenever the other Children told an exaggerated version of the story in the presence of a Mentor—adding a sentence or changing The Ghost's wording—the Mentors and the clerics-in-training would just about pull out their hair in aggravation and then sharply reprove the storyteller.

On Rest Days the Children were allowed more time for fun. After morning worship in the makeshift Temple, the boys held obstaball practice games and the girls danced—on their own respective sides of the peninsula, of course. Soon a tradition developed. After the banquet at each Monthly Feast, the boys played a real game of obstaball and the girls presented a new dance they had created.

***

On Work Days Savot spent all his time with Galen except for the one week out of the month that King Jorash visited the peninsula. During that week each month all Jorash seemed concerned about was teaching Savot how to appear kingly. He focused on Savot's attire, how he carried himself, what he was to say and not say as king, and so forth.

Jorash, of course, didn't really care about teaching Savot how to be a successful king. And, though Savot tried to learn from his monarch, toward the end of the Year of Preparation he considered his weeks with Jorash mostly valueless. By contrast the young king sometimes wondered how he would ever function without Galen's wisdom.

Teran served Savot well as his secretary. He took meticulous notes for Savot and, most importantly, kept all he heard strictly confidential—quite unlike Antony. Galen advised Savot to keep Teran on as his secretary when they arrived at New Atlantis.

Aria relished her time with Sophea. The queen had stayed the entire first month with Aria on the peninsula. She left for three weeks during Month Two but Aria missed her so much that she had begged her father during the Month Two Feast to allow her mother to stay there the rest of the year. Jorash compromised and let his wife stay on the peninsula two out of every four weeks.

***

Pairs of eunuchs supervised each area of the society under the tutelage of their Mentors, who were King Jorash's own Palace Guard soldiers.

"This is such a joke," Win commented to Nat one Work Day as one of their Mentors gave orders to the palace staff. "*We're* the ones who are supposed to keep everybody in line once they leave us on New Atlantis."

"Yeah, so?" Nat retorted.

"Aw, c'mon, do you really think these kids are going to suddenly start obeying us like they do the adults? I mean Lian practically bows down to Sovius, but when I tell him to do something he has such a rotten attitude."

"Just watch me, Win," boasted Nat. "If you act like you've got authority—like you know what you're doing—they'll follow your orders. Lian treats *me* with respect. And have you noticed how scared Billius is of me?"

"No!" Win snapped.

"Well, he is. He knows I could beat him up if I wanted to. Even Lian knows it. They know we're tougher than them even if we are a little shorter." Nat spoke boldly as if trying to believe himself. "You have to be more intimidating, Win."

So Win tried. He even got a little obnoxious sometimes. The palace staff Children often rolled their eyes when they saw him coming. "Power sure has gone to his head," Stacia told Caris one morning after Win barked an order at them.

The two generals over all the military, Cain and Sensia, were engaged to marry each other but showed no attention to each other at the feasts, each for different reasons. Cain, of course, had no real plan to marry Sensia. And Sensia had never been that interested in boys. The biggest tomboy of all the girls, she seemed consumed with her military job.

Every Work Day Sensia ordered Dayra (the girls' Navy captain) and Lalera (the girls' Army captain) to impose increasingly strict workouts for the girls. The strenuous exercises of marching, fencing, drilling, wrestling, spearing, and climbing intensified as time went on.

At the end of each Work Day most of the military girls were so exhausted they could hardly stand. They all hated Sensia now. But the result of her seemingly sadistic regimen was that by the end of the year, when the Mentors called for fencing matches between military boys and girls, the girls won as often as the boys. Cain had been strict with the boys' training too but, ultimately, the military Mentors agreed that Sensia had worked the girls harder.

Amedis and Thea, fiancés also, studied to become the high priests in the Temple of the Unknown God. The eight other priests—four boys, four girls—received similar lessons. Their jobs included making weekly animal sacrifices on Rest Days and servicing the Temple and the holy utensils.

The priests and priestesses spent at least half of each day on their memory work. More than a thousand years' worth of messages from the Unknown God comprised a book about two inches thick. They also spent much time in foreign language study. The priests were also to be considered the experts in other tongues. They had already learned quite a bit of Greek, Hebrew, and other

Mediterranean languages from their fathers, who had also been priests, but they still had much to learn.

And one of the two high priests would also be required to attend King Savot if and when The Ghost ever appeared to him. That priest would need to record every word precisely as The Ghost spoke it. Amedis and Thea invented a speedy form of shorthand to make sure they'd be able to take down the messages accurately.

One afternoon in the half-completed Temple Thea and Aurora were helping each other review the latest message from The Ghost from memory. It was the one King Jorash had written down (but was not the true message). After an hour or so of quizzing each other, Thea put her book down.

"You know," she started hesitantly, "it's always bothered me that this is the only one of The Ghost's messages that was recorded by a king of Atlantis. All the others were written down by the attending high priest."

"But, Thea, we all know what happened," Aurora defended. "The Ghost just scared poor Evran to death—literally. I mean, he was really old, remember? King Jorash had no choice but to write the message down himself."

"Yeah, so I've heard." Thea looked uncertain. "But, for that very reason, I'm wondering whether Amedis and I shouldn't both plan to attend if The Ghost ever appears to Savot."

"Don't you think that's a bit too much, Thea? And besides, there's no way to tell when The Ghost is going to show up," Aurora argued.

Thea continued disregarding Aurora's thought, "Not that I don't trust King Jorash to tell the truth, but I wouldn't want Savot to ever be in a position like that. You know, I'd hate for any of the Children to think Savot made something up if he was the only one to hear The Ghost speak."

Thea was known to be ultra conservative in everything she did. Aurora finally convinced her that both she and Amedis were young and healthy—unlike the ancient and frail Evran—and the need for both of them to be present was completely unnecessary.

***

Parius and Bena headed up the judicial system for New Atlantis. While the priests labored over their memorizing and language study, the twelve lawyers did even more difficult brain work learning the vast body of Atlantean law.

They also conducted daily mock trials, experimenting with how Atlantean laws applied to everyday civil conflicts. At times, during the Year of Preparation, the lawyers were even called upon to conduct real trials regarding small violations.

The boys' medical Area Head, Calum, expressed concern over his job to his official fiancée Phaedra at the Month Five Feast.

"There are too few of us," he complained. "And we've only treated minor conditions like cuts and broken bones. What if somebody gets really sick? And, I don't know about you, but my only experience in delivering babies was helping the midwife when my little brother was born."

"I've never even *helped* with a childbirth!" Phaedra exclaimed. "You know, it doesn't really matter how much they teach us from books about the more serious conditions. We won't really learn it till we have to deal with it in real life."

Calum continued her thought. "I mean, what if somebody gets a really bad fever that won't break? So far our herbs have been able to cure most fevers, but I've heard of epidemics—even plagues—in other lands. Thank the Unknown God that's never happened on Atlantis."

"But what if it happens on New Atlantis?"

Callum's question went unanswered.

Phaedra, Calum, and the eight other doctors, raised by parents who were physicians, knew how to treat the sick and injured more than any of the other Children. But their apprehensions continued to mount as they approached the time when they would be the only medical resources in their future society.

Medo and Fara, the head architects, worked diligently on blueprints for the capital city of New Atlantis. The city's plans were based on drawings of its prototype—the capital city of Atlantis. The Children would build New Atlantis City twice, once on the peninsula and again on their islands. The blueprints for the original Atlantis City had to be scaled down substantially. The completely round capital city of Atlantis, inclusive of two moats surrounding it, was twenty miles in diameter, but their New Atlantis City would span only five miles due to the island's size and the smaller population.

Medo and Fara had only two fellow architects, Travus and Kezi, and the four worked closely with the six civil engineers, headed by Artur and Joesy—the Mentors working with the boys and girls separately. The architects' and engineers' Mentors were highly qualified and had supervised a reconstruction of Atlantis City some twenty years earlier after an earthquake. And the Children working in architecture and engineering had been trained all their lives 'on the job' by their parents. They made quick progress.

Jaran and Baylee, Area Heads for construction, led their thirty-six fellow builders in the actual assembly of the mock city. According to King Jorash's command, every building within the central part of the city—inside the innermost moat—was to be overlaid with gold—even the practice buildings on the peninsula. And the more luxurious the building, the more the construction Children vied to work on it. As a result, the job of building the actual palace was fought over the most.

Conversely, all of the construction workers dreaded the grueling labor of digging the circular moats around the city. It was finally decided that moat work should be rotated so that no one group got stuck with the unpleasant chore all the time. The female construction workers grew to be as physically strong as the military girls.

The farmers provided the backbone of the food supply system. Farmland lay in the more remote areas on the peninsula, reaching as far as nine miles beyond the city. Averil and Brisa oversaw eighteen other peers as they learned from their Mentors how to farm grain crops, root crops, and tend orchards and vineyards.

It occurred to Averil during Month Five, when autumn was coming on, that the climate probably would be different on New Atlantis.

"What if our crops won't grow on the northern islands?" he inquired. His Mentor had, of course, considered this. But he was at the disadvantage of never having visited the triple islands that would house New Atlantis and could only speculate.

"You could be right," the Mentor replied. "I was wondering when that possibility would occur to one of you. It may indeed be too cold there to grow these same fruits and vegetables, Averil. But that's why we're staying with you for six months. Arriving in early spring should give us the advantage of trying our seed through an entire growing season. You're right, we probably will have to make some adjustments."

That Mentor reported the head farmer's foresight to Galen. At the next feast, Averil received a special commendation, and he deserved it. Averil was a conscientious leader.

Fiancés worked together—through their Mentors—in like manner throughout the other occupations as well. Beldin and Lavena headed the smiths. Arden and Meli oversaw the millers. Adom and Vida led the carpenters. Pendil and Sunni, Area Heads for the fishers, knew their techniques well. They, however, spent most of their time making sure the boats and nets were operational so the others could do most of the actual fishing.

Durrill and Brina were the head merchants. Buying and selling in Atlantis involved the exchange of currency but also, at times, took the form of barter. Having gone to the marketplace daily with their parents, all ten of the merchants had already refined the arts of bartering and haggling. Everyone agreed the merchants had the easiest jobs.

The miners' task, on the contrary, was the filthiest. All the Children felt sorry for them. The Area Head for the boy miners, Ambros, devised a motivational contest utilizing his peers' competitive natures. After getting his Mentors' approval, Ambros announced his plan.

Whichever boy mined the greatest weight of orichalcum each day would get to be first in line for supper and could eat as much as he wanted. That usually meant that the winner was called a pig, but that didn't stop everyone else from competing to be the 'pig' the next day.

The girls were not as motivated by food. Lusi, the girl miners' Area Head and Ambros' intended, tried to maintain a positive attitude. But more complaints arose from the miner girls than from any other group of workers. Mining was even more exhausting than the labor of construction.

Following Ambros' incentive strategy, Lusi soon came up with a similar plan to reward her girls. After each weigh-in of orichalcum, the winning girl could refrain from digging the following day and serenade the other miners on her instrument of choice. The daily music seemed to offset the bitterness of the miners' jobs and all seemed to benefit. After that, singing was often heard coming from the mines during the girls' shifts there.

The months progressed swiftly and sooner than anyone could believe it was Month Eleven.

Chapter 8

A Shocking Report

"Look!" Billius whispered loudly into Savot's sleeping ear. Savot's eyes opened and squinted in the morning sunlight. He focused first on Billius, then on the object Billius was pointing to.

"It's back!" said Billius.

Savot slid out of bed and crawled slowly toward the large blue and red bird that again perched on his windowsill. "Don't fly away this time," he begged the bird.

"Fly away, fly away," squawked the bird. It fluttered its wings.

"No, I said 'don't fly away'," Savot clarified.

"Don't fly away," agreed the bird.

Lian growled as he rolled over in bed, rubbing his eyes. "What's going on?"

"The bird's back," answered Jamin softly, sitting up carefully in his bed. "Let's catch him this time." Jamin sneaked out of his bed silently and just as silently opened the front door and tiptoed out.

Lian sat still in bed, wide-eyed. "The pirate bird!" he whispered.

"Get that laundry basket," Savot ordered Billius, pointing to a basket in the corner that was as big around as two boys put together and almost as tall. Billius obeyed quietly.

"What's your name?" Savot asked.

"What's your name?" the bird asked Savot. Savot tried not to laugh.

"Savot. My name's Savot," answered the king as he stole carefully closer. The bird cocked its head and watched Savot approach.

"Memphis is a fine-lookin' birdie," said the bird.

"Memphis? Your name is Memphis?" Savot questioned.

"Memphis is *sooooo* handsome!" boasted the bird.

Just as Memphis revealed his name, Jamin sprang up behind him on the outside of the window and shooed the bird into the house. Billius rushed to clap the basket over Memphis in mid-flight. Wings still flapping and squealing like a screech owl, the bird was trapped under Billius' basket within seconds.

"We've got ourselves a pet!" Lian roared, jumping around the basket in a circle like a monkey. Memphis shrieked and fluttered under the basket until Savot felt sorry for the trapped creature.

"Maybe we should let him out," Jamin suggested.

Savot thought about it but then reconsidered. "No, I'll get a nice, big cage for him. I'd like to have a pet. I'll need someone to keep me company when all of you get married and leave me." He tried to laugh when he said this but wasn't successful.

That very morning Savot sent Billius to the farming boys and had him retrieve the largest chicken crate they had for Memphis to live in temporarily. He also commissioned the smiths to make a huge, golden cage for his bird.

And so it was that Memphis came to be Savot's pet.

***

Lalera still flirted with Savot even through the Month Eleven Feast. Savot gave her as little attention as possible. Jamin had pretty much given up on Lalera ever caring for him at all, much less loving him as much as he loved her.

He often cried on Savot's shoulder about his heartache, mostly figuratively but sometimes literally. Jamin didn't even understand why he felt so strongly toward Lalera. She not only flirted with Savot but with just about every other boy at the feasts.

At this last regular feast on the peninsula, Savot noticed a definite change in Aria. The princess let Savot see her glances at supper. And though she sat with her parents at the meal, she came to sit by him for the obstaball game, which was a first.

Aria's behavior so shocked Savot that he barely noticed everyone looking their way during the game. The princess laughed and joked with her fiancé as the couple watched the boys smack each other around the field.

This was how Savot wished Aria had behaved toward him all along! *Have all the flowers, gifts, and poems finally gotten through to her? Have her feelings toward Cain changed?* Savot wondered.

Aria stayed by Savot's side all evening. King Jorash, passing her at the dessert table commented privately, "Good show, Daughter! This will help the Children feel more secure about leaving Atlantis."

When Savot was caught momentarily in conversation, Cain took Aria aside and scolded her. "You don't have to overdo it, you know?" Aria just smiled and returned a wink to him and then joined Savot in a dance.

Before the princess parted from Savot that evening, she whispered to him, "I have something important to talk to you about at our next meeting." Then she held out her arms, inviting a hug from her fiancé. Savot, though confused, didn't dare pass up this opportunity. As he held her briefly, all he could think was, *Man! She feels good!*

"Good night, Savot," Aria said in the most heart-melting tone he'd ever heard. It took him the entire walk back to his quarters to focus on anything but the memory of her voice and the delicious embrace. But, finally . . . *something important?* What could she mean by that? Savot only half-slept all night, his thoughts floating back and forth from enchantment to trepidation.

***

Before their next weekly meeting, however, when she was to talk to Savot about the 'something important', Aria received an unexpected visitor. Antony—the newest farmer and ex-royal secretary—appeared at her door two mornings after the feast.

"Thank you for seeing me, Your Highness," Antony began, entering Aria's house and almost tripping over the corner of her rug. He fumbled to regain his composure and then continued. "You know I wouldn't request such a meeting with you unless it was an emergency." Antony now wrung his hands nervously.

"All right, Antony, what is it?" Aria humored him. No one ever took Antony seriously anymore.

"Well, I was working in the field yesterday," Antony said in his fast-paced manner, "and I got tired and laid down to rest—just for a minute. I guess I fell asleep 'cause the next thing I remember was hearing voices near me."

"You fell asleep on the job? Don't you know I could have you punished for that?"

Antony dropped his head, looking like a puppy that had torn up his master's shoe. But then he straightened up and fixed his eyes on Aria's. "Yes, Your Highness." Antony's voice took on a theatrical tone. "But I thought what I overheard was urgent enough to take the risk. Punish me if you must."

With concern now, Aria instructed in a lowered voice, "Go ahead, Antony, tell me what you heard." She checked the window to make sure no one was around to eavesdrop.

"They were walking through the field right past me, but I stayed on the ground. They didn't see me because the grass was so tall. They were talking—almost whispering—but after a few seconds I could tell it was Cain and Toren.

"Toren said, 'But what if, once we get there, she wants to marry Savot?' Do you know what he was talking about, Princess? Of course you're going to marry Savot. Or, maybe he wasn't talking about you. Does somebody else want to marry Savot?" Antony looked perplexed.

Aria stood as still as a statue. "Go ahead, Antony. What else did you hear?"

"Well then," Antony continued, apparently feeling encouraged by the princess' interest, "this is the part I *really* didn't understand. These were Cain's exact words." Antony spoke slowly and distinctly, "'Then she would have to share Savot's fate.' I don't know what that meant exactly, but it sure didn't sound good to me. Your Highness, do you think Cain could be planning to hurt Savot?"

Aria remained rigid, her gaze stuck to a spot on the floor. When she finally spoke, it was with a confident tone.

"I know that couldn't be the case. Cain has always been extremely loyal to Savot." Then she asked condescendingly, "Antony, are you sure that's precisely what you heard?"

"Well, y-yes," Antony stuttered. "I know those two voices when I hear them, and . . ."

Aria interrupted. "I'll do my own investigation into this. Thank you for coming to me, Antony." The informant looked bewildered.

"But, Your Highness . . ." Antony argued as Aria escorted him to her door.

"Have you told anyone else about this?" Aria inquired.

"Well no, but . . ."

"Good. Make sure you don't. But if you hear anything else that concerns you, please don't hesitate to come to me again," Aria instructed him. "Goodbye, Antony," she concluded and shut the door behind him.

Aria stood with her back pressed against the closed door until her knees became too weak to hold her up any longer. She slid to the floor. No one heard her next words, which she spoke in a feeble whisper, "He's planning to kill Savot. And me too if I change my mind."

***

King Jorash had decided he would stay on the peninsula the entire last month of the Children's training. Aria went to her father immediately with Antony's story.

"Oh, Aria, please. That's simply ridiculous!" Jorash laughed. "We all know you can't believe anything Antony says."

"But he risked punishment to tell me, Father. Shouldn't we be concerned?"

"Daughter, Antony will do just about anything for a little drama," Jorash assured. "Just think how bored such a busybody must be out working in the fields all day, mostly alone, no one to gossip with!" Jorash chuckled again, and this time Aria echoed his laughter a little. The king studied his daughter carefully.

"Besides, I have the utmost confidence in Cain's integrity. Antony was just making that story up to get attention," Jorash assured Aria. "The best way to handle it is simply to ignore him."

She nodded, and then giggled. "Oh, that reminds me of the time he made up the tale about fighting a lioness when he'd really scratched up his face by stumbling into a bramble bush!"

"Yes, my dear. You see, that's just the way Antony is." Jorash laughed with his daughter. Then the king became serious. "Aria, you do know how much Cain loves you." She nodded. "The very thought that he would ever hurt you is utterly preposterous."

Aria nodded again, more assuredly this time.

"So you have no need to worry," Jorash comforted. "I promise you, Aria, neither you nor Savot will ever be harmed. All you need to be concerned about is sticking to our plan and everything will be all right. For you, for Savot, and for New Atlantis." Aria's father spoke with finality. Then, as though in afterthought, Jorash added, "Let's not even mention this to Cain, all right? It would just hurt him to know someone was trying to spread such vile rumors about him." Aria agreed. "You did tell Antony to keep his story to himself, didn't you?" asked the king.

"Yes, I did."

The conversation ended abruptly when the queen entered Jorash's private quarters. After a brief conversation among the three of them about something else entirely, Jorash excused himself from his wife and daughter and went to find Cain.

"I think I've convinced her there was nothing to Antony's story," the king told Cain. The young insurgent's brow wrinkled, and he fidgeted in his chair.

"In the future, Cain, you must make absolutely sure no one is anywhere close to you when you discuss the takeover with Toren," Jorash admonished Cain.

Cain took the reproof staunchly. "I will, Sir. I promise."

With a huff, as if shaking off the whole mistake Cain had made, King Jorash went on to a related subject. "We'll both watch her closely during our next meeting. Women aren't good at hiding what they're feeling," said the king.

"And what if she acts like her loyalties aren't with us anymore?" Cain wanted a solution.

"Then we'd have to make a drastic change to our plan. If we feel she can't be trusted, I could arrange for her to stay on Atlantis. My wife is already mourning about Aria leaving her. People would understand that."

"But not having the princess on New Atlantis? That would be strange. Are you sure everyone would accept that?" Cain asked.

"They would if I ruled it so!" declared Jorash harshly. "But we don't have to make that decision until after our next meeting with her." Then he added with a cocky grin, "Cain, have you ever known of any situation in which I didn't hold absolute sway over my people?" Cain agreed that this was Jorash's history.

Aria couldn't sleep at all that night. And the next day her regular meeting with Savot had to be cancelled. New Atlantis' first fatality had occurred.

***

The farmers had found Antony's body during the night in the field where he worked. He hadn't come in for supper the evening before, and three boys had been sent back out to look for him. To their horror, they discovered the inexperienced farmer had apparently fallen on the large plow blade he had been working with earlier that day.

King Jorash summoned Savot and several of the Mentors to an early morning meeting.

"This is a dismal day in the history of New Atlantis," King Jorash began, his head hanging remorsefully. "The first death among the Chosen Children. It was bound to happen sooner or later. I regret that it has happened this soon." He stood silent a moment, allowing for appropriate sorrow. "Perhaps it's better in a way, though, for this to have happened while the Children still have adults around to comfort them."

Savot summoned all his courage to ask the question that he was astonished no one else had thought of. "Your Majesty, are we sure Antony's death was an accident?"

Jorash eyed Savot with an intimidating glare. He fired back at the fifteen-year-old king. "Of course it was an accident. Antony was a novice farmer. I could question your judgment, Savot, in having him assigned to work with dangerous equipment with which he was unfamiliar."

A thorny silence froze the meeting as a face-off appeared possible between the two kings. Galen spoke up, breaking the tension,

"This is a terrible tragedy, Savot, there's no doubt about that. But it does seem prudent at this point to conduct Antony's funeral with as much dignity and as little controversy as possible. For the sake of the Children. It's best for them to stay focused as much as they can on their work."

Savot's head dropped in resignation. *If Galen won't even support an investigation,* he reasoned, *I guess I'm just outnumbered here.*

"And our visitors will be coming in less than two weeks," one of the other Mentors reminded. "If we're going to be ready, there's a lot more work to be done." Family members and government officials were scheduled to arrive in ten days for a brief reunion and a presentation of the completed city. Though he felt quite defeated, Savot deferred to the judgment of his elders. He didn't mention the matter of an investigation again.

Antony's family was contacted immediately and came within two days to the peninsula for the funeral. King Jorash generously consoled the grieving parents. And Savot tried to show the sincere sympathy he felt for them. But he found himself distracted by broader and even more disturbing thoughts.

My people are going to be dying, he kept thinking. *From accidents like this, from disease, from . . . who knows what else?* It's not that he had never thought of death among the New Atlanteans before, but Antony's death forced the somber reality of the fact on Savot sooner than he expected. And it set him to wondering how he would handle such situations when he, not King Jorash, would have to be the one to set the tone for each funeral. Savot had Teran make a note to have the priests to create a generic funeral service to be used on New Atlantis. But later. They shouldn't have to think about the details of that right now.

All the Chosen Children attended the memorial service. Meril, Antony's fiancée, appeared to be in a state of pure shock. She didn't even cry but sat gazing at Antony's coffin the entire funeral, trembling. When Meril had learned of her fiancé's death, she had gone into a full-blown panic, wailing to her roommates that she'd be the only single girl on New Atlantis now. Not that she had been in love with Antony, but as her roommates knew, he had represented security to Meril.

After the funeral, Antony's parents requested that they be allowed to take their son's body back with them to Atlantis City and bury him in their family cemetery. King Jorash gave permission and the family left right away. The elder king then commanded the grief-stricken Children to rest for the remainder of the day.

***

Though delayed by three days, Aria and Savot did finally have their last private meeting on the peninsula. Savot wondered how Antony's death had affected Aria. He was still curious, too, about the 'important' subject she had wanted to discuss with him.

Entering her quarters, accompanied as usual by Nat and Win, Savot immediately turned to his two eunuch escorts. "Guys, give us a minute. Okay?"

They argued dutifully—again—but at length left the two alone for the second time. Savot felt his heart skip a beat as he stood opposite Aria, remembering her hug and tender words to him just a few nights before. Neither Savot nor Aria sat but remained standing facing each other at a distance.

"Hi," Savot ventured, hoping for the warmth he'd received from her at the feast.

"Hi," Aria answered faintly, not letting her eyes meet his. Feeling the same old frustration rise inside of him, Savot got straight to the point.

"You wanted to talk to me about something important?" Savot asked.

Aria's forehead ruffled. She seemed at a loss for words. Finally she said, "Well . . . it's just that I'm concerned about . . . umm . . ." *Is she afraid to tell me what it is?* Savot wondered as he watched her awkwardly hesitating. Aria smiled nervously, looking out of the window. "With all that's been going on, I guess I forgot what I needed to talk to you about."

Savot struggled to identify her mood. It wasn't friendly like it had been at the feast. But neither was it cold as it had been all year. Studying her countenance carefully, Savot thought, *Maybe this is the sadness Galen was talking about.* But no, she wasn't sad. Savot could tell her mood was more one of anxiety. He also felt she was trying to communicate something to him nonverbally. Something was definitely wrong. He asked her about it.

Aria answered with an unexpected and abrupt stare, the first eye-to-eye contact she'd given Savot during this encounter. And the stare was intense.

"No, I'm fine," she replied. But her eyes definitely betrayed her words. She held his gaze longer than she had even at the feast, as if anticipating something. Her breathing was shallow.

"Is it that you're upset about Antony?" Savot guessed.

This question seemed to ignite an idea in Aria. "Yes," she replied hastily, turning away from Savot and pacing quickly around the room. "That's it. Oh, Savot, Antony's dead!" Savot got the clear impression that she was acting.

"Yeah. I'm really shocked about it," Savot commiserated. "But a death among us was bound to happen sooner or later. Your father reminded me of that right after it happened."

"My father?" Aria stood still and turned to look Savot in the eye again. Her interest had apparently piqued. "What did my father say?" She watched Savot intently, waiting for his next words.

"When we met—the Mentors, your father, and me—he said maybe it was better that our first loss happened while we were still on Atlantis, while there were adults to comfort us . . ." Savot was going to continue but Aria impatiently broke in.

"Galen told me you wanted an investigation." Aria rushed her words, pacing again. She shot message-filled glances at Savot.

"Yes, I did," Savot admitted, feeling his own cowardice at not pressing harder for the examination. "But all the adults thought it was unnecessary. It probably *was* just an accident."

Aria stepped nearer to Savot—uncomfortably nearer. She stared more intently than ever into his purple eyes. He could almost see rapid thoughts passing through her mind. She seemed to be begging him to say more. But he couldn't think of anything else to say in his defense. *If I'd been totally in charge, I'd have insisted,* he thought, beating himself up inside.

After a few unbearably anxious moments, Aria forcefully let out the breath she'd been holding in. She walked to the window with an icy countenance. Savot was totally baffled by Aria's peculiar behavior.

Before he could think of what to say the princess had marched to the door, opened it, and callously announced, "I believe our meeting is over, Savot." Now it was clear to Savot that Aria was angry.

Nat and his brother, who'd been trying to listen through the keyhole, stumbled backward and traded puzzled looks as the door flung open. Even the eunuchs apparently recognized the extreme shift in Aria's mood since Savot had first entered the house. Taking the unmistakable hint, Savot walked toward the door.

"Well, I guess I'll see you at the feast," was all Savot could think to say.

Aria only glared at her husband-to-be as he passed her on his way out of her house.

Savot was perplexed and drained. He could have stayed and pressed her for an explanation but he was tired. Very tired. So he said goodbye and left.

***

The mock-up of New Atlantis City was completed by the next week. It was right on time, even though the Chosen had had to work extra long days making up for the time they'd lost with Antony's funeral.

The city was stunning. It sparkled in the sunlight like a multifaceted diamond. Silver, orichalcum, and gold overlaid every building in the central part of the city and adorned most buildings on the concentric islands surrounding the palace.

Luxurious tapestries donned the pavilions that surrounded the feasting area outside of the palace. Both Mentors and Children had now turned their attention to setting up tents for the coming visitors—their families and the officials of Atlantis.

The day before the visitors arrived, the Chosen Children packed all their belongings tightly into trunks to be shipped with them to New Atlantis. In just a little over a week they would set sail. Hidden among the clothing items in almost every Child's luggage was nestled a tattered blanket or a well-loved doll or toy.

Aria took her precious figurine out of its cabinet. She held it to her chest and closed her eyes. A tear slipped down her cheek as she wrapped the crystal treasure in several layers of soft cloth and then settled it carefully in its sturdy wooden box

Chapter 9

Goodbye to Atlantis

The night before the visitors arrived at the peninsula, the last and most critical midnight meeting between Jorash, Cain, Toren, and Aria took place. And, as they had discussed, after that meeting Jorash and Cain would determine whether Aria went on to New Atlantis or stayed on the continent with her parents.

Both Cain and Jorash scrutinized Aria's every move. They listened judiciously to the undertones in her voice. Had Jorash convinced her to disregard Antony's story? Was she demonstrating continued commitment to their plot against Savot? No one mentioned Antony.

The four conspirators reviewed the insurrection plan yet again. Had solid friendships been built with the Area Heads so they would easily accept Cain as their new leader? Check. Were Cain, Aria, and Toren all agreed about the timetable of events? Check. Had plans for the appearances of the mysterious ships been arranged? Check.

Jorash peered at Aria when the topic of Savot's kidnapping was discussed.

When the princess showed no signs of reluctance about any element of the conspiracy, the king and Cain exchanged coded glances that said, 'she's still with us'. Aria went on to review exactly how she would pretend great fretfulness when the 'pirate' ships appeared on the horizon seven months into the Year of Construction—after all the adults will have left.

The appearance of the inexplicable ships would become common knowledge on New Atlantis and they would be investigated for the following four months. This would be Cain's job as general of all the military.

Aria would express convincing shock and grief, she said, at Savot's disappearance during Month Ten on New Atlantis. And she would dispatch ships immediately to find him. She would order a thorough search of the three islands. Then, when Savot could not be found, Aria would conclude that pirates had abducted and probably killed him.

After some time for her to mourn, she would become concerned (after a week or so) that 'the government must be stabilized'. Next, she would follow Atlantean protocol and name Savot's second-in-command as the new king. That would put them close to the Month Ten Feast and two months before the beginning of the Year of Merger. And Aria would be the first of the Chosen girls to be married . . . to the new king, Cain.

At the end of the meeting, Princess Aria volunteered a final pledge to Jorash, Cain, and Toren.

"None of you need worry about my part in this," Aria stated as resolutely as she'd ever spoken. "I know this is the only way New Atlantis can thrive. I know it's what you want, Father. And fulfilling your wishes for New Atlantis is my primary goal."

Then she spoke directly to Cain, "And, just in case you ever wondered, I only want to marry you, Cain. That's extra motivation for me!" She giggled when she spoke these words but then her face changed to a bitter look. "The thought of marrying Savot makes me sick."

That was all Cain and Jorash needed to hear. The two agreed after the meeting that they were safe to proceed with the plan as it stood—with Aria fully included.

***

The Children's families and a host of Atlantean officials and other citizens arrived the first day of the last week on the peninsula. A week-long feast followed, the most elaborate one ever, celebrating the end of the Year of Preparation.

King Jorash had created a celebratory atmosphere for the first full day with the visitors—music, dancing, and many other festivities—so that only a few passing references were made to Antony's death. The day after that, the visitors toured the newly built government buildings, farms, homes, marketplaces, the Temple and, of course, the palace.

All the visitors, especially the proud parents, were amazed at what this group of 268 young people had been able to accomplish in only one year. The citizens who would inhabit the model city thereafter as an Atlantean outpost marveled as well. King Jorash planned to use the peninsula as a vacation spot for himself after the Chosen Children's departure.

Savot hadn't seen his parents in a year, and he had many times longed to see them. But when he did, to his surprise, he felt awkward in their presence. His mother and father seemed almost like pleasant strangers to Savot. After a few hours with his family, Savot realized what was making him feel uncomfortable. Over the past year New Atlantis had become his whole world. And his parents, dear as they were to him, were outsiders to that world. This was a strange and unexpected feeling for the now-fifteen-year-old Savot.

However, as the last week on the peninsula progressed, New Atlantis' king began to feel his attachment to his parents return.

"I think it was wise of King Jorash to make our time together brief," his father said on the last day, seeming to read Savot's thoughts.

Aria stayed closer than ever to her mother that week. After all, Sophea had not only served as her daughter's Mentor during the Year of Preparation but—in a less formal way—she had been Aria's mentor her entire life.

Aria's separation from her mother would be equal in some ways to the other children's absence from their parents. But there was also a big difference. Aria would be the only Child without her mentor for the first six months on New Atlantis.

Savot saw Aria several times that week and each time he could tell that the girl he loved had been crying. She still didn't speak to him unless she had to. And he noticed a new coldness in her sad eyes.

***

The last day of the week, the day before the Children were to leave the peninsula, King Jorash, Galen, and Savot gave speeches. Jorash's speech was politically correct in nature as always. He praised the Children. He praised Savot and Aria. And he exalted the purpose of the New Atlantis mission.

Galen, in his jovial style, presented a true and glowing report about the Chosen Children—the maturity he had seen develop in all of them over the course of the year and the superb nature of their finished work. Extending his speech longer than the allotted time, the Overseer went on and on about what a fabulous group of youngsters they were and said he'd concluded they were quite possibly all geniuses. The parents loved that part, and their children sparkled at the compliment.

Savot's speech was predictable too, sounding much like his other speeches. Of course that would be the case, because the speech had been written by King Jorash as had all Savot's orations. Though his spirits were low in general, at least Savot had gotten over his stage fright and felt more at ease addressing his peers. He sounded confident even though he still wasn't.

***

Very early the next morning, their possessions loaded on the same wagons that had brought them a year earlier, the Chosen Children left the peninsula. Parents and Children rode together in carriages. Only the citizens slated to inhabit the peninsula stayed to move their own possessions into the abandoned houses and to make plans for their future in the remote colony.

The day-long journey allowed the reunited families to catch up on the main events of the past year. The Children especially wanted to brag about their new skills. Without exception, however, the Children's conversation kept drifting toward their future on New Atlantis.

Cain and Aria—in accordance with the insurrection plot— had buddied up to the Area Heads. And Cain had cleverly planted ever-so-subtle seeds of doubt in the minds of the

Area Head boys about Savot's fitness as king. Those reservations had spread to many others as well. A few Children expressed their insecurity about Savot's leadership to their parents on their trip back to Atlantis City.

Savot's natural opponents—Shay, Toren, Dolius, and Marcum—held back nothing. They told their families how weak and indecisive Savot was. How he had tried to sound like King Jorash all year in his speeches. All the Children knew that Jorash had written Savot's speeches for him.

"Can't he speak for himself? How is he ever going to make any big decisions for New Atlantis if he can't even write his own speeches?" Toren asked his father. Of course, with Toren knowing all about the insurrection now, his expressed concern wasn't real. He was just talking to be talking.

But deep concern showed on his father's face. "Son, don't you see anything good at all about Savot?" Toren's father inquired.

"No, nothing! He doesn't have any backbone! I don't see how he's going to rule us." After that Toren's entire family lapsed into an uneasy silence.

***

Twenty-four large schooners awaited the Children when they arrived in Atlantis City. After a brief night's sleep in their old quarters near the palace, the fifteen-year-olds dressed and gathered their overnight belongings to be loaded onto the ships. King Jorash conducted a commissioning ceremony for the New Atlantis Project shortly after dawn.

The eastern sky broke red and storm clouds threatened the northern horizon. With this being noticed by all, King Jorash delivered his speech as concisely as possible and quickly concluded the service. Then only a few minutes were permitted for the Chosen Children to say permanent goodbyes to their families.

Some of the Children were able to keep their composure, mainly the military Children who had been psychologically trained to be stoic. But most wept and clung to their family members. Parius and Kelen, the other set of twins beside Nat and Win, had to be torn from their parents' arms to board their ships.

Observing the families' agony at the separation distressed some of the Mentors.

"I thought we had prepared all of them for this," one commented to Galen.

Galen answered, "We did all we could. No matter what, this hour was bound to be bitter. Remember they are still children." The last of the Children had just reached her fifteenth birthday, and it was evident that most of them felt unprepared for real adulthood.

Savot felt the oddest mixture of emotions he'd ever experienced. His parents couldn't stop weeping despite their bravest efforts. Knowing he would probably never see them again, Savot joined them in expressing their sadness. He cried as much as any of his peers.

But strangely, at the very same time, his heart raced with exhilaration over the monumental venture he was embarking on today. Both his parents gave him mementos and, after a long final embrace, Savot boarded the lead ship.

Aria trembled with weakness as she embraced her mother for the last time. Tears poured like rivers down the young princess' cheeks. The queen nestled her face in her daughter's long, soft hair as she too wept profusely.

When Aria finally composed herself enough to speak she said, "You can be proud of me already, Mother. You can be assured I will strive to be as good a queen as you have always been," she pledged.

Jorash then wrenched Aria from Sophea's arms. He forced her arm through the crook of his own and made her walk with him to her ship, instructing her not to look back. Escorting Aria onto the third schooner, King Jorash spoke in code to her about her future reign with Cain. He said nothing about his own separation from her. Then, while he was in the middle of a sentence, Aria interrupted him.

"Will you miss me at all, Father?"

The question apparently took Jorash by surprise. He stammered a bit. "Well, of course, Aria. You are my only child . . ." Aria flung herself on her father in a clutching embrace, sobbing shamelessly.

Then she whispered, "I will miss you, Father. I hope I'll see you again. But if not, I want you to know that I *will* be the queen you've always wanted for New Atlantis."

Then, fixing her soft golden eyes on her father, Aria vowed slowly—every word deliberate, "I will not let you down." With that the future queen of New Atlantis let go of King Jorash and turned to enter the hold with one of the Mentors. After that she saw neither of her parents again.

Trumpets sounded and round flags of blue, green, and yellow flew at the dock as the twenty-four, fully loaded ships embarked from their mother continent. The Children stood at the sterns and waved 'goodbye' to the families they never expected to see again. There were many tears and wailings as the ships sailed farther and farther away from Atlantis. Aria stayed below so she wouldn't have to see her parents disappear from sight.

That night most of the Children retrieved their cuddle blankets and ragamuffin dolls from their trunks. Though their Mentors tried to comfort them, the CHildren suffered a weepy bedtime in every ship.

***

The voyage would consume the first full month of the Year of Construction, actually adding a month to it. With strong east winds blowing across the Atlantic at the end of that winter, the 267 Children and their 100 Mentors braced themselves for a rough crossing.

During the month-long voyage the girls occupied eight ships and the boys another eight. A few Navy Mentors supervised each vessel. But most of the adults traveled together on two large ships at the head of the convoy. Building materials and extra supplies filled the other six vessels. When the seas got rough, the twenty-four ships had to slow down to stay within sight of one another.

Savot journeyed with the Mentors in the lead ship. His roommates and best friends, Jamin, Lian, and Billius, accompanied him. Teran, his secretary, also traveled with him to write down the many new ideas Savot generated each day for New Atlantis.

Savot had also insisted that Amedis travel with him on the lead ship, and for a specific reason. He wanted the priest to pray with him. Amedis had been surprised at Savot's request for joint prayer every morning during the voyage, but he was also pleased that the new king took prayer seriously.

The high priest told Savot, "It's really encouraging to have a king who's so interested in religious things." Eveyone knew King Jorash never had been.

Savot explained, "It's not just interest. I mean, not just in an intellectual sense. This is very practical. To be completely honest with you, Amedis," Savot confided, "I don't know how we're going to do by ourselves once the Mentors leave us. I really need guidance and strength from the Unknown God." So Savot and Amedis prayed every morning of the journey for Savot to have divine wisdom during his reign.

Memphis also traveled with Savot in his deluxe cage. The bird had practically learned to carry on conversations by now. When the seas were particularly choppy, Memphis had learned to say, "Oh man, am I ever seasick!" and "I'm about to lose my lunch," which were common phrases of Lian's.

And, also imitating Lian, Memphis learned to make repulsive gagging and vomiting sounds that he used at the most random times, usually making the boys cackle, or the really seasick ones to go ahead and throw up. The bird himself, though, never seemed to actually mind the movements of the ship. And Savot began letting him out of his cage from time to time when he knew the door to his cabin was locked for the night. Memphis loved to sit on Savot's shoulder and chatter.

With the Mentors totally available to Savot and his four peers for that month, Savot instructed his friends to take

full advantage of the time to learn all they could from
their elders.

"Guys, these adults are a goldmine of knowledge! Ask
them any questions you can think of." Savot especially
relished his long conversations with Galen, ranging in
subject from battle strategies to theology to the ongoing
figuring-out-women topic.

***

Aria grieved for many days after leaving Atlantis. But
when she finally re-entered social life with the girls on her
ship, she began showing her lighter side again.

"Now, this is the old Aria," Caris told Stacia. "I'd almost
forgotten how funny she is!"

The young princess was an expert when it came to
making faces. Her face seemed to be made of rubber.
She could contort it in just about any imaginable way.
And she loved to impersonate the various Mentors, especially the quirky ones. Aria laughed so contagiously
that others laughed too, even when they didn't know
what was funny.

For that one month at sea, Aria seemed to have found
a reprieve from the pressures of her rank. But what the
other girls didn't know was that almost every night the
princess silently cried herself to sleep.

King Jorash had arranged for Aria to travel with the girls'
Area Heads and Cain with the boys' so that they could
keep building alliances for the takeover. Cain wasted no
opportunity in developing an even deeper camaraderie
between himself and the boys' leaders. Wanting to remind
them as well that he was second-in-command, the general exercised his authority subtly but often. Still he confided only in Toren about the plan to overthrow Savot.

***

The voyage served the purpose of further education as
well as transportation for two groups in particular: the
sailors and the eunuchs.

Five Navy Children managed each schooner under the supervision of two Navy Mentors per ship. Their Mentors had taken the sailors out on similar ships during the Year of Preparation but the waters around the peninsula had been much calmer than here in the open Atlantic.

Though this intimidated the young sailors—both girls and boys—the rough ocean proved the best training ground yet for the New Atlantean Navy. The girl sailors decided after a few days to shorten their ankle-length pants and their long skirts.

"These skirts are so much easier to work in being shorter," Dayra told Narsis. "We should just forget ever trying to work in long skirts."

Narsis agreed. "I bet we're the first girls in the world to ever sail ships! And I guess we've just invented a new uniform too!"

The voyage also provided the eunuchs with their first real experience overseeing their peers. With only two Navy Mentors on each ship, the eunuchs—dispersed among the vessels—had to assume much more supervision of the Children.

With boys and girls on separate ships, the eunuchs' jobs were easier than they would be once on New Atlantis. Here they didn't have the mixing of boys and girls to deal with. Most of the eunuchs performed their roles exceptionally and their peers obeyed them. But the Children would probably never respect a few of the eunuchs, like Eton and Rik, because these two constantly behaved so impishly. The Mentors' decision to put both of these eunuchs on the same ship, the lead one, had probably been a mistake.

By the end of the first week the boys—led by Lian— had already played several pranks on Eton and Rik. The two victims retaliated generously in response to the boys' pranks.

When the occupants of the lead ship surprised Rik with a cupful of oatmeal in his shoe one morning, Rik and Eton emptied buckets of shellfish slime into all four boys' beds the following night and covered it over with their blankets. The quarters had to be aired out for days afterward and Savot, Billius, Jamin, Lian, and Teran had to sleep on deck.

And the two eunuchs' misbehavior wasn't limited to their peers. Once, early in the voyage, one of the two Navy Mentors on their ship also got a taste of their mischief. Eton and Rik had stolen into the Mentor's cabin while he was sound asleep. The eunuchs carefully painted the palms of the sleeping man's hands with thick green paint and then tickled his nose with a feather.

That Mentor awoke the next morning with a green face and green-smeared bedclothes. Lucky for Rik and Eton this was a good-natured Mentor and they were not punished, just rebuked. The worst part of that escapade was that, since all Atlantean paints were permanent, it took the Mentor practically the entire month-long voyage scrubbing his skin with sea salt before the green paint was all gone.

The two pranksters got more than paid back though. The boys captured and threw Eton and Rik overboard every time they anchored, each time yelling, 'SHARK!' And each time Eton and Rik squealed and thrashed, begging to be rescued. Everyone on the first ship agreed that some people must be created sheerly for entertainment.

Chapter 10

New Atlantis, At Last!

One stormy day at sea, two weeks into the journey, monstrous waves bumped some of the cargo overboard. Bundles of valuable cut lumber were lost, as were a good deal of the remaining foodstuffs. Rationing had to be imposed.

During that storm so many got seasick that all the passengers needed baths afterwards. Savot was the last on his ship to actually vomit. But even this storm did not bother Memphis. Not in the least. He just imitated the gagging sounds Lian had taught him and then talked about how pretty he was. He lightened the mood for the sick boys, making them laugh.

The Mentors had given the boys permission not to shave for the entire month-long voyage. Atlantean men kept themselves clean-shaven as a rule. But the boys had never had a chance to see how much facial hair they could grow. So Cain had proposed the beard-growing contest for the voyage. He knew he could grow a much thicker beard than Savot, so he had told King Jorash this would give him more clout among the boys—and girls as well.

After all the throwing up, though, the boys regretted having grown any form of beard. It made the experience all the more smelly and messy and gave them more to clean up.

The method of bathing while at sea was for the Children to take turns climbing down a rope ladder into the ocean and soaping up when the ships anchored for brief periods. Bath times on the voyage normally came only once a week, but the Mentors made an exception in this case. Accustomed to bathing daily back on Atlantis, the sparse hygiene schedule thoroughly disgusted most of the girls. They were glad the boys couldn't see them with 'such nasty, greasy hair'.

The third week on bath day, a shark was spotted on the horizon. Only a few of the boys—and one girl, Sensia—ventured into the water that day to bathe. Fortunately the shark attacked no one. Sensia taunted all the girls on her ship after that, calling them 'big babies'. Later her Mentor reprimanded the girls' general for her unwise daring.

At last, one morning late in the fourth week, the sailors on Savot's lead ship caught their first glimpse of the islands. Yellow flags were raised, signaling the sighting of New Atlantis. Elation erupted on all twenty-four schooners. But the strong winds speeding them toward their destination soon accelerated into another massive storm.

The sailors quickly lowered all flags and sails. This turned out to be the worst squall the company had faced the entire month. Lightning hit the mast of the last ship. Hail knocked one sailor completely unconscious and left most of the Navy Children bruised. The other passengers hid below deck, exercising every trick the Mentors had taught them to fight seasickness. By mid-afternoon the storm had cleared, but everyone and everything on all the ships was thoroughly soaked.

Regaining sight of the islands in the distance, Savot commanded the sailors on his ship to raise their sails again. The other ships followed suit and within a couple of hours all twenty-four ships came ashore on the largest island of New Atlantis. The Chosen Children had finally reached their new home.

The sailors dropped anchors and secured the landings of each ship. Gangplanks were lowered into the shallow water. Military personnel—the first Children to disembark—took a large Atlantean flag on a pole and planted it firmly in the wet sand.

The rest of the Children then clambered down the planks, competing to beat each other in setting foot on New Atlantean soil. Even though they all looked and felt like drowned cats, the Children shared their first moments of wonder surveying the beach together.

Then, spontaneously, all began celebrating. Cheering, running, jumping, and hugging went on for quite a while. The watching Mentors chuckled through their own tiredness. Here they were at last on New Atlantis, having survived the long voyage and several frightening storms. Savot watched from his ship as his subjects reveled in the moment.

Aria and Stacia had remained on their ship as well. "It's so cold here," Aria complained to Stacia, both girls standing at the ship's bow. The princess' responsibilities seemed to have robbed Aria of her natural jollity once more.

"Here, put on your shawl, Your Highness." Stacia handed Aria a wrap. "Don't you want to go down and join the party?"

"Not just yet," Aria answered. She turned her gaze toward the lead ship, fixing her eyes on Savot who stood at his ship's helm watching the Children play on the beach. It was the first time she had seen him clearly in a month. He had grown a nice beard.

"He looks taller, doesn't he?" Stacia asked when she noticed Aria watching Savot.

"No," stated Aria frigidly. "Just as short as ever." But she didn't take her eyes off of him. Stacia remained quiet.

Once everyone had disembarked the ships, the soldiers started a giant bonfire to dry and warm the wet company. Farmers opened barrels of food and passed out supper. Savot went over to where Aria hunched beside the bonfire and greeted her awkwardly. She greeted him back awkwardly. Not wanting to extend the uneasiness, Savot went to find Galen.

After everyone had eaten, Galen climbed up on one of the empty barrels and addressed the assembly.

"Welcome to New Atlantis!" Galen boomed. The Children burst into applause and cheers. "Congratulations to all of us! We made it!" exclaimed Galen, grinning wearily but contentedly. "And you all know what comes next." The Overseer got down off his barrel and nodded toward

Savot which meant it was his turn to speak. Savot stood up on the barrel.

"I don't really have a speech prepared," Savot began. Galen looked at him questioningly. "But first, I would like to say 'thank-you' to the New Atlantean Navy for getting us all here safely."

Everyone clapped for the sailor boys and girls who took multiple bows. Savot thought he should say something significant now but didn't know what. Then the obvious—the practical—occurred to him. He should just instruct his peers what to do next.

He asked Galen in an aside to make sure he didn't forget anything. This took his Mentor off guard, but Galen grabbed another barrel, scrambled back up on it, and aided Savot—tag-team fashion—in delivering directions for that night and the next day. Savot noticed that Aria's eyes were glued on him the entire time he spoke. *What is she thinking?* passed through his mind momentarily, but he had to keep his focus on instructing his citizens.

The Children began to yawn and slump by the time Savot and Galen finished giving the directions. Everyone gathered necessary items from their ships for the night and claimed preconstructed quarters with their same peninsula roommates.

And, just as on the peninsula, boys' houses had already been built on one side of the island and girls' on the other. Again, Mentors and eunuchs were in between. Within a half-hour the entire island went silent except for the sounds of native night creatures.

Before Galen retired he questioned Savot, "Didn't you have a speech King Jorash had written for you to give tonight?"

"It just didn't seem to fit the occasion," was all Savot answered. Then, without waiting for a response, he bid Galen goodnight. Once inside his house, Savot reached into his duffle bag and pulled out the speech Jorash had written for him. He held it pensively in his hand for a moment. Realizing King Jorash's permanent absence, Savot became aware that his sense of duty in delivering the prefabricated speeches had faded.

He walked outside to where the bonfire had burned most of the day but had now died down to embers. The king of New Atlantis placed the papers written by King Jorash on top of the smoldering coals and watched until they turned to ashes.

***

Cain didn't waste any time preparing for his takeover. The second evening on New Atlantis, he met secretly with Aria in a heavily wooded grove. Initially, his girlfriend seemed standoffish. Cain looked quite different, but still handsome, with a full beard. He was quick to turn on all the charm he had ever learned.

He told Aria how much he had missed her during the month-long voyage. He wrapped his arms around her and kissed her tenderly. His moustache tickled her and she giggled. But Cain soon moved past the romance to the subject that was most important to him.

"We have six months until the adults leave us, Aria," Cain began. "How do you feel about that?" Some of the boys had taught Cain to always ask about girls' feelings.

"Fine. I feel fine about it. That's always been the plan," Aria answered matter-of-factly.

"We'll be so much better off when they leave," Cain added. "You and I will hold much more sway over our people then. And, once they're gone, it'll only be four more months 'till Savot's gone. Then two months later we can be married!"

At this comment, Cain slid his arm around Aria's waist from the side and tried to kiss her again. She shivered and moved away from him quickly.

"What's wrong, Aria?"

"It's just . . . we haven't seen each other in so long," the princess responded.

"You do still want to marry me, don't you?"

Aria answered quickly and indignantly. "Of course I do. It may just take me a while to get used to us being together again," she replied. "And I wonder if we should be meeting this often. I mean, what if we got caught? It could ruin the whole plan."

"But I want to see you," Cain whined pretentiously. "Let's just keep meeting like we did on the peninsula, all right? We'll meet every other night—right here. It's important for us to let each other know how it's going with the Area Heads. I made a lot of progress with the guys on the voyage. How about you?"

"The Area Heads?" Aria's mind seemed to have been elsewhere. "Oh, yes. It went well between me and the girls, too. None of them would oppose my wishes." She was right. All the girls liked Aria.

"Excellent! Just keep up the good work then. The critical allegiances are with the boys anyway." Cain didn't catch the glare Aria shot his way when he made that statement.

He continued, "And I think I'm winning most of the guys over. Of course, Toren is with us. He's still the only one who knows. Shay, Marcum, and Dolius will be with me . . . I mean us, when it's time to tell them. The only guys I'm really concerned about are Jamin, Billius, and Lian. And Amedis. Savot seems to have really gotten close to him."

Aria yawned as Cain kept talking. "How about the girls? How about Sensia?"

"I think Sensia will go along with whatever I say," Aria answered, turning away from Cain.

"Do you think she'll be upset?" Cain asked. "I mean, she *is* my official fiancée. But she doesn't seem to like me much." Aria stood at a distance from Cain now.

"No, I don't think she'll be upset at all. She told me she thinks it's stupid that we all *have* to get married. I really think she'd rather just stay single and focus on her military career."

"Good," Cain said, obviously finished with the subject of Sensia. "What about the other girls?" Cain walked to Aria and put his hands on her shoulders. She pulled away from him.

"I don't want to talk about this now," replied Aria bluntly.

"Oh . . . of course not. I'm sorry, sweetheart," Cain spoke softly and slipped his arms around her waist again, this time from behind her, and he held her tight.

"I'm tired, Cain. I'd really like to get some sleep now." Aria yawned again and stretched her way out of his embrace.

"Well, all right," Cain retorted, a little irritated. "I'll meet you night after next then." Already walking away from him, Aria turned and bid him a quick goodnight.

***

The Children and Mentors had spent most of the second day on New Atlantis unloading the ships and settling into their temporary quarters. Galen ordered the boys to shave their faces before the third day—the day the Chosen Children were to start working. They would build New Atlantis City and its outlying areas . . . again, beginning on the big, middle island. Only this time their buildings would house them and their families for the rest of their lives.

The highest priority, Savot had commanded, was the Temple. So, after the city and farming fields had been staked out, the architects, civil engineers, and construction workers put their energies into building the Temple, which would stand near the palace on the main island.

New Atlantis City would occupy the largest—the middle—island, the one they had landed on. The city would accommodate all the government and religious buildings as well as most of the recreational fields and a huge amphitheater. Atlanteans loved to produce plays and hold concerts. The amphitheater would be the stage for their artful events as well as for a variety of other national meetings.

The next priority, according to Savot, was to get started on the permanent homes the newlywed couples would live in beginning during the second year, the Year of Merger.

Medo and Fara, the Area Heads for architecture, and Jaran and Baylee, the Area Heads for construction, were allowed to meet weekly to discuss progress. Their Mentors also attended the meetings but only to observe and encourage the four Area Heads, not to direct the project.

Medo, Fara, Jaran, and Baylee decided on the placement of the 114 family homes that would be built on the residence island to the west, which was the second largest of the three islands. They also planned for the eighteen eunuch homes to be assembled on the main island.

The third and smallest island, due east from the big island, would be divided into thirds. A third of it would be used for garbage collection and recycling. Another third—suitable for mining and farmland—was reserved for those two purposes. On the easternmost third of the small island a prison would be built . . . just in case the need for one arose.

Savot told Galen he hoped the prison wouldn't have to be used much. But he knew better. It wouldn't take long before violators of the Separation Rules would have to be sent to the prison, just as they had on the peninsula.

Many more hardwood trees grew on New Atlantis than on the mother continent. The engineers and architects loved that, because hardwood made for stronger structures than the trees their buildings had been made of on the peninsula. And it made up for the lumber they had lost while at sea.

But the carpenters, who also served as the lumberjacks of the society, complained about the extra work. The girls decided that they should do more of the actual carpentry and that the boys should fell the heavy trees.

Averil, the boys' Area Head for farming, had guessed right. The climate was quite different on New Atlantis. From early spring when they arrived through late summer the farmers found that some of their fruits and vegetables didn't grow well. Trees like mango, banana, and coconut didn't succeed at all. On the other hand, their wheat, barley, and rye crops thrived in the cooler weather.

The first few months seemed to pass quickly, and progress was made swiftly in all areas of the New Atlantean development projects. The Mentors began feeling more at ease about leaving the Children alone after Month Six. Savot, too, gained more confidence in his ability to rule his peers.

***

Monthly Feasts were held just as during the previous year. King Jorash had written speeches for Savot to give at each feast. Out of respect for Galen's expectations, Savot decided to at least use them as outlines.

He asked Galen to help him modify the addresses to include commendations for specific accomplishments each month. The language of the speeches began sounding more like Savot's normal conversation, and Galen didn't seem to mind.

The feasts took on a different atmosphere too. They became more sophisticated. The girls' dances evolved into musical plays staged on the obstaball field, at first, and later in the amphitheater. Dancing, singing, and acting accompanied by an orchestra soon became the norm each month.

Determined not to be outdone by the girls in any area, the boys had a play to present at the Month Four Feast. And thus, theatrical competition between boys and girls began. A few of the Children eventually developed into accomplished playwrights.

The boys' and eunuchs' obstaball skills improved each month as well. Everyone agreed that Jamin was proving himself to be the most valuable player. The guys always fought to get him on their team.

After all Jamin had no reason not to play. Lalera never showed the least interest in him even though he had copied Savot's flower and gift campaigns. Lalera gave up on Savot and now played up to many of the other boys at every feast and earned herself the reputation of 'biggest flirt in the new kingdom'.

During the fifth month, though, Lalera came to Aria late one evening in private. She had a shameful admission to make.

"Your Highness, I have something to tell you. And I know I'll be punished for it," Lalera started, her voice quivering. Aria put down the blanket she'd been folding and gave Lalera her full attention. "I could even have to die for what I've done." Worried, Aria sat down and invited Lalera to sit as well.

"Lalera, what is it?"

"I'm pretty sure I'm pregnant," Lalera confessed.

Aria's eyes widened and she stiffened. Finally she managed to ask, "Who?"

"I'm not going to tell," Lalera said. "The only thing I'll say is that it wasn't Jamin."

"Well, of course not Jamin!" Aria retorted with a nervous chuckle. She stood up and started pacing with her arms folded.

"I want everyone to know that it's not Jamin even though he is my fiancé. I plan to tell everyone it's not him."

"That's good of you to spare Jamin, Lalera. But you must tell me who it is," Aria demanded. "The law calls for punishment of both parties you know."

"I told him and he doesn't want to admit to it. So I won't tell—not ever. If he wants to come forward, that's up to him. But I will not tell on him." Clearly Lalera had made up her mind.

"I guess I should have thought about this happening," Aria mumbled in short, shallow breaths, thinking out loud and still pacing. "But I . . . I just never did." Then, directing her words back to Lalera, she told her, "You know I'll have to tell Savot. I don't know what he'll decide for your punishment."

"I understand," said Lalera quietly, her head down. "Whatever the penalty is, I'll bear it. I knew what I was doing."

Chapter 11

No More Grown-Ups

Aria had to wait five days until her next meeting with Savot. And she didn't tell a soul about Lalera's situation. When she told him what Lalera had confessed, all Savot could think of at first was Jamin. *He loves Lalera so much. This is just going to kill him!*

"Please, Savot, don't be too harsh with her punishment," Aria implored. "I mean, I know she needs to be punished, but I just can't stand to see her suffer a lot. Not in her condition." Savot understood what she was saying. Although Aria and Lalera had never been close friends, Savot respected Aria for her compassion in this case.

For a few moments Savot sat in pensive wordlessness. Then his answer came. "The Mentors don't need to know," he had decided. "They probably won't notice that she's . . . you know . . . before they leave us."

Aria held her breath, waiting for Savot to say more.

"Let's see, who does need to know?" The king was thinking out loud. Still Aria waited. "The Area Heads for priests and lawyers. Amedis and Parius." Aria sat motionless to see what else Savot would decide. "We should enter a plea with them on Lalera's behalf and then let them take it to the Combined Court."

"We?" Aria asked with a confused look on her face.

Savot answered quickly. "Yeah. These are the kind of hard judgments that I need your wisdom on," Savot told the soon-to-be-queen. Aria stared at Savot in disbelief. "We'll have to make these kinds of judgments together from now on, Aria, by ourselves, without the Mentors. So it's really important that you and I be in agreement on big decisions like this."

Now Aria looked more than perplexed. She looked surprised.

Savot didn't understand her puzzlement. He continued with the obvious subject. "What plea do you think we should enter?"

Aria stammered, "Uh . . . well . . . whatever the lightest sentence is, of course."

She still looked befuddled so Savot asked, "What's the matter?"

"You said you and I should make decisions together. My father never included my mother in any decisions," Aria informed him.

"Really? Well, I don't want us to operate that way."

Savot watched the thoughts dart behind Aria's eyes. He could tell the new concept of joint decision-making was hard for her to envision. Aria had never seen such an arrangement in action.

It was the most natural thing in the world to Savot though. His parents had always made decisions together, even little ones. So Savot couldn't imagine ever lording his authority over Aria as Jorash had Sophea. It just wasn't who he was. And his guess was that he cared much more for Aria than her father had ever cared for her mother.

As this thought entered his mind, Savot felt sad for his princess. Finally she spoke.

"And . . ." Aria started, then hesitated.

"And what?" Savot prompted her.

"Could we not tell anybody else either. I mean besides the officials? Till the Mentors are gone? Could you . . . I mean, *we*, ask them to keep it secret?"

"Yeah, I was thinking that too. I'll order Amedis and Parius to keep it to themselves." Savot reached over and patted Aria's hand, which rested on the arm of her chair. "I'll talk to them tomorrow. I'll let you know how it goes." Aria nodded, pursing her lips in a slender smile.

"I'll see you next week then," Savot said as he rose from his chair and wandered toward Aria's front door.

"Yes, My Lord," Aria responded as she rose and walked him to the door. This time Savot didn't react to her use of the royal title. She hadn't spoken it sarcastically this time, or even awkwardly. Besides, Savot's mind was preoccupied with the crisis at hand. And when he thought again of Jamin, his heart sank.

***

That evening, right after supper, Savot took Jamin out for a walk. The late summer sun was just setting and a warm breeze rippled the boys' clothing. They walked along the beach together in poignant silence. Jamin reached down every so often to pick up a shell. The quiet finally got to him.

"Savot," he ventured, "this is something serious, isn't it?"

"Yeah, it is, Jamin." Savot hated to continue.

"Well, go ahead. You've got to talk about it sooner or later." Jamin rattled the shells around in his hand.

Savot could not think of an easy way to say it so he just started talking. Jamin looked somber but kept striding at a steady pace. Though Savot could see tears welling up in his friend's eyes, overall Jamin didn't seem to be taking the news as hard as Savot had thought he would.

Savot ended with, "Under the law, you're not obligated to marry her—in a case like this."

"But I still *want* to marry her!" Jamin responded without hesitation. "I love her, Savot."

The statement surprised Savot, but then he nodded in understanding. He was thinking, *what if Aria was in the same situation?* He'd marry her too. He'd rather provide a home for her and her child than to see her dishonored and ostracized. He'd rather be thought of as immoral himself than for Aria to be shamed alone. And he'd rather be her husband than to not be—even under such conditions.

"You said you're going to ask for an easy sentence for her, right?" Jamin looked Savot in the eye as he asked this question.

"I'm going to see what the lightest possible punishment could be."

"Thank you, Savot," Jamin whispered. "When can we get married?"

"If she's allowed to live . . ." Savot cringed as he started. At this Jamin abruptly stopped walking and stood still, facing Savot.

"*Allowed to live?* Savot, they wouldn't kill her, would they? *Oh, they just can't!*"

"Jamin, I don't think they will," Savot replied, trying to calm his now-panicked friend. "I promise I'll do everything I can for her."

There seemed nothing left to say so the two friends resumed their walk along the peaceful shore. Savot was miserable. And he knew Jamin was even more so. The ocean breeze brought salt air into Savot's nostrils. It seemed to calm his nerves. Then he remembered one more thing.

"I'm meeting with Amedis and Parius tomorrow. The law calls for both parties to be punished, but Lalera won't tell who the guy is."

"Good. I don't want to know." Jamin choked with what Savot thought was anger as he said this. Then he wiped his eyes with his sleeve.

"I'm so sorry, Jamin." Savot was really hurting for his buddy but 'I'm sorry' was all he could think to say in commiseration.

***

Amedis and Parius, once they got over the initial shock of the news, read Savot all the laws that pertained to Lalera's transgression. No one even raised the question as to whether Jamin might be the baby's father. They all knew he wasn't.

The least severe penalty for Lalera, according to Atlantean religious law, was imprisonment until the birth of the child. Savot was glad to hear that. He then commanded Amedis and Parius that Lalera's secret not be revealed until after the Mentors had left New Atlantis. The priest and lawyer agreed.

They wanted to take the matter to their Combined Court without the Mentors' involvement. They agreed with Savot that they should handle this themselves. Only after the Children were left alone on New Atlantis would the Combined Court become involved, they decided.

So it was agreed that the only Children to know of the situation until after the Mentors left would be Savot, Aria, Jamin, Amedis, and Parius. And, of course, Lalera. The agreement for confidentiality was made among the six of them. But Parius was really angry.

He talked to Savot about it later. "As soon as the adults are gone, we've got to demand that the guy confesses. This just isn't right—for Lalera to carry all the guilt herself!" Parius was the right boy for his position as justice-keeper. He had always possessed great zeal for following laws, and great indignation when rules were broken.

***

Jamin arranged—through Savot—to visit Lalera the next day.

"Will you marry me, Lalera?" asked Jamin forthrightly.

Aria had told her he was going to ask. Lalera was prepared.

"I can't, Jamin," the mother-to-be responded. "It's so kind of you to offer, but I just couldn't do that to you."

Jamin was set to argue. "You wouldn't be doing anything to me. I've always wanted to be your husband—under any circumstances." Lalera looked puzzled and then ashamed.

"I don't understand you, Jamin. You really should hate me."

"No, I could never hate you," Jamin replied softly. Then he pleaded, "Will you at least think about it?"

Lalera began to tear up. She could only nod her compliance to his request. Jamin had brought a gift for her, so he handed it to her now. It was a stuffed animal he had made himself—a cat, her favorite animal. The rugged (and definitely unprofessional) needlework on the cat made Lalera smile.

"Sleep with it and let it always remind you that . . . somebody really loves you." Jamin put his hand under Lalera's chin and raised it so their eyes would meet. "And that will never change."

***

The Month Five Feast came and went. The tone of it was not as festive as the others. Both Children and Mentors knew this would be the last 'normal' feast together and the next would signal the imminent departure of the adults.

Amedis and Savot spent many mornings after that intensely praying. The increasing weight of responsibility on Savot as New Atlantis' king made him feel more and more inadequate each day. Lalera's situation wasn't the only thing that occupied Savot's and Amedis' petitions to the Unknown God.

As the girl doctor Phaedra had predicted, some serious medical problems had arisen during the first five months on New Atlantis. An unfamiliar-looking snake had bitten one girl. Since the fang marks were large, the doctors treated the bite as they had treated viper bites back on Atlantis. They cut shallow slits in the girl's skin where each fang had entered and sucked the poison out. The girl still lost consciousness and almost stopped breathing. But this soldier girl was strong, and after several days of high fever and delirium she had recovered.

At one point about half of the Children got horribly sick to their stomachs and most couldn't leave their beds for an entire week. The cause of the illness, the doctors concluded, must have been an unfamiliar leaf used in supper preparation the evening before. The cooks thought they recognized the gray-green herb as one common on Atlantis, but it apparently had been a poisonous New Atlantean look-alike. The food poisoning caused vomiting and diarrhea. So even when the Children could return to work, it took several more days for them to fully recover their strength.

Another problem—though not a new one—was the discovery of more couples than ever breaking the Separation Rules. After Billius and Caris had been caught and punished twice on New Atlantis, Billius decided they should stop their illegal meetings.

Shay and Narsis, on the other hand, met even more often and were also caught more often. Narsis, though probably the most competent of all the Navy girls, was demoted to the lowest possible rank by Sensia. A similar fate did not befall Shay, however. He retained his position as the Navy Head. Cain made sure of that despite Sensia's insistence to the contrary.

***

The Mentors had planned to have an official cononation for Savot and Aria at the Month Six Feast. Savot, however, had requested that the ceremony be delayed until something could be resolved about whether he would marry Aria or not. Galen understood and convinced the other Mentors to simply reiterate Savot's election as king by the lot and announce that the official ceremony would take place at the beginning of the Children's Year of Merger. Galen told Savot he felt sure Aria would come around by then. Though Savot still felt that was doubtful, he agreed with Galen in order to put it off.

The Month Six Feast was a cheerless one for both Children and Mentors. Even though the usual festivities had been planned, they were executed with what seemed to be a storm cloud looming over the feasting area. Galen gave his last official speech and reiterated King Jorash's wish for the Children to wear their bracelets always to remind them of those that they loved on Atlantis.

Then the sad day arrived for the Mentors to depart from New Atlantis. The 100 men had worked tirelessly helping the Children get their construction as far along as possible before leaving them to finish it.

Now it was time for the youngsters to start living their lives completely independent of all adults. Each Child gave his Mentor a gift upon their parting. They also sent presents with the Mentors for their families back on Atlantis.

The Mentors boarded their ships weeping, every one. And their protégés shed almost as many tears as when they had left their parents seven months earlier, some even more. Savot had had a stunning diamond ring made for Galen. It was only a small symbol of the immense gratitude he felt toward his invaluable Mentor.

Beyond all the political skills he had taught Savot, Galen had spent the past nineteen months opening up his whole life and pouring it into his protégé's—counseling, coaching, instructing, and encouraging. Savot knew he could never repay this man who had essentially become his surrogate father. But the ring was at least a symbol of his great appreciation.

Their actual parting was much more difficult than Savot had ever imagined. Before Galen boarded the ship, he and Savot seized each other and froze in a long, tight embrace. They sobbed shamelessly on each other's shoulders.

"Well, my boy, you're on your own now," Galen blubbered as he tried to look the now sixteen-year-old Savot in the eye. "I have a gift for you too." It was a diary Galen had been keeping for Savot. Though bound in thick leather, the book looked already well worn. The royal Mentor had made an entry in this diary every night for the entire nineteen months he had been training Savot.

"It's not all advice. Sometimes it was just observations about different Children. Observations about you and about Princess Aria. I hope it will help you somehow. Encourage you a bit after I'm gone." Savot clutched the leather-bound book to his chest and then dropped his chin on it as tears fell straight to the ground.

After one last, strong handshake, Savot's beloved teacher boarded his ship.

The autumn breeze swept the shiny, black hair away from Savot's face as the king of New Atlantis turned to walk away from the dock. The New Atlantean sailors helped the Mentors set out. Waves and shouts of 'goodbye' and 'thank you' continued until the Children were sure their Mentors couldn't hear or see them anymore. They squinted in the bright new sunlight that had appeared to their left as the ships disappeared over the southern horizon.

The Chosen Children, the New Atlanteans, were alone.

No one made a sound for a long time. They all just stood staring at the abandoned ocean.

Then a sharp whistle pierced the crypt-like silence.

"Assembly at the palace gate!" bellowed Win. Savot and Galen had decided the king should address his people as soon as the Mentors left.

Once the Children had gathered near the palace gate, Savot took his place on a ledge at the top of the half-built wall. He stood flanked by the princess and the two high priests, Amedis and Thea. Everyone expected another modified Jorash-written speech. But the address Savot delivered surprised everyone—even Aria.

Savot now spoke to his subjects for the first time in the absence of any adults.

"Citizens of New Atlantis," he began. Those familiar four words were as far as Savot got into the long speech Jorash had written for this occasion.

"Well, here we are. We're on our own at last," Savot began. The Children fell quickly into quietness. They already recognized this speech as very different from his others. Even Savot's demeanor was much less formal, much more genuine. Savot improvised the rest of his oration.

"The work is going well," the king encouraged. "The buildings look great!" Savot continued. "And when the city's finished, I'm betting it'll be even better than the one we built on the peninsula," King Savot exclaimed. His audience looked around at one another with bright faces.

"Our fields are almost ready for harvest." The Children welcomed their king's every word now. "Our houses are nearly all finished . . ."

Savot paused and deliberately changed his upbeat tone. "But my main concern isn't our ability to build buildings and grow healthy crops."

Savot searched the faces of the Chosen Children. At this last statement, the Children's eyes had widened and were now glued to their monarch.

"Look you guys . . . and girls," Savot spoke to his peers now with unusual ease. "All the confident words you've heard from me in the past, about how successful we're going to be here on New Atlantis. Well, the truth is, I don't really know what'll happen to us now."

This confession clearly unsettled some of the Children. Low murmurs rippled throughout the assembly.

Savot went on, "We are really going to have to pull together on this. I'm in charge because the Unknown God chose me. But I can't make New Atlantis work without you." He scanned the faces of his competitors—Toren, Dolius, Marcum, and Shay.

"*All* of you."

Cain stood beside Sensia on the ground in front of Savot. Both generals had stoic, military nonexpressions on their faces.

Although Savot had not prepared what he was going to say word for word, he did know that he wanted to speak from his heart to his people. And he had braced himself for a protest. About what, he wasn't sure.

The audience was tense, but only Toren fidgeted noticeably. Savot couldn't probe Aria's face because she stood beside him. The Children observed her as placid and almost motionless. The young king continued.

"I want to tell you all something. I know it's the job of priests to pray, not kings. But I've been praying to the Unknown God for us." Some of the Children looked puzzled.

"Amedis and I have prayed together every day, and I've prayed by myself many other times each day." The New Atlanteans stared at Savot curiously.

"I figure it this way," their king explained. "If The Ghost directed us to build New Atlantis, then the Unknown God must be planning to help us. I mean, there must be something he wants us to accomplish through this mission."

Savot then turned to the high priests standing beside him for confirmation.

"Amedis and Thea, you've studied what The Ghost said to King Jorash seventeen years ago. He *did* appoint our generation to build New Atlantis, didn't he?" Both Thea and Amedis nodded emphatically.

"Yes, Your Majesty," they replied, almost in unison.

Turning back to his audience, King Savot went on. "So that's why I pray now. Beginning the first day of our voyage, Amedis and I have met every morning to pray for help and wisdom. For me and for all of us."

"If you take that as a sign of weakness on my part, then so be it. But I'm not going to claim that I have enough wisdom or power to rule this new kingdom all by myself. I need the help of a power and a mind greater than my own."

Surprising whispers of satisfaction, smiles and nods spread among the Children. Aria stood on the ledge beside Savot, observing the transformation of the crowd. She looked completely stiff now.

Savot then added with deliberate emphasis, "And, as much as anything, Amedis and I have prayed for unity as we work together to build New Atlantis." Here he stopped and eyed his opponents again. Stares from several of them signaled resistance.

"I think it's best for us to keep right on with our work, even today," King Savot commanded. "Obey your supervising eunuchs as you did your Mentors. Show them as much respect as you ever did the adults. We're right on schedule to finish all the construction by the Month Twelve Feast. Then the Year of Merger can begin."

At that statement the Children's faces and voices heralded a broad spectrum of emotions. Those who had always been pleased with their fiancés and even those who had grown fond of their appointed mates found each other's eyes, smiled, and some even blew kisses. Those still unhappy with their marital arrangements avoided eye contact with their fiancés. Only about a third of the Children actually looked happy. And Princess Aria lowered her eyes.

Again Savot couldn't see her reaction, and he dared not turn to look at her. He concentrated on concluding his address.

"I really want New Atlantis to work. I want us to grow into a kingdom of men and women . . . and eventually children . . . who follow the Unknown God and live in peace. Just the way our forefathers always have." The New Atlanteans listened attentively.

"It's important to me for you to know that I, as your king, am putting confidence in a stronger authority than myself." Savot wanted his people to know full well of his devotion to the Unknown God. "I'm trusting that, if the Unknown God regarded us highly enough to call us to this undertaking, he will help us carry out our destiny. I'm asking each one of you today to join me in that trust."

And that was the end of Savot's speech. No fanfare, no pageantry. The Children were finally seeing the real Savot. *It kind of feels like being clean,* the young king thought to himself. As he turned from the ledge to descend the stone wall, a spontaneous surge of applause rose from the audience. Savot looked at Aria. She smiled, but he saw anxiety on her brow.

"Hail to the King! Hail to New Atlantis!" As the chant began, the Chosen Children raised their right arms high in the air, displaying their wristbands. Cain shot a nervous glance toward Aria. She returned the same.

After Savot disappeared into the partially built palace, like dutiful warriors the Children dispersed themselves toward their assigned areas of work. Their eunuchs led them and order seemed secured. At least for the day.

Chapter 12

Disturbing Discoveries

Cain wanted to meet with Aria and Toren that very midnight. They had been meeting weekly as the new mutiny team in King Jorash's absence since they first arrived on New Atlantis. Now Cain was disturbed by the Children's amiability toward Savot's speech. The general wanted to hear his cohorts' reactions. Especially Aria's.

"Well, Savot sure gave us a different kind of speech today," Cain started, fishing for a response.

Toren answered first. "Yeah, I didn't think he had it in him to make a speech using his own words." Toren chortled in a tone that belittled Savot. Aria didn't say anything so Cain asked.

"What did you think of it, Aria?"

"I thought it was pretty good actually. I mean, unpolished, but I was watching the Children. I think they liked how he was being so open with them."

Cain grunted. He stepped up on a large stone in the heavily shrouded grove. "The more they like him, the more upset they'll be when he disappears."

"We'll just have to match their mood," Aria added. "Maybe extend the mourning period." Cain raised his eyebrows and looked at her curiously.

Toren chimed in, "I talked to lots of others after the speech. They were surprised at the change in him, but they liked what he said. I didn't think he could come across as such a good leader. That's kind of scary."

Aria scolded Toren. "Oh, Toren. Don't let him fool you. He's not a good leader. My father knows his weaknesses. He might be able to talk a good talk, but his actions will eventually betray him." She shot authoritative glances at both Toren and Cain. "He's a coward!" Aria continued. "When he's put under pressure he'll buckle. He could never be the leader you are, Cain." Cain's wide mouth broadened into a smile. He sat down on the rock.

"Oh, absolutely," Toren agreed readily. "But if Savot's popularity keeps growing, I think we should move the timetable up for the kidnapping."

Cain and Aria agreed. "Let's just see how it goes though," Cain ordered. "Today may have been his only shining moment. He'll show his true colors before long, and the Children will see it. When the first crisis comes up, they'll see it. He's just too soft to be a king."

***

Savot had decided—along with Amedis and Parius—to delay the Combined Council meeting about Lalera until some sort of daily routine without the Mentors was established. And so the next day, their first full day without their Mentors, proceeded almost as smoothly as if the adults were still there. Savot was pleased.

Heavy rain began just before supper that evening. After their meal, the Children retreated to their houses to stay dry. Savot and his roommates played a card game as Memphis perched on Savot's shoulder. The boys sat in a circle on the floor by the fireplace.

The bird entertained the boys with his comments about the game or about random things that had nothing to do with the game. Every once in a while Memphis would recite expressions from his pirating days.

"*Hoist the anchor, you mongrels! They're after us!*" he blurted when Lian won the first hand.

"Memphis, you scared me today," Savot reprimanded his bird friend. "I thought you'd left us for good this time."

"I still can't figure out how he lets himself out of that cage!" Billius pondered.

"Smart bird," Savot replied.

"SMART BIRD!" Memphis agreed loudly. The boys laughed and called Memphis big-headed as Jamin began dealing the next hand.

"At least he always comes back," Lian said. Then, as if talking to a baby, he addressed the bird. "He knows who loves him. Don't you, Memphis?"

Memphis responded as he sometimes did at hearing Lian's voice. "Oh, I feel so sick! I'm gonna barf . . ." Lian swatted at the bird. Memphis squawked and fluttered to the ground, but Lian had stopped him before he made the vomiting sounds. Savot retrieved the bird back onto his shoulder.

The roommates hadn't talked about their Mentors leaving. Savot wondered how the other three were adjusting. He asked Jamin first, then Lian, then Billius. All seemed encouraged with their respective jobs—even empowered—since being left alone. The boys under their charge were cooperating as expected. No major complaints. But Jamin confessed missing the Mentors.

Now on to touchier matters. This time Savot started with the safest, Billius.

"How's Caris, Bill?"

"Cawis?" Billius asked as he grinned widely. "Well, she's amazing, as usual! I can't wait to be her husband." The boys chuckled at Billius' typical honesty.

"How 'bout you, Lian?" Savot probed. "What's the latest with Stacia?"

Lian didn't answer right away, seeming to study his hand of cards. He had moved from sitting to lying on his belly, propped up on his elbows. At last he answered, "I apologized to her for acting like a jerk. She forgave me, but . . ." Lian laid down a card that was not a wise choice.

"But what?" Billius asked.

"It was just weird after that. I don't know. She seemed like a cold fish at the last feast. Wouldn't even let me hold her hand." At this Lian put his cards face down on the floor and plopped his forehead on top of them.

"What?" asked Jamin in genuine concern.

Lian raised his head and slouched his cheek into his fist. "What if the problem is . . ." he hesitated.

"*What?*" Billius insisted that Lian continue.

"What if it's just that I really *am* a jerk? I mean—you know, Savot—I didn't even realize I was saying something wrong when I was kidding her about children. I didn't have a clue! But she got so upset." Lian puffed and slammed his head back down on his cards.

"Maybe it's just one of those giwl things. You know . . ." Billius tried to assure Lian. "It'll probably pass."

"We'll find out soon. The next feast is coming up," Jamin added.

No one said anything for a while after that. Even Memphis. The boys played another hand in relative silence. Savot could feel the tension. No one wanted to mention either Aria or Lalera.

Finally Jamin looked toward Savot for reassurance, and then spoke up. "Okay. I know you're all thinking, 'What about Lalera?' Well, I sent her some flowers and some sweetbread that Dayra made for me to give her . . ."

Lian interrupted, "Jamin, why do you want to marry her? She's so skanky."

Lian had no way of knowing how hard that comment would hit Jamin. The only two in the room who knew so far about Lalera's pregnancy were Jamin and Savot. Jamin's face reddened, and he bolted across the circle to attack Lian. But Savot grabbed him around the waist, tackling him and scattering cards everywhere.

"Don't you *ever* say anything like that about Lalera again, Lian!" Jamin warned, still restrained by Savot's grasp.

"Whoa! Okay," Lian returned, having jumped to his feet to dodge Jamin's lunge. "It's just, you know, the way she acts around all the other guys . . . I mean, if it were me, I'd write her off. But, hey, it's your business!"

Savot intervened. "Yeah, it *is* his business. So let's just drop it, all right?"

That ended the card game. Jamin left the house and went for a walk out in the cold.

***

Savot had decided he would read Galen's diary every night before he went to sleep. Tonight he read a lot of it. The phrase of advice that stuck with him through the night was:

> *Savot, always trust a man's history more than his present actions.*

Savot was certain that Galen had been thinking of Cain. Galen had never trusted Cain much. He had argued with King Jorash about appointing him as second-in-command. And Galen, too, had been suspicious of Cain's new expressions of allegiance toward Savot.

***

Through the first week after the Mentors left, the Children's work continued as before. Savot was just beginning to believe that he might, after all, be able to rule New Atlantis successfully. But that hope was soon threatened. The last Work Day of that first week the miners discovered something in a cave on the smallest island that no one could explain.

"Look at THIS!" Quint hailed his fellow miners. He had been the first to notice the mouth of the cave and had entered on his own. Standing inside the cavern now, Quint held his torch out over a huge fabric-covered pile of . . . something.

Both boy and girl miners crowded each other through the small mouth of the cave. Several of them lit torches and held them over the mound. The miners whispered guesses as to what could be under the sheet and who had left it there.

Ambros, the head miner, stepped over to Quint. "Well, uncover it," he ordered his underling.

Quint cautiously took hold of a corner of the fabric and tugged it off the mound.

The miners gasped. Glistening in the torchlight before them stood orderly rows of large, blue-silver bricks—orichalcum.

"Where did this come from?" Jiana questioned. "Atlantis is the only place in the world that mines orichalcum."

"The people who built our buildings before we came. They could have brought it here," Quint volunteered.

"I've got to report this to the king right away," Ambros announced. But just at that moment, Collan called to the others from further inside the cave.

"There's more over here!" he shouted. That announcement bade all twelve miners, plus Arni and Burl (the eunuchs who supervised them), to spread out inside the larger-than-expected cave. All torches were lit now and soon seventeen heaps of orichalcum bricks, similar to the first, were uncovered.

"Lusi, take Arni with you and go tell Savot about this," Ambros commanded.

***

Upon hearing Lusi's report, Savot dispatched Cain and several Army officers to the eastern island. The soldiers gawked at the piles of riches that they found. The general quickly put forth a theory, agreeing with Quint, about the presence of the bricks.

"Well! Another gift from King Jorash," Cain said, smiling confidently. "I wonder how many other surprises he's left here for us." But Cain knew how the stockpiles of orichalcum had gotten there. And he knew what he was supposed to do with them.

The news of the discovery spread quickly throughout New Atlantis. And Cain made sure that his hypothesis about the orichalcum being King Jorash's 'gift' accompanied the news. But Savot was leery about Cain's assumption. Galen's suspicions of Cain had begun to grow on him.

***

During Month Seven something else alarmed Savot. One clear night the Navy spotted lights on the northern horizon. The alien flickers appeared almost every night for two weeks after that, but the ships never got close enough to be identified.

"See Toren, our plan's working," Cain snickered to his confidant when the two were in private. "He's scared to death about those ships. I try to act scared, too, but it's so hard for me not to just laugh!" He laughed now. "If he only knew it was just you and me out there!"

"Man, everybody's so spooked now that you told them it might be pirates!" Toren enjoyed this ruse as much as Cain did.

In reality Savot doubted Cain's theory about pirates just as much as the one about the orichalcum. But he decided not to mention either subject to Aria if she didn't bring them up.

At the end of the week, Aria went to Savot's house for their regular meeting. Now they were taking turns holding their meetings in each other's temporary houses. Savot began the conversation.

"You were uneasy with my speech after the Mentors left, weren't you?" he asked after handing her his weekly flowers and gift. This time the gift was a new perfume made from the buds of a native bush.

"No, it was a great speech," Aria answered carelessly, but not convincingly. She applied a dab of the ointment to her wrists and then sniffed it. The luscious aroma filled the room. "It just sounded so different from your others." Savot had been hoping for some comment that resembled more of a sincere compliment. But he didn't get one.

Aria placed the perfume bottle on the table and then sat down in the chair beside Savot. She changed the subject.

"Wasn't it generous of my father to surprise us with the orichalcum?" she asked, smiling.

Savot, realizing she had believed Cain's premise as much as anyone, thought it best for the moment just to pretend to agree. "Yes, very generous."

Aria changed the subject again. "Now . . . I'm dying to know," she said, "what was decided about Lalera?" Lalera had been avoiding everyone since she had revealed her news to Aria. So none of the girls had heard of Jamin's proposal. But Lalera's pregnancy was beginning to show, and the girls had started quietly gossiping about it.

"Parius is taking the matter to the Combined Court at the beginning of next week. He agreed to put in a plea for leniency," Savot answered, again hoping for a positive reaction from Aria. Instead she sprang up and scowled at Savot.

"Leniency? What does that mean? *How* lenient?" Aria paced back and forth now on her oriental rug, frequently flashing golden eyes at Savot.

"Only a short time in prison. Until the baby's born," Savot answered. He got up and stepped toward the princess to block her pacing.

"That's four or five months!" Aria sputtered, turning and almost running into Savot. She moved back a step and then continued pacing—this time around him. "Savot, the girl is pregnant! And winter's coming on! You're going to make her stay in a cold, lonely prison for five months— pregnant?" The princess was furious. She fiddled with her long, blond braid and then tossed it over her shoulder. Her face was turning pink.

"Aria," Savot said firmly as he stopped her again and took her by the shoulders. "She could have gotten a death penalty for this. Five months in prison—or until the birth of the baby—that was the lightest possible sentence." Aria's stiff body relaxed a little at the touch of Savot's warm hands on her shoulders. She took a heavy breath.

"And I've told Jamin," Savot added.

Aria's eyes got big. "How did he take it?" she asked with genuine concern.

"He still wants to marry her."

Aria looked shocked and then impressed. "Oh . . . dear Jamin! I think that's the sweetest thing I've ever heard!" She instinctively threw her arms around Savot's neck. Then, realizing she was in a tight embrace with him, she pulled away.

"He really loves her," Savot explained, trying unsuccessfully to ignore their hug. "He'd rather raise someone else's child than not have Lalera as his wife." Aria looked dazzled, shaking her head as she drifted away from Savot. Then a flood of other questions came.

"When do we have to tell everyone? And how soon can they get married? But what if she doesn't want to marry Jamin?"

"Wait, wait," Savot snickered at her energetic burst. "One question at a time! First of all, if she doesn't want to marry Jamin, that's her choice. But it'd be better for her if she did. Otherwise, the law says she'll have to stay single."

Aria then broached a sticky subject. "Can't we *change* a few things about the law? I mean, now that it's just us?" She bit her lip, and Savot could tell she expected him to reject this suggestion. But he didn't.

"Actually, I've been thinking about that," Savot began. There was one rule, in particular, he had been giving a lot of thought to changing. "If we ever change any Atlantean laws, it wouldn't be done without good reason. And we'll never change any of our religious laws."

"Is Lalera's case decided by civil or religious law?" Aria wondered.

"Religious law," answered Savot.

Aria looked disappointed.

"I don't understand you, Savot. Why are you so firm about religious laws and not so much the civil ones?" she grumbled.

Savot's answer was both simple and complex. "Because I believe in the Unknown God. I believe he's real," he answered. Then he wondered, "Don't you?"

"Well, of course I do!" the princess snapped.

"Then how could we possibly go against anything he's commanded?"

Aria didn't answer for a minute. *Maybe she's never thought this through,* Savot surmised. Then at last she spoke. "If our laws here are Atlantean and we would consider changing some of them, our religion is also Atlantean. And we're *New* Atlantis . . ." Savot could tell where this was headed.

"No, Aria. Men made the Atlantean laws. And men can make mistakes."

"How do you know the Unknown God doesn't make mistakes?" Aria countered.

This was a weighty question, and Savot gave Aria the conclusion he'd come to on that.

"Because there's got to be someone who doesn't make mistakes."

Savot's answer stumped Aria. But then she came back with an even more disturbing query.

"How do we know there's really such a thing as The Ghost? Or the Unknown God, for that matter? Couldn't the kings and priests have made it all up?"

Savot couldn't believe what he was hearing. "So, you don't even believe your own father? That The Ghost appeared to him? That the Unknown God really appointed our whole generation for New Atlantis?"

Aria didn't answer and a look of uneasiness engulfed her.

"Aria, I'm surprised at you. Either the Unknown God is real or we're all fools to be here doing what we're doing!" Savot had never expected Aria to be so faithless.

She deflected his comments by returning to her original subject. "Savot, Lalera's waiting to know something."

A bad feeling was rising inside Savot toward Aria, probably the first bad feeling he'd ever really had toward her. The tension in the air was almost palpable, but Savot managed to answer Aria calmly.

"There are several possibilities for Lalera's punishment within our religious laws. And you know I've requested the most lenient of them. I think the Council will agree on the penalty we proposed. I'll announce the Council's verdict at the next feast."

Aria looked halfway satisfied.

Savot continued, "Between now and then, you should have Lalera get herself ready to move to the prison." Aria's face fell. "Don't worry. The eunuchs guarding the prison are good guys. They'll take good care of her," Savot added.

Finally, though reluctantly, Aria agreed they had done all they could to help Lalera without totally ignoring her misdeed. Savot watched as the princess picked up her flowers and bottle of perfume.

"I'll see you at the feast," Savot concluded as he walked Aria to the door. After she left, Savot closed the door and slumped down into a chair. His roommates were not home. The young king dreaded the announcement he would have to make at the Month Seven Feast. He was thinking he didn't like this part of his job at all. And he was thinking Aria wasn't as perfect as he had once supposed.

***

The Month Seven Feast arrived. The time had come for Savot to tell everyone the news about Lalera's pregnancy and her penalty. He had rehearsed with the Combined Court of priests and lawyers what would be said and when. Feasting, dancing, an obstaball game, and a theater production proceeded as usual. At the end of the play, when all the Children were assembled, it was time for Savot to deliver the unpleasant report.

"I have an announcement to make," he started. His words and countenance instantly ended the light mood of the crowd after the humorous play. It seemed as though the Children were expecting bad news.

As Savot unfolded the report, volumes of varied emotions showed themselves on the Children's faces and in their hushed mumbles. Some even stood and objected to Lalera's prison sentence. Cain motioned for his guards to deal with the protesters. With soldiers moving in on them, the dissenters grudgingly sat back down and hushed.

Lalera sat on the front row of the theater—stone still—between Aria and Risa, one of the girl doctors. She had told Jamin not to sit near her. Aria bit her fingernails as she listened to Savot's words. When he announced the sentence, tears trickled down Aria's cheeks, washing powder off them to reveal her persistent freckles. When Savot finished, several hands went up to ask questions.

"I thought death was the penalty under Atlantean law for having sex outside of marriage," shouted one strict engineer.

"I just want to know—who's the *coward* who got her pregnant and now won't admit it?" another boy challenged, turning to face the whole crowd. No one answered. So, ignoring the two questions, Aria rose and spoke.

"I've arranged for Risa to stay with Lalera in prison to keep her company and to tend to any medical needs she might have," the princess announced. Risa was also Lalera's best friend. "And anyone can visit her who wants to."

Questions and objections continued. Savot, Amedis, and Parius handled each interrogation skillfully. But the Children wanted to talk about the issue for quite a while and especially after Aria and Risa escorted Lalera out of the theater.

"You all have legitimate concerns," Savot said after he thought the debate had gone on long enough. "This is our first big problem together and I want you to know that I'm really proud of the way Parius, Amedis, and their Combined Council have handled this decision. They've been both professional and compassionate."

By the time he dismissed the meeting, the crowd's agitation had died down enough that Savot wasn't worried about any more unrest for the night. But he thought, *what a way to end a feast!* Lalera was moved that night to the newly built prison on the eastern island with Risa accompanying her.

Aria made sure both girls had comfortable bedding in the prison and, since winter was approaching, she had one of the eunuchs constantly tending a fire in Lalera's cell. Lalera still had to decide whether or not she would marry Jamin once the Year of Merger began. The baby was due just before that. She had nearly five months ahead of her—in prison—to consider Jamin's proposal.

***

Savot missed Galen. He took his Mentor's worn leather diary out from under his pillow that night and opened randomly to an entry toward the end. By candlelight he read some more of Galen's thoughts about Aria:

> *She's a complex person, Savot. Something's definitely eating at her. Maybe when we Mentors leave New Atlantis you'll be able to discover what's going on in her mind.*

And I hope by the time you read this the princess will have come to her senses and will have realized how lucky she is to be marrying you.

I don't think there's any chance of that, Galen, Savot answered in his thoughts. Sadly, he closed the diary, put it back under his pillow and miserably drifted off to sleep.

Chapter 13

Savot vs. the Court

Savot's next meeting with Aria didn't go well at all. For no apparent reason the princess acted more aloof toward her fiancé than ever before. And after the srained meeting Savot was more discouraged than ever before. He concluded that she really must hate him, and he told Amedis, Billius, Lian, and Jamin so. Though his friends tried to hearten him, Savot decided it would really be better for him to give up on ever winning Aria's affections rather than continue holding on to false hope.

He called a special meeting with Parius, Bena, and all the lawyers in the middle of Month Eight. Savot had thought and prayed a lot about the radical proposition he was about to make.

"I'm thinking we should consider changing the Marriage Rules," Savot announced. "Maybe we should let the Children decide who they want to marry." The group of lawyers gawked at him in disbelief. This was not like Savot—to make such a drastic suggestion. A heated debate ensued.

After everyone had presented his argument, someone reminded the group that the king had the prerogative to override any judgment made by the civil legal system. It was only at that point that Savot fully realized what he was facing. He would have to rule against the majority of lawyers in order to implement the change if they wouldn't agree. His chest felt heavy.

Only one lawyer agreed with Savot about amending the Rules. That female attorney was Stevana who didn't want to marry Garwin, her intended. Garwin, on the other hand, fought ardently to keep the Rules. He cared deeply for Stevana and knew he'd never stand a chance with her if she had the right to choose.

"I'll think on this for a few days and then we'll meet again. I want this settled before the next feast, though,"

Savot concluded. "Until our next meeting then, this sub-ject needs to stay completely confidential," he instructed. The king dismissed the formal meeting, but many of the lawyers stayed after, trying to reason with him.

"You have a personal motive for wanting to change the Rules, don't you, Your Majesty?" asked Kelen, an insight-ful female lawyer. "I bet I can guess what it is."

Savot knew he was cornered. He fought inside his own head to rationalize while he delayed giving Kelen a reply. He remembered all the Children who had come to him, unhappy with their fiancés, begging him to change the Rules. They were his main consideration . . . weren't they? An awful sense of irresponsibility swept over him.

But what about upholding the laws of Atlantis . . . and now New Atlantis? Isn't that more my responsibility than just doing what pleases the Children? And maybe Kelen's right—I might be just acting out my own self-pity.

The king was so deep in thought that the impatient Kelen gave up on getting an answer and spoke again, this time in a mock dialogue with herself.

"'Oh, so you think you know, do you, Kelen?'" she said, imitating Savot's voice. "Yes, I'm pretty sure I do, Your Highness." She continued this imaginary interview until it made Savot laugh. He looked around to find that, by then, everyone else had left the meeting room.

"All right, Kelen, tell me what you think my personal interest is," Savot humored her. Kelen nailed the issue straight on. He didn't want to make Aria marry him when she obviously didn't love him.

"Kelen," Savot confided in a lowered tone, "okay. You're right, but only partially. I do want her to be happy. But I *am* also thinking of the other Children." He paused. "You and Kanin are settled on marrying each other. Of course it's fine with you two not to change anything."

"Yeah, I guess we lucked out," Kelen agreed.

"But what about other couples? Like Stevana and Gar-win?" Savot posed. "You know she doesn't want to marry him. Both of them would end up miserable if she doesn't love him. What would be the harm in letting everyone just choose? You and Kanin would still choose each other, right?"

"Well, I'd choose him," Kelen replied. Then, with a hint of insecurity, she added, "I hope he'd still choose me."

"Wouldn't you like to be sure he would, though?" Savot had made a good point; he could tell by the contemplation on Kelen's face.

"Yeah. Actually, I would like to be sure," Kelen agreed. "But what about you and Princess Aria? Would you still be king even if the princess married someone else?" Kelen was thinking like a lawyer now.

"Yes," Savot returned unreservedly. He had already thought that one through. "But I thought maybe she and . . . whoever she chooses . . . could rule the residence island. She should still have some position of authority. She *is* the only one of us who is of royal blood."

"I don't know if she'd go for that, Savot—I mean, Your Highness," Kelen corrected herself. "She might want to rule all of New Atlantis herself, being King Jorash's daughter."

"I know. I've thought of that, too," Savot answered, feeling pretty disheartened over the knotty problem. "We'd have to come up with some kind of compromise. I guess I should talk with her before I make a final decision."

***

So he did. And he didn't wait until their next weekly meeting. He had Nat and Win escort him to Aria's quarters that very night. This time the princess came outside to talk with Savot and he sent the eunuchs inside.

It was a warm evening for autumn, and Aria wore only a light shawl draped over the crooks in her bare arms. She looked especially lovely tonight in her pale yellow pant dress. The color of the shimmering fabric complemented her blond hair, which she had already taken out of its braid. The golden waves draped softly over her delicate shoulders. *She would have to look this beautiful tonight*, Savot thought.

"This must be important, Savot. It's not like you to change our regular meeting schedule." Aria's usually loud voice sounded silky this evening. *Why do I have to love her voice so much?* Savot wondered, now feeling tortured. His thoughts drifted back to the one and only time on the peninsula she had been friendly toward him. Her voice had sounded the same then. It had such a warming, soothing effect on him. Then he realized he had been asked a question.

"What? What did you say?" Savot hadn't really heard the words Aria had spoken, just the melody of her voice.

"I said this must be important," Aria repeated.

"Oh, yes. It is," faltered Savot, overcome by his attraction to her. As she walked past him he got a whiff of the intoxicating perfume he had given her. His head was absolutely swimming. *Great timing for me to have to tell her this!* But he forced the words anyway.

"I think maybe we should change the Marriage Rules," Savot stated directly, while at the same time mentally slapping his hormones back into line.

Aria stared at him in dismay as she repeated his last four words as a question. "Change the Marriage Rules?"

"Yes, I've given it a lot of thought," he answered.

"Why would you want to do that?" Aria asked, now sounding alarmed.

"Well," Savot began his prepared answer, "so many of the Children have asked me to change the Rules. I figured, why not? Maybe we should just let everybody decide who they *want* to marry."

Aria didn't speak but was obviously thinking hard, her eyes lowered. So Savot kept talking.

"I know we were paired the way we were for a reason: so that the couples would be working in the same areas and could train their kids and all that. But if more than half our people don't like their chosen partners, they'd be unhappy." Aria was still reflecting when Savot admitted the other part of his motivation.

"And *you'd* be unhappy."

This jolted Aria out of her pensive daze. "I—I'd be unhappy?" she said, seeming surprised. "Savot . . ." she started, but Savot interrupted.

"I know you're in love with Cain. This way you could marry him."

Aria deflected his comment about her feelings for Cain. "Are you saying you'd abdicate the throne and let Cain be king?"

Savot had wondered how long it would take her to bring that up.

"No. I don't think that would be the right thing to do. The Unknown God had a chance to choose Cain as king and he chose me. So I think I should stay king even if we change the Rules. You and your husband could rule the residence island." Aria didn't even seem to hear Savot's last statement.

She quickly asked, "Then who would *you* marry?"

"I don't have anyone in mind." This really tore at Savot's heart because he was thinking, *you're the only girl I've ever wanted to marry.*

"Savot, I know the final decision on this is yours. And I appreciate your involving me in the process, I really do. But I just don't know what I think of it. It's such a strange thought to me."

"Well, how do you *feel* about it?" Savot asked her.

"I don't know that either," she said. Now that answer surprised Savot. He could tell she really didn't know how she felt. She was genuinely confused. And nervous. She bit her fingernails.

"Let me sleep on it and I'll give you my opinion tomorrow," she said.

They parted quickly, the scent of her perfume still lingering in the air. The sight of her golden hair and the sound of her soft voice stuck like a spear down deep somewhere inside of Savot. It hurt.

Aria couldn't sleep that night so she wrote her thoughts down on paper. By morning she had distilled and transcribed the words into a letter to Savot. Delivered by Nat to the king, the letter read:

Savot, I disagree with your idea. I understand you have the right to change the Rules at your will, but unless the position of king could be transferred to the husband of my choosing, I will oppose your decision to change the Marriage

Rules. Just as the Unknown God has chosen you to be king of New Atlantis, he chose me to be born into the royal family of Atlantis. I was also chosen to rule. It doesn't matter who I love. My responsibility as King Jorash's daughter comes before my personal feelings in all matters. I will object to your decision publicly if you change the Rules without also abdicating the throne. —Aria

Nat studied Savot's face as he perused the letter. A growing frown wrinkled the king's forehead the further he read. When he finished he put the paper face down on the table in front of him.

"What's the matter, Savot?" Nat asked.

Savot minimized. "Just a snag between me and my fiancée."

"Yeah, that seems to go with the territory," Nat answered with a chuckle.

"Nat, just get out of here, would you?" Savot barked at the eunuch.

"Whoa! She really got to you this time, didn't she?" teased Nat.

"OUT!" Savot shouted, which he rarely ever did. Nat left apparently aware that this was not the time to tease with Savot.

All that day Savot thought. He analyzed the decision every which way. He called on Amedis to pray with him. Amedis didn't know what decision so haunted Savot, but he knew by the intensity of the king's prayers that it must be something big. Finally, Savot decided. That night he wrote Aria back.

Since the sun rose on the first day of my life I've been incomplete. Since I was old enough to know the difference between male and female, it has been you who has defined 'female' for me. All the soft, beautiful, tender and wonderful things there are in this world.

I've worked puzzles and all the pieces fit. I've solved problems and the answers made sense. I've painted pictures and all the colors balanced. But you I cannot balance, I cannot solve, I can't seem to make all the pieces fit of the puzzle that is you. You are totally other than me, yet you alone make me complete.

Since the sun rose on the first day of my life I've been only partial. And now I know that I'll always be unfinished since I won't be made whole by you. You are the colors lacking in my painting. You're the answers to all the problems I try to solve. You are the piece that finishes my puzzle.

There is no other. My first treasure is my Unknown God. My second is you. And there are no other treasures in my soul.

I must change the Marriage Rules. I will not take your body if you won't give me your heart as well.

Savot

Chapter 14

The Rules Change

Aria received Savot's letter the next morning and shut herself up in her house for the rest of that day. She didn't eat or drink. And she commanded Win to make certain that no one was allowed in to see her. At bedtime Caris and Stacia tried to talk to their reclusive roommate but Aria wouldn't answer them a word.

Savot made the legal arrangements with the lawyers for the Rule change before the Month Eight Feast. He regretted having to overrule the lawyers, but he felt strongly that this was the right decisions for many reasons. Rumors of the revision leaked out so all of the Children knew before the official announcement.

Shay and Narsis were elated. So were many other couples who hadn't been matched but who had mutual attractions. Now they would be able to marry each other. And some who had been pleased with their fiancés under the original plan began to have second thoughts.

The night of the Month Eight Feast the Children didn't want to wait until the normal speech time at the end of the evening to hear the details of the change. During supper—at the beginning of the evening—a delegate from the lawyers requested that Savot address the marriage issue while the Children dined.

The king had already been asked so many individual questions that he agreed he might as well go ahead and make the announcement now. And he had prepared himself for what he thought would be an unpleasant showdown with Aria in front all the Children. He dreaded that part the most. She had warned him that she would object publicly if he changed the Rules. Savot stood to speak and the audience hushed.

"All right, everybody," Savot began. "I'm officially announcing that the Marriage Rules have been changed. All previous engagements are now nullified." Before he could speak another word, a massive cheer ascended from the crowd and most of the Children rose to their feet with applause. A few, however, remained seated and silent. Motioning for the crowd to settle down, Savot continued.

"Wait a minute! I know a lot of you like this change, but you need to understand exactly how things are going to work now." The Children quieted, for the most part, and listened.

"The Court has outlined how the changes will affect our calendar," Savot explained. "The Year of Merger will still begin just as we'd planned, at the end of this year— four months from now."

"According to the old calendar, we were supposed to have one wedding a day, except for Rest Days, until all 115 couples were married," he announced, but then his eyes fell on Meril who had been Antony's fiancée. Instead of correcting the number to 114, so as not to draw attention to Meril, he continued, "But under the new Marriage Rules, we'll slow things down." The Children looked a bit worried until their ruler clarified.

"The first day of the Year of Merger will still mark the beginning of the weddings. When new engagements become official, you'll need to register your betrothal and set a wedding date," Savot instructed. The Children waited with anticipation while Savot unrolled the new plan.

"If you'd still like to marry your previous fiancé, the two of you must register a new engagement and sign up for a date. Is that clear?" Most of his peers nodded that they understood.

"Before we had planned for all weddings to be performed during the Year of Merger. Now there won't be a time limit on when . . . or even if . . . we all get married." These were two parts of the new Rules that surprised everyone . . . 'no time limit, and IF?' Many of the Children, especially the boys, were clearly pleased to hear they didn't have to be in a hurry to get married. Or to ever get married at all.

Sensia now made a bit of a scene. She stood up and stabbed her knife into the table with a big grin broadening her ruddy face. She shouted her hearty approval of the change. Everyone had always known Sensia didn't want to marry at all. Muffled snickers sounded throughout the crowd of seated Children. Though he didn't actually say anything, Cain made sure everyone saw the vivid (though fake) indignation on his face, because he had been Sensia's official fiancé.

"Parius will explain the rest of the details," Savot announced, sitting down.

Parius, apparently not having expected Savot to give him the floor, wiped the roasted boar grease from his mouth with a napkin as he stood up.

"Well, New Atlanteans," Parius started, swallowing his last bite of meat. "Laws on New Atlantis may change some, as this one has, but we plan to keep most of the laws as they were handed down to us by our forefathers." It was no secret to anyone that Parius, if he could have his own way, would never have changed a thing. But he was clearly supporting Savot's royal right to change civil laws.

"King Savot felt this change was desirable because so many of you have been dissatisfied with your appointed fiancés."

At this Parius glanced at Bena, his now-former fiancée. She quickly turned her gaze away from him. Savot could tell this unnerved Parius, but the head of all the lawyers kept speaking in an official tone.

"So, as of today, all original engagements are broken." Although Savot had already said this, something about the executive tone of Parius' announcement precipitated a reverent hush across the feasting area.

"You may reaffirm your former engagements by registering them—starting tomorrow morning—if you'd like," he continued, trying to catch Bena's eye again. She still wouldn't look at him. "Or you may choose to marry someone else," he said in somewhat of a monotone.

Savot could almost feel Parius' agony. It was much like his own. The lawyer's love for Bena was widely known. But, as Savot could tell, Parius continued speaking—through sheer discipline—to fulfill his official responsibilities.

"When a couple registers for a wedding at the Court, both partners must sign the contract. The marriages will be scheduled in the order they are registered. In other words, whoever signs up first will be first to be married when the Year of Merger begins, the second will be next, and so on." Billius and Caris winked at each other across the table.

As soon as Parius concluded his oratory and sat down, dozens of hands shot up.

"What if somebody still wants to marry his fiancé but she doesn't want to marry me? I mean . . . him," Harus asked. His buddies near him stifled their snickers. Parius stood back up.

"No one gets married until both are in favor of the marriage," Parius clarified.

Harus' head dropped.

Then someone asked the crucial question. "Will Princess Aria still marry King Savot?" At this all the Children went quiet and Savot held his breath. *Here it comes*, he told himself, bracing for the worst.

But much to Savot's surprise, and before Parius could answer, Aria rose from her seat and announced,

"Yes. Our arrangement will not change." It took Savot a moment to gather his thoughts. Then he reasoned, *it's all about the right to the throne*. He glimpsed at Cain who didn't look at all fazed by Aria's declaration.

Nothing went normally for the rest of the evening. The eunuchs ended up playing obstaball by themselves. Hyperactive New Atlanteans intermingled until late into the night. Some had the courtesy to confirm the dissolution of unwanted engagements face to face with their ex-fiancés. Others didn't even bother but, rather, made a beeline for their already-chosen replacements.

Savot looked all around for Aria but couldn't find her. He asked Stacia where she was. The princess had asked to be alone, Stacia told him. Respecting her wishes, Savot settled into a hammock on the outskirts of the feasting area. He felt miserable.

Half-mindedly, the king surveyed the other Children's activities. Most of them clumped together for conversation in gender groups. Savot gathered that the boys were finally leveling with each other about which girls they each liked. One group stood close enough for him to hear.

Alek said to Jaxen, "I don't even want to decide yet. Since there's no deadline for when we get married, hey! Who's in a hurry?" Jaxen and the other boys around him laughed, and most agreed.

"Yeah, I need to think about this a while. Lots of great girls have just become available tonight. To be honest, Jaxen admitted, I've liked several of them at different times."

"Me too!" Vidor responded, acting surprised as if Jaxen had read his mind. "But I never thought about who I'd choose if I had the option." Savot wondered how many of the Children felt that way.

Among the groups of girls Savot heard giggling and saw frequent looks aimed at the boys. But he couldn't hear what any of the girls were saying.

The lawyers answered questions for the rest of the evening. Some of the newly formed couples were so eager that they asked Parius to go ahead and sign them up for weddings that night. But the attorney reiterated that the registration of marriage contracts would begin the next morning and not before.

***

Aria had disappeared from the feast because Cain had wanted to speak with her. The Rule change had come as a total surprise to the general. Aria had never told him anything about the possibility or about the letters between herself and Savot. But Cain told the princess that he was pleased with Aria's announcement that she would still marry Savot—even though they both knew that would never happen. It kept up their ruse very well.

"Quick thinking! You were just so composed!" he complimented her. Cain was delighted that Aria had kept up her deception so unflaggingly even though Savot had thrown this twist into the formula.

"And you too!" she complimented back. "You didn't even flinch! I thought the people needed to hear me pledge my loyalty to Savot at that point," Aria explained.

"You know, to make my grief more believable when he disappears."

"Brilliant!" Cain praised the princess again. The two stood in the same clearing where they usually met in secret—far away from the feasting area.

They now sat down on a tree stump and Aria settled backward into Cain's arms. They discussed the implications of the Rule change and concluded that the mutiny plot need not be affected by the amendment. But Cain did express his concern, once again, about waiting almost two more months to remove Savot from the throne.

"Savot's popularity with the people just keeps building," he explained. "I heard one of the boys say he's already a better king than your father was."

Aria gave a laugh, a bit of a nervous one. "That's crazy! No king could ever match my father. Except maybe you . . . someday," Aria teased. "Who said that about my father anyway?"

Cain couldn't remember. His mind was apparently fixated on changing the timetable for the insurrection.

"Maybe you're right," Aria agreed. "The more the Children like Savot, the harder it'll be for them to transfer their loyalty to you."

"Let's do it right after the next feast," Cain suggested. Offering no resistance, Aria agreed. Cain said he'd inform Toren.

"Until then," Cain instructed, "you go ahead with your 'plan' to marry him."

***

The next day thirty-nine couples registered for weddings with the Court of New Atlantis. Billius and Caris beat everyone else there, arriving before dawn, to make sure they would be first on the list. Only eighteen of the original pairs had remained engaged by their own choice.

The other twenty-one were new engagements. Within the first hour of the registrations, the wedding dates filled the first month of the Year of Merger and spilled over into the next month.

Aria went to the Court that morning and signed the registration paper to marry Savot. That fulfilled her part of the requirement for an official betrothal. She then dispatched Win to deliver the news to Savot, requesting him to come sign their registration also.

Aria waited at the Court, but Win returned alone, reporting to the princess that Savot refused to sign the contract. Upon hearing this news, Aria kicked sharply at the dirt. She insisted on seeing Savot immediately . . . and this time she went directly to his house unannounced.

"Savot!" Aria demanded, marching inside without knocking. "I understood from your letter why you don't want to marry me. *But you have to.* That is, if you refuse to abdicate your power."

Savot said nothing. He couldn't even look at Aria.

"I won't marry Cain," the princess told him. "Or anyone else. If you're going to be king of New Atlantis, then I have to be queen. Don't you understand?"

Still Savot didn't speak.

"Savot, say something!" So finally he did, with a great amount of control.

"I was thinking you and Cain could rule the residence island," Savot said with his back to Aria.

Aria puffed in exasperation. She moved around to where he could see her. "You obviously haven't thought that through, Savot. Don't you know that would end up dividing the kingdom?"

Savot had indeed thought that scenario through. And his trust in Cain's loyalty wavered more each day since he had read Galen's caution in the diary. Previously cloaked evidences of Cain's self-service had become apparent since Savot had been watching for them. He now rebuked himself in his thoughts for his generalized trust in people. But, on the other hand, he didn't want to exclude Aria from holding a position of rule either. And ruling was undoubtedly vital to her.

This is a no-win situation, he thought. He still wouldn't look at Aria. It was just too difficult.

"I don't want to marry any of the other girls. Maybe there could be another solution," Savot pondered aloud.

The two argued about the potential for another arrangement for a while, but came to no agreeable conclusion. After a while Aria stomped her foot and then turned on her heel and stormed out of the house.

As Savot watched her trudge away, Nat—standing guard at the door—opened his mouth to say something. But the king caught him. "Not a word from you, Nat." Nat clamped his mouth closed and rolled his eyes.

***

Aria called for yet another meeting with Cain that night. Secretly, of course.

"He won't sign the papers," the princess announced. "He says you and I could get married and rule the residence island." This idea seemed to hit Cain sideways. He took a while to consider it. Then a slow, sinister smile spread across his handsome, sun-tanned face.

"Well, let's do that then," Cain proposed. Aria looked startled.

"Yeah," Cain said. "Let's just go ahead and sign up to get married. That way people will already be used to you and me being together instead of waiting till later."

"But . . . but wait, I don't understand . . ." Aria sputtered. Even in dim torchlight it was clear that all the color had faded from her face. She sat down on a stump. Now Cain looked puzzled.

"What's wrong, Aria? Doesn't that make sense to you? The reality of us ruling the residence island won't even be an issue once 'the pirates' kidnap Savot."

Aria gathered her composure and spoke. "Umm . . . yes, I suppose that makes sense," she answered tentatively. Then with growing determination she added, "Yes, it does make sense. I just hadn't considered that we could handle it that way." She got up slowly and strode to the other side of the clearing.

"But how do we make that announcement after I've told everyone I was still going to marry Savot?"

"We'll make the announcement at the Month Nine Feast and then we'll register," Cain answered her. "Most people know you don't really have any feelings for Savot . . . and that you do for me."

"That'll make Savot look so bad, though. We don't want him to look bad, do we?" Aria reasoned. Cain eyed her suspiciously.

"What do you care how he looks?"

"Well, I mean . . ." Aria stumbled over her words. "We still want the people to respect him, don't we?"

"Just because you don't choose him as your husband, you think people won't respect him?" Cain argued.

Back and forth they went along those lines until Aria and Cain came to the agreement that—if they explained their engagement in careful words—Savot could maintain most of the admiration from the citizens that he now held. They left each other agreeing to announce their engagement at the Month Nine Feast and register the following day.

But they parted that night without their usual kiss. And Aria didn't tell Savot about her change of plans, though she had told Cain she would. She didn't tell anyone.

***

Toren spotted lights on the northern horizon about a week into Month Nine. And he knew it couldn't be Cain in their secret ship, so he was quite alarmed. Cain was asleep in his house. Toren rushed to awaken the general.

Cain wasted no time in investigating the mystery. He took a trusted group of Navy personnel with him, paddling quietly in two unlit skiffs toward the strange vessels. The boys got close enough to see by the light of the full moon what roughly resembled four Atlantean-style ships, but no flags were raised. The occupants of the foreign ships apparently sighted the boys' small boats and sailed further away from them.

"Maybe they really are pirates!" Toren proposed to Cain. The two conspirators were in a boat by themselves. Three other sailors occupied the other skiff.

"Maybe, but I doubt it." Cain's mind seemed to be wandering. Then he said with a spark, "This could make our mission more complicated. Or . . ." A crafty smirk invaded Cain's face. "It could make it easier."

"What? I don't get it." Toren wasn't the fast thinker that Cain was.

Cain explained—with annoyance—that if the ships kept their distance, the lights from those ships could eliminate the need for the clandestine outings he and Toren had been making. And that would eliminate the risk that either of the two would ever be caught posing as pirates themselves.

"All right," Toren agreed, finally understanding. "But what if those pirates are here to make trouble for New Atlantis? What if they're going back to get a hundred others to come attack us?"

"You *idiot!*" Cain shouted in a whisper so that the boys in the other boat couldn't hear. Toren cowered. "Don't you know anything about pirates? They hardly ever travel in groups of more than two ships." Cain practically spat his words at Toren. "Those aren't pirates!

"I'm betting they're just trading ships anchoring at night before traveling on." He spoke more evenly now. "But even if they are pirates, we've been trained to fight them off."

After that night Cain appointed himself to the nightly shore guard for a while. He didn't have to watch long to spot the lights again. They appeared the very next night. The general took Shay and Marcum out on a small boat to try to identify the vessels again. The three returned with a dreadful description.

"We were able to get pretty close," Cain told Savot the next day. "Our Navy Mentors taught us what kind of ships those are."

"What kind?" Savot asked.

Cain answered with trepidation and drama. "They are *definitely* pirate ships, Your Majesty." Shay and Marcum, who had accepted Cain's confident statement as fact, confirmed the information.

Savot knew the stories of pirate attacks on Atlantean naval missions. Perhaps Cain had been right all along about the lights indicating pirates.

"Prepare the Navy to double up on their shore guard both day and night," the king commanded his general.

"I've already done that," Cain replied. "We're ready for them, Your Highness."

Chapter 15

The Ghost Appears to Savot

As Month Nine progressed, Savot's prayer appointments with Amedis lengthened. Meeting in the now-completed Temple, the king and high priest prayed about the pirates. They prayed about the dilemma between Savot and Aria. They prayed about the new marital plans the Children were making.

One sunny morning, they prayed for an unusually long time. Both knelt facing the altar as usual. Neither Savot nor Amedis had any inkling that New Atlantean history was about to be made right before their eyes.

Savot was praying aloud when the altar before him seemed to burst open with a penetrating brightness. A sweet but bulky aroma filled the room. Savot and Amedis instinctively covered their eyes for protection from the glaring light. While sputtering and coughing in the heavy incense-like air, they heard a man's voice. They both began quaking uncontrollably and fell to their knees.

"King Savot of New Atlantis," the powerful voice echoed in the vaulted chamber.

Savot allowed his fingers to part while still covering his eyes. Blinking in the dazzling glow that emanated from the obscured altar, he could barely make out a figure standing in the light. Amedis ventured to peek too. As Savot's eyes strained to adjust to what seemed like direct sunlight, he guessed at what this apparition might be.

He whispered to Amedis, "It's The Ghost!" Amedis covered his eyes again and yelped with his mouth closed.

The ominous form stepped toward them. The boys couldn't rise to their feet though they tried. It seemed they were held down on their weak, trembling knees by some invisible force. As The Ghost came closer to them, the heavy holiness in the air grew even stronger. Savot fought to breathe.

But his rapid heartbeat strangely calmed as the alien came to stand right in front of him. Savot suddenly felt warm and stopped shivering, but the invisible weight on him still wouldn't allow him to stand. Amedis finally dropped his hands from his eyes and gawked at the legendary Ghost.

The specter that stood before Savot and Amedis looked like a normal man in many ways, except he had no beard. His hair was brown and shoulder-length. He wasn't human, though, because his eyes shone as brightly as stars and his robes emanated a bright radiance in the otherwise unlit chamber. Savot strained his eyes to focus on the radiant shape.

"Are you . . ." Savot dared to ask, "The Ghost?"

A split second passed and then a hearty laugh came in reply. Savot and Amedis stared at each other, befuddled. *The Ghost laughs?* Savot thought. And then the shining figure answered him.

"Yes, King Savot. I am the one your people have called 'The Ghost'. Some among your race have wondered whether I am real or not," The Ghost said, seeming amused.

Amedis shook his head mechanically as if to answer, "Not me!" The Ghost laughed again. Then Savot remembered that the priest was supposed to be writing down The Ghost's words.

"Get some paper," he ordered Amedis out of the side of his mouth. The young priest crawled laboriously to a nearby table and, with wobbly hands, retrieved a quill, ink, and a piece of parchment. Amazingly, The Ghost waited for Amedis to return to Savot's side before speaking again. Amedis started scribbling, trying hard to remember exactly the words he had missed.

Still The Ghost waited until Amedis had finished writing. Then he announced with a smile, "The God of Heaven has sent me with an important message for you, King Savot." Savot was so awestruck that he didn't answer. He could hardly believe he was in the presence of the fearsome Ghost he'd heard about all his life. He sat back on his feet in wonder. Amedis had to hold his right wrist steady with his left hand as he resumed his frantic scrawling.

The Ghost repeated, "I have a message for you from the God of Heaven."

"Oh!" Savot blurted out, realizing The Ghost had been waiting for a response from him. "I'm very honored, My Lord. Just tell me what he wants me to do and I'll do it."

The Ghost smiled as if pleasantly entertained by Savot. Then he straightened his expression and addressed the young king formally.

"King of New Atlantis . . . Savot, the message I delivered to King Jorash seventeen years ago has been related to you many times. But each time you have heard a false report," The Ghost revealed. Savot and Amedis were taken aback and confused, but The Ghost kept on speaking.

"I have been sent to correct the message in your minds and in your records."

The Ghost then announced that he would redeliver the message just as it had been conveyed to King Jorash seventeen years prior—word for word. But before he did so, he warned the boys that there was bad news to come. So Savot and Amedis braced themselves as they waited to hear it. Amedis had his quill ready to write on the parchment that he had placed on the floor.

"'King Jorash,'" The Ghost began, quoting himself from years before, "'your charge to rule the great kingdom of Atlantis has been deplorably violated. Though you knew full well of your requirement to deal justly with weaker lands, your greed and pride have overcome you.'"

Savot and Amedis looked at each other in dismay. This was quite different from the message they had always heard. *What violation is he talking about?* Savot wondered. Amedis struggled against his weakness to scribble down The Ghost's words using the shorthand he and Thea had invented.

"'Your heartless slaughter of countless innocents has been witnessed by Heaven's God. You have acted only in accordance with your own unbridled avarice. By your orders you have sent your soldiers to ravage the Mediterranean lands—a severe crime against Heaven. And not only have weaker peoples perished at your hand, you have also sent many of your own military men to their deaths.'"

"Ravage?" Savot mouthed silently. Things were starting to come together in his head. *Uncle Thad?* he thought as he remembered his mother's brother who was killed on one of King Jorash's 'missions'. Many pieces of this grotesque new puzzle flew through Savot's mind. There were too many for him to assemble all at once. He felt sick to his stomach.

"'What you have done is unforgivable, King Jorash,'" The Ghost continued soberly. By the contortion of his friend's face, Savot could tell that Amedis was also absorbing the vile reality of the situation. Things were badly askew in Atlantis and had been all their lives.

Both boys began trembling again as their minds raced to comprehend the horror. Though by this time they had finally been able to stand, they both now crumpled to the floor in pitiful heaps. Many times as The Ghost continued revealing his report, the boys collapsed. But each time they wilted to the floor, the glowing form came to them and placed his right hand on Savot's head and his left on Amedis'. Instantly, each time, the king and priest were strengthened enough to continue listening and for Amedis to keep writing.

"'Your golden palaces are covered with blood, King Jorash.'" The Ghost persisted. "'Your silver opulence is detestable in the sight of Heaven. Though the wealth of your orichalcum could have greatly benefited less fortunate lands, instead you withheld your resources, stole theirs, and butchered their men, women, and even their children.'"

The Ghost paused as if grieved. Then a deafening crack of thunder sounded, though the day had been cloudless. This sent the boys to the ground again. *Retaliation*, was the only word Savot could think of at this point. *All those people; they're going to want vengeance.*

"Orichalcum!" Amedis whispered, looking wide-eyed at Savot. Savot understood the priest's thoughts. The orichalcum bricks the miners had found on the smallest island were evidence that Jorash had hoarded the precious metal instead of trading it with other countries as the Unknown God had instructed him. And he had plundered their gold and silver, bringing them back to Atlantis. The beautiful stolen metals now covered all the buildings on Atlantis.

And the buildings on New Atlantis were in the process of being veneered with the gold and silver as well! *Our buildings might as well be covered with blood,* Savot realized with repulsion.

The Ghost had even more bad news. This time he spoke directly to the boys, pausing from repeating the original message to Jorash.

"King Jorash himself murdered Evran, his high priest, so that the truth of this message would never be revealed to the people of Atlantis," The Ghost told Savot and Amedis.

So their lifelong monarch was a prolific liar, a first-hand murderer, and had commanded massacres and worldwide thievery. Savot felt as if a giant had just punched him in the gut. He covered his face in shame. But his next thought was of the princess. *Aria. Oh, my poor Aria!*

The Ghost took an unusually long, deep breath. Then he said, "The final announcement I was sent to deliver to King Jorash was this." An ominous silence followed, and Savot suspected what was coming.

"'Three times I have been sent to warn you, King Jorash,'" said The Ghost. "'But you have not ceased your treacherous dealings with the Mediterranean peoples. The God of Heaven has decreed punishment upon you for your evil deeds.'"

Then The Ghost uttered the most ghastly words the boys had yet heard.

"'Because of your hard-heartedness and impenitence, Atlantis will be destroyed.'" Savot and Amedis gawked at The Ghost in terror.

Then both king and priest heaved themselves flat on the ground and wailed. The supernatural being stood silent before them. At last Amedis dutifully, though feebly, lifted his head and hand to record this last fateful pronouncement.

But Savot was completely overcome with grief. Still lying face down, his tears made puddles on the stone floor of the Temple. He couldn't make himself stop sobbing.

The Ghost went to Savot and knelt beside him. Placing one hand on Savot's head and the other on his shoulder, the heavenly messenger simply lingered there with Savot until the boy-king's weeping began to subside. When Savot finally sat up, Amedis had quit his writing. Both of their faces were white and completely wet with both sweat and tears.

Then, in a thin voice, Savot asked the obvious question.

"Our families. They will all be killed, won't they?"

The Ghost hesitated, "Yes, they will. A ruler bears the responsibility for the fate of his subjects. Their destruction is the consequence of King Jorash's persistent malevolence." Then Amedis put his face to the floor and wept loudly. Savot had no strength left with which to cry.

But finally the dark report had come to an end.

"Now you may wonder why you are here on New Atlantis," The Ghost said. Savot just stared at him too tired now to answer. "This next part of King Jorash's report was mostly true. As I told the king, 'Because of the earnest faith of King Thorean, to whom I first spoke five hundred years ago, and because of the faithfulness of all the other kings of Atlantis, the God of Heaven has ruled that a remnant of your people shall be preserved.'" At this Amedis looked up.

Savot momentarily forgot that he was in the presence of a heavenly being. "So . . . we're not here to 'expand the great glory of Atlantis' as King Jorash had always told us? We're just here to be preserved?"

"Atlantis was great only because the blessing of Heaven's God rested on it," The Ghost answered. "And the God of Heaven has desired to give the Atlantean people one more chance to honor him."

Savot's mind swam with questions, but The Ghost now proclaimed, "Rise up, rulers of New Atlantis! Your task is before you. The God of Heaven has shown mercy to you and to your generation. There is yet hope to preserve your race."

Savot, the king, at that very moment, realized—as if a lightening bolt had hit him—that not only the fate of the Chosen Children but also the destiny of the whole Atlantean legacy lay upon his shoulders. He raised his head. Surprised that now they had more than adequate strength to stand, Savot and Amedis rose to their feet and stood before The Ghost.

The young king spoke to The Ghost in a frail, almost-whisper, "Will you help me? Will you ask the Unknown God . . . I mean, the 'God of Heaven' to help me?"

The Ghost smiled brightly. "King Savot, this is why *you* were chosen. And I have been restrained until now from coming to you because you were being tested. But now, Heaven's God regards you as a man of great preciousness. You are highly esteemed by him, King Savot. Your submission to him has been recognized and honored. Your humility has been recorded and your faithfulness will be rewarded."

This made Savot feel immensely thankful, but also surprised. *I can hardly believe the Unknown God values me so much*, he thought. He suddenly felt both elated and empowered. And, beyond that, The Ghost had referred to him as a man. No one had ever called him that before. Amedis dropped his quill to gaze at Savot as if he was someone really famous.

"But . . . what else could I have done, My Lord? It only makes sense that I needed to humble myself before the . . . the 'God of Heaven'. My prayers and his help are the only way I know to survive the weight of this position."

"Very good, King Savot," The Ghost replied, with delight in his voice. "That is all he requires. I only regret that King Jorash did not see it that way." Savot wanted to ask many more questions. But The Ghost wasn't finished, so he continued speaking.

"Now that you are aware, at last, of the complete and true set of instructions the God of Heaven has given your people, obey them, and New Atlantis will prosper."

"Could I ask you something, Sir?" Savot ventured.

"Yes, King Savot. Ask."

"We have only known you as 'The Ghost'. What is your real name?"

The Ghost softly laughed. "If I told you, you wouldn't understand."

Savot struggled inside himself about whether or not to argue. And just as he had gathered his courage to, the heavenly apparition changed the subject.

"Atlantis will be destroyed. The God of Heaven commands you, King Savot, and Amedis, high priest of New Atlantis, to keep this revelation sealed until it becomes clear that your former homeland is no more."

Then The Ghost vanished.

***

Savot and Amedis swore to each other that they wouldn't say anything to anyone—not even Thea—about The Ghost's visit or his message until the tragedy manifested itself. Each boy, independent of the other, mourned and fasted for many days after their encounter with The Ghost.

Holed up in their rooms, both refused to see anyone. Amedis carefully hid the papers on which he had written The Ghost's message. Everyone on New Atlantis speculated about what could be wrong with the king and the priest.

Savot even cancelled his next meeting with Aria.

"This is really strange, Your Highness," Caris commented upon hearing of the cancellation. "Savot usually makes up reasons to have extra meetings with you. Is he sick or something?"

Aria puzzled over the question. "I doubt it. Savot's as healthy as a horse. He never gets sick."

"I'd have thought he'd be more excited than ever about seeing you since you announced you're still planning to marry him," added Stacia. Aria didn't answer. Instead she shifted the focus of conversation to her attendants' love lives. Both had reaffirmed their engagements with their former fiancés.

"I'm glad you two still want to marry your fiancés too," she diverted.

Caris' face lit up. "You mean double-fiancés! That's the way Billius and I like to look at it." She giggled and clapped her hands in a sudden burst of excitement. "We're first on the new registration list! I'll miss you, Aria—but living with Billius . . . as my husband! Oh, it's just what I've always wanted!"

"I'm glad to see you so happy," Aria said sincerely. "And you, Stacia, you and Lian. I know you've had your ups and downs. But I'm happy for you, that you've decided he's really the right one for you."

Stacia glanced sheepishly from under furrowed eyebrows at her two companions.

"What?" Caris asked. "Did something happen?" Aria's full attention turned to Stacia as well. Stacia stammered a bit with 'well' and 'you see' until finally she came out with it.

"I broke off our engagement last night," she confessed. Then she plunked herself down on Aria's bed and erupted into weeping.

"Stacia! I thought you two had everything settled," Aria blurted in surprise. "You registered and everything. You were celebrating just yesterday!" Aria spoke with chastisement in her voice. That made Stacia cry even more. Caris sat down beside her and put an arm around Stacia's shoulders. But almost immediately after her gesture of sympathy, Caris' tone changed to match Aria's.

"Listen to me, Stacia," Caris admonished. "You've got to quit jerking that boy around. He's always loved you. And I know you love him. What's the matter with you?"

Through sniffles and tears, Stacia explained. "After we registered the other day it just hit me. Before I didn't have a choice, and now I do. I couldn't sleep at all night before last thinking of all the selfish things he does. How every conversation we have is all about him." The words spilled like a waterfall from Stacia's lips.

"He hardly ever asks about *me*," Stacia continued, "and if he does it's just 'cause I tell him he's supposed to. I mean, I do love him—how can I help it? He's so charming. And he's so much fun . . ."

"And cute!" Caris interrupted in a persuasive tone.

"Yes, of course, cute," Stacia agreed. "But living with him the rest of my life? I'm just not sure I could put up with him."

All three girls now sat on Aria's bed, thinking. Stacia repeatedly wiped tears from her cheeks and whimpered. After all, she was right. Lian's juvenile behavior had been a source of annoyance to everybody at one time or another.

"Well, I guess you're right, Stacia. Better not do it if you're not sure," Aria concluded.

"Maybe Lian just needs to grow up some more," Caris speculated. "Maybe in a year or two he'll realize he's not the center of the universe."

In the end, after Stacia had cried on both her friends' shoulders until they were thoroughly wet, Aria and Caris promised to support her decision. But the two roommates afterward decided to write Lian separate letters. Caris and Aria now knew that Stacia was determined to hold out for a more mature version of Lian, or someone else she could love who was more ready for marriage. In their letters Aria and Caris urged Lian to hurry up and grow out of his childish self-centeredness if he ever wanted Stacia as his wife.

$$***$$

The work of building during Month Nine progressed faster than anyone had expected. The eunuchs took all the credit for this. But in reality, it happened because the Children had already done the very same work once on the peninsula and had learned from their mistakes.

Savot could see no end to his grief over Atlantis' pending destruction. But after a solid week of isolation, he decided he should at least try to return to his routine schedule. He gave no one an explanation for his seclusion.

The first thing he felt he should do was visit the work sites. He made special notes for commendations he would give at the Month Nine Feast, now only a week away. But The Ghost's words rang in his ears almost incessantly. And he constantly worried about how Aria would take the news.

***

Since the first night the anonymous lights (the truly unknown ones) had been sighted on the horizon, the military generals—Cain and Sensia—drilled their troops harder than ever, preparing them to fight pirates.

Though the military girls still despised Sensia for what they considered her 'torture' of them, they all had to admit they felt well-prepared for combat. Besides, the military girls had begun challenging the military boys to duels at the feasts. And the satisfaction of beating them at least half the time was almost worth Sensia's rigorous training even if they never had to battle pirates.

The night before the Month Nine Feast, Savot read Galen's diary again.

> *I'm sure there will be unexpected challenges. But you are wiser than you should be for your age, Savot. Consult with Amedis and Parius. They seem to be insightful. And they perceive many things that others miss. Jamin is also wise and unselfish. These three should prove good advisors for you. I pray for you often, and you can be sure I will continue when we're apart . . .*

Savot had to close the diary at this point. He dropped his forehead down onto the leather. Deep sadness again swallowed him as he thought about Galen perishing soon along with his parents and everyone else he loved on Atlantis. He wasn't sure how long he wept, but the next thing he knew it was morning, the day of the Month Nine Feast.

Chapter 16

Fire in the Sky

The Month Nine Feast was held in the coldest weather the Children had ever experienced. Snow had fallen the week before and hadn't melted much and there was continuing cloud cover. It was the first snow the Children had ever seen. Savot had even cancelled a day of work so that his peers could play in the new white phenomenon. The boys and girls—though separately—discovered how to make snowmen and snow angels, and they also engaged in many snowball fights.

Now bundled in their warmest clothes, the Children began the Month Nine Feast with the customary massive spread of food. Only the thirty-nine officially engaged couples sat together. The others mingled and flirted as never before. Aria sat with Savot, but the king barely spoke to her. He didn't know what to say to her about any subject right now, considering all The Ghost had told him. Cain and Sensia, having called off their engagement, ate with their military inferiors.

Risa, who had been reluctant to leave Lalera, spent part of the evening with her fiancé Peri before she went back to the prison; but all she wanted to talk to him about was Lalera's condition. The kindhearted girl doctor was concerned that Lalera wasn't eating much and looked pale. Peri cared—as a fellow doctor—but he also pouted, wanting some of Risa's attention for himself. Still Risa went on and on about Lalera's health, both physical and mental.

After the dinner the eunuchs convinced some of the boys to play obstaball. The boys welcomed the chance to warm themselves with exercise. A lively game began on the field despite the inch of snow that still covered it. The players scampered and slid around the field like puppies. Instead of participating, or even watching the game, this time Savot walked around by himself. He avoided talking to anyone.

Next on the agenda, after the game, was a new musical play. Small camp-type fires had been built up and down the aisles of the amphitheater to help keep the Children warm. The boys presented a play that Blane and Vidor had just written. The story was about King Jorash and Atlantis. Blane played King Jorash and had put the traditional story of The Ghost's appearance to song. *Why did tonight's play have to be about this?* Savot thought, a sharp pang running him through like a sword.

"'I, King Jorash of Atlantis,'" Blane sang, "'was visited by The Ghost last night.'" Savot cringed as he listened to the melodious lie. He wondered how this play was affecting Amedis. Inconspicuously scanning the audience, Savot caught sight of the priest sitting toward the back of the outdoor theater. He was perched on a stone bench with his head ducked into his coat not even watching the play.

The sky was at last beginning to clear and, since the sun had set, the sharp chill in the air intensified. The stars shone brighter than usual with no moon to outshine them. *I'll just look at the stars*, Savot told himself. *That way I won't think about what Blane's singing.* He gazed up at the black, star-dazzled sky.

"'Atlantis the Great, too vast for containment . . .'" Blane warbled in his finely-grained tenor voice. The music was so beautiful. It struck Savot as ironic that such wonderful music could be married to such horrible deception.

"'Two hundred and sixty-eight yet unconceived, chosen by the Unknown for the glorious, glorious mission . . .'" sang Blane. The lyrics were artfully constructed even though mostly untrue.

Blane had just taken another deep breath to sing more when it happened.

The ground beneath the theater jolted. Then a slow, ominous quivering started under the Children's feet . . . and it grew.

"Earthquake!" someone yelled.

The Children instinctively scattered in all directions, screaming and rushing as quickly as their unstable legs would carry them toward sheltering structures. Some accidentally stumbled into the nearby campfires, setting their clothes ablaze. Nearby Children rushed to put out the flames before their friends were too badly burned. Amid the chaos, Cain, Savot, and Nat made their way to the stage.

"Wait!" Cain shouted at the top of his lungs so that all the Children could hear. "Stay here!"

"Don't go into any buildings," Savot yelled the warning. "This is the safest place to be. Everybody sit down." The crowd obeyed the king.

"Try to stay calm," Nat added. "This should be over soon."

The Children, now crouching or sitting on the ground, held onto the theater's stone benches for stability. They had experienced a similar earthquake on Atlantis when they were much younger. Now they huddled together in clumps, trying to contain their alarm. The ground's trembling persisted.

Halfway finished buildings nearby broke apart from the top down. Both goals on the obstaball field shook until they tumbled over. Boys crept carefully toward clusters of panicky girls.

The boys placed their outspread arms around the girls, trying to protect them. Many Children followed Amedis' and Savot's examples of calling out to the Unknown God to make it stop. Still the earth beneath them kept vibrating violently.

Savot made his way on wobbly legs to where Aria, Stacia, Caris, and Billius sat. He knelt behind Aria and cradled her in his arms. Amedis made his way to the same area to be near Thea.

Cain refused to sit down. Rather, he staggered around the theater stationing guards at its exits. He also took it upon himself to reinforce Savot's command.

"NO ONE LEAVE THE AREA!" Cain shouted many times as he struggled to remain upright on the joggling ground.

Looking again toward the stars, Savot tried to calm himself. But the dark sky he had viewed so clearly only moments earlier was now obscured by a dull, gray haze that grew thicker toward the southern horizon.

All eyes soon turned toward what quickly became a horrific display in the sky behind the stage. A growing semi-circle of orange light rose slowly from the haze like an enormous half-moon on the vista to their south.

"Atlantis!" several shouted. "Atlantis is on fire!" The girls' whimpers ruptured into frantic shrieks. Even the boys and eunuchs cried out in terror at the ghastly spectacle.

Savot and Amedis agreed with a single look that the time had come to inform the Children about The Ghost's visit. The two made their way, with difficulty, to the stage.

"Don't be afraid," Savot called out to his subjects.

"We're going to be all right, I promise," Amedis added.

With the crowd still panicking, Toren shouted over the noise, "How do you know we're going to be all right, priest? Looks to me like we're all gonna die!"

"I know for sure that we're not going to die. The Unknown God said we'd be all right," Amedis assured. This got several Children's attention. They eyed Amedis suspiciously.

"Wait until this is over and we'll explain," pledged the king.

Though Nat had assured the Children the earthquake would be over quickly, it wasn't. For nearly ten minutes it continued. But at least the tremors didn't get worse. The Children, jumbled in groups, tried to calm one another. Still, they couldn't keep their eyes off the fiery southern sky. Most wept as they watched, not only from fright but now—Savot could tell—also from the realization of what was happening to their mother continent.

At last, and suddenly, the earth beneath them went still.

The Children sat cautiously frozen, fearing the quake would begin again. But after a few minutes when it didn't, the stark awareness of what had happened fell on the group as though they had been conglomerated into one person. All burst into loud, unrestrained weeping.

Clinging to each other, some even collapsing from the trauma, the Chosen Children seemed to Savot like a group of helpless infants. For quite a while the wailing and bawling went on. Then words began to emerge from the Children. Soon the front of the stage was crowded with citizens seeking answers from Savot and Amedis.

Lian's question was the first the two leaders could really hear.

"Atlantis has been destroyed, hasn't it?" His question was followed instantly by Toren's.

"Amedis, what did you mean the Unknown God told you we wouldn't die?"

Amedis looked toward Savot. The priest and king had prepared a joint announcement, and now was the necessary time for them to reveal what The Ghost had said. Savot especially dreaded Aria having to hear it. But he nodded for Amedis to begin.

Amedis spoke calmly and steadily. "Two weeks ago, as King Savot and I were praying together, The Ghost appeared to us." Thea was the first to gasp. And her gasp rolled like ocean waves throughout the tightly bunched mass of Children.

Amedis continued, "He told us that Atlantis would soon be destroyed."

Tears flowed anew at the official confirmation of what they had already guessed. But soon some of the Children became irate and objected.

"Why didn't you tell us if you've known for two weeks?"

"Yeah, maybe we could have warned our families!" Anger was growing within the crowd.

"No, there would have been no way we could have gotten to them fast enough to warn them," Amedis answered. "Believe me, Savot and I tried to think of a way, but we finally concluded it was impossible."

"You could have at least warned *us* it was going to happen!" Shay complained.

"Yeah, why'd you let us all go through this scared to death?"

Savot held up both hands, motioning for quiet. "The Ghost commanded us to keep his visit secret until it was evident that Atlantis had perished."

Nat and Win cried out almost in unison, "Our families! They're all dead?" This question turned the divided mood of the crowd back into pure grief. The distressed Children bawled even harder now. Savot knew how they felt. They were now experiencing corporately the immense sorrow that he and Amedis had suffered for the previous two weeks in solitude. Aria wept harder than Savot had ever seen before.

"Let them cry," Savot instructed Amedis. And the two leaders joined their countrymen in mourning. They didn't move, however, from their locations on the stage. Savot knew his stance there above his subjects was crucial at this juncture. Standing as firmly and confidently as he could, Savot represented to them the only stability New Atlantis now had.

Savot looked around for Cain who had been noticeably absent since Amedis had announced The Ghost's appearance. He spotted the general sitting at the back of the theater, standing against a stone wall. The expression on his face was markedly different from every other Child's. Instead of being grief-stricken, Cain was unmistakably terrified. Savot had never seen Cain frightened about anything.

What in the world is going on with him? Savot wondered. But now was not the time to find out. Savot's subjects needed comfort from him. He wiped his own eyes with his fists and mustered up all the courage he could find inside himself.

"Yes. Our families have perished," he answered the needless question. Savot maintained the bravest countenance he could for the sake of the Children, but his heart fluttered hopelessly in his chest felt like a wounded moth.

"Everything will be all right. We'll all be fine. The Unknown God will help us." He tried to think of other words of assurance but then he looked toward Aria. She had thrown herself on the ground in a prone position, face-down. She was sobbing despairingly.

When he saw Aria's condition, Savot could not keep holding back his own tears. So what he was about to say stuck in his throat. He stepped away from center stage and nodded for Amedis to take over again. The king and priest had planned beforehand for Amedis, not Savot, to be the one to reveal Jorash's wickedness.

"The Unknown God decreed judgment on Atlantis." Amedis cautiously glanced in Aria's direction. She didn't raise her head. Amedis reluctantly proceeded to unfold the saga of her father's corruption. Savot bit the inside of his cheek and clenched his hands behind his back. When Amedis first mentioned Jorash's disobedience, Aria finally looked up. As he went on the princess sat up, staring in disbelief. Savot cringed as he watched her stunned reaction. His beloved princess' face turned a ghostly white as she learned the full extent of her father's crimes.

Aria became so weak that both Caris and Stacia had to wrap their arms around her to hold her up. Several times the princess appeared to be hyperventilating and came close to passing out. Savot had never seen her look more fragile. As agonizing as he knew this must be for Aria, just watching her was killing him.

When Amedis finished, the audience was in a state of absolute shock. Savot took the floor again without delay. With the worst of the news behind them, he was anxious to finish reporting The Ghost's instructions.

"I understand how you're all feeling. My family is dead too. I know we had hoped to see them all again." He paused, unsuccessfully blinking back huge tears. "Amedis and I have had a while to think about this though. The Unknown God could have just destroyed us along with our families. Or he could have destroyed Atlantis before we were even born."

Amedis broke in, "But he didn't. The Ghost told us that . . ." Amedis stopped just long enough to retrieve the parchment scroll from its container that hung at his side. Reading now, he continued, "'Because of the earnest faith of King Thorean, to whom I first spoke five hundred years ago, and because of the faithfulness of all the other kings of Atlantis, the God of Heaven has ruled that a remnant of your people shall be preserved.'"

Amedis then looked up from the parchment and addressed the Children. "That's what The Ghost said! The Unknown God wants to give the Atlantean race one more chance." Then he added with emphasis, "And we're it!"

The Children now appeared awestruck. The boys, even with fresh tears on their cheeks, stood straighter and some even puffed their chests out. Most of the girls' splotched faces still looked helpless, but now inquisitive. Savot knew it was time for him to deliver the most important challenge he'd ever voiced to his people. He stepped up beside Amedis.

"So, you see," he told his subjects, "this means we're even more special than anyone ever thought. When we should have been killed—or not even born—because of the sins of our leaders . . ." He had to say it this way, because it was true, but he noticed Aria's frail wince at this statement. "we were chosen to preserve our race. We *must* continue with this assignment!"

"The Unknown God is good!" Amedis encouraged. "He hasn't given up on us." As the Children struggled to absorb this reality, some began responding.

"We're all that's left on earth to represent Atlantis," Vigo summarized, looking flabberghasted.

"We were spared because of King Thorean and the other kings?" questioned Maya. "But we didn't even know them. I don't understand."

Rapid-fire questions pelted Savot and Amedis.

"What did The Ghost look like?" asked Thea.

"Did our Mentors know?" Jaxen inquired.

"Did our parents know what was going to happen?"

"You mean King Jorash knew all along?"

There was silence after that question. All eyes turned to Aria. And that took her last bit of strength away. Giving in to her lightheadedness, the princess fainted.

Savot started down off the platform toward Aria. But Cain beat Savot to where Aria lay in the arms of her attendants. Savot noticed that the general had somehow shaken the fright from his countenance and now seemed very gallant.

Cain ordered guards to carry Aria to her house. That broke up any formality the meeting might have had left. The Children flocked to the stage, barraging the king and priest with more questions.

***

When Aria became conscious again, Cain was kneeling beside her. He ordered everyone out of the room before she could speak.

"Aria, we need to talk," Cain said, taking her hand and stroking it.

"My father . . . did he lie to me, Cain?" Aria asked with passionate dismay.

"Did *he* lie?" Cain retorted indignantly. "You know your father would never lie to you, Aria. It's Savot who's lying. Apparently, he's bribed Amedis into lying too."

"Really? Do you think Savot could have come up with a lie like that so quickly? During an earthquake?" Aria questioned. "And . . . why?"

"Well, I have to admit, he's quicker than I'd given him credit for. But it's the only thing that makes sense. I saw him talking to Amedis soon after the earthquake started."

"And then," Cain went on, "when he went over to you during the earthquake, I saw Amedis writing something on his little parchment. As for why, well . . . Savot's obviously shrewder than we'd thought. He's trying to ensure the people's loyalty to him."

"So you don't believe The Ghost really spoke to the two of them?" the princess asked. As Cain shook his head strongly, Aria asked another question. "Do you even believe there is a Ghost, Cain?"

"Of course I do," Cain answered crossly. "I believe he appeared to your father. And I believe the message we've always heard was the *real* one he gave your father. But—think about it—why didn't Savot tell us earlier if The Ghost had really appeared to him?"

"I don't know," whimpered Aria. "Oh, I'm so confused." The princess abandoned herself to weeping again so Cain pulled her in and settled her head on his shoulder while she cried.

"That traitor!" Cain declared while he held Aria. "Why, I'm ready to depose him right now!" Aria sat up and pulled away. Her eyes probed him suspiciously. Then, carefully, she stood up.

Slowly, pensively, and at first unsteadily, Aria began pacing around the periphery of the oval carpet she stood on. She was obviously gathering her thoughts to speak.

"If you're right about him, then yes. I believe—now more than ever—that our plan is the only right thing to do for the good of New Atlantis," Aria replied calmly.

"My father was a good man and a good king. And he was right about Savot being unfit. He's even more unfit than Father knew. The sooner he's gone, the better," Aria said.

At this Cain stood and grabbed her shoulders, audibly sighing in relief. "Aria, you are amazing! I've never known a stronger woman than you."

"Thank you," Aria answered, seeming a bit irritated. Then she broke away from Cain again. "Now. I need some time to grieve the loss of my family . . ." Her brow wrinkled. "My mother . . ." The princess burst into uncontrollable crying again. Cain held and comforted her once more. He even forced a few tears out of his own eyes.

By the time he left the princess, Cain had made arrangements for Aria, himself, and Toren to meet that night at midnight.

Chapter 17

Aria's Confession

Savot declared a week of mourning for Atlantis and the Children's deceased families. He desperately wanted to talk to Aria but she refused to see him. So he sent her a letter every day of that week, expressing his sympathy and describing The Ghost's visit in more detail. Aria never wrote him back except once and the note was short. All it said was:

> *I'm having a hard time believing my father was that wicked.*

No work was allowed during the week of mourning so most of the New Atlanteans stayed inside of their houses. Savot knew they each needed to deal with their losses in their own private ways. But many of the Children, especially the Navy boys, asked Savot for permission to sail back to Atlantis to see if anyone or anything had survived the catastrophe. The king assured them he would dispatch ships after several weeks had passed. He felt it would be too dangerous if they went right away. He also wanted the mission to occur only after the Year of Merger began so that the citizens of New Atlantis would then have a sense of moving forward before any more bad news could be procured.

Amedis, Thea, and the other priests and priestesses prepared a memorial service to be held in the outdoor theater at the end of the week. Everyone agreed that they needed this service to have closure on the official mourning period, though they all knew their grieving was not over.

As the Children assembled for the service, Savot noticed that they all looked worn out. It had been a horrible week for them. The priests and priestesses delivered a long eulogy for the Children's lost families, friends, and Mentors. The Children sat reverently and many silent tears were shed. After the eulogy ended, Savot had some important words for his subjects.

"Our mission has taken on new meaning," Savot announced as the ministers sat down on the stage behind him. "We now owe our families and our forefathers an even deeper debt than we had thought before." The Children listened attentively to their sovereign. Savot felt bonded to his people now far more than ever before.

"We are not in control of how history will record Atlantis. But we can control how history will remember New Atlantis. We have our own history to make now, separate from that of our motherland." The crowd looked serious.

"And I firmly believe that the future record of New Atlantis will depend almost solely on our willingness to follow the commands of the Unknown God. Or, as The Ghost called him, the 'God of Heaven'". Savot surveyed his audience carefully to see if his words were resonating with the Children. He couldn't tell. They all just looked tired.

"As I've told you before," he continued, "I have committed myself to following all the laws the God of Heaven has given us. Now I want to know . . ." Savot allowed a long silence before he asked, "will you make that same commitment with me?"

Savot waited again until the Children recognized that this was not a rhetorical question. The king really wanted an answer. Breaking protocol for audience behavior at a king's formal speech, a hand went up to answer. After Savot called his name, Jamin answered.

"I am with you, King Savot," he pledged. Then Jamin sort of chuckled which seemed quite out of place for the sober moment. Children around him gave him odd looks.

"I have to confess though," Jamin explained, "all the stories about The Ghost and the Unknown God, well . . . they seemed a little bit like fairy tales to me before last week," he paused and when he continued his mood was back to a serious one, "But now I know it's all real."

Shay was the first to argue. "Oh, Jamin. Earthquakes happen. Volcanoes . . . or whatever it was that destroyed Atlantis . . . they happen. We don't know that any 'God' caused it."

This comment kindled a mass, chaotic dispute among the Children. Some agreed with Shay, some agreed with Jamin. Some just watched the two polarized camps argue. Savot recognized the acceleration of the quarrel as impending mayhem so he motioned to his second-in-command. Cain joined the king on the stage and shouted for the Children to be quiet.

"I realize some of you may not agree with me," said Savot after the crowd had settled down. "But the fact remains that I'm your king. And I plan on leading you, my citizens, according to the design that Heaven's God gave us to follow." The opponents grumbled. The allies clapped and cheered.

Savot went on. "I'm going to rule the way it's been planned all along. But I need to know. Will you support me?"

Savot knew that whatever response came from the Children right now would determine what kind of government he would head. If many dissented, New Atlantis would have to be ruled by martial law. But if the majority followed Savot, the nation could exist as a benevolent monarchy. This was big.

Spread out across the theater, the New Atlanteans watched one another for initial reactions. Then King Savot pushed his request even further.

"Those of you who will make this commitment with me, move to the right of the theater," he commanded, sweeping his left arm outward. Several of his fans marched readily to the right side of the theater. Jamin, Billius, Lian, Amedis . . . and then even some who surprised Savot . . . Sensia, Medo, Averil, Dayra. These were strong leaders and opinionated so more followed them. Aria also moved to the head of the crowd as quickly as she could.

But Savot was most nervous about the boys whom he knew had never favored him. Marcum, Toren, Shay, Dolius, and about a dozen others all had their eyes on Cain. After a quick, message-filled glance to Toren, Cain strode resolutely to where all the other Children already stood—on the right side of the theater. On Savot's side.

Toren led the dissenters in following Cain, but, seemed disgruntled. Several, however, threw Savot grudging glances as they straggled to join the rest of the Children.

Soon all the Children stood to Savot's left, indicating a unanimous vote to follow his leadership, and a unanimous vote to obey the Unknown God. Cain was the first to raise his right arm in the air.

"Hail to the king! Hail to New Atlantis!" he boomed. Right arms shot up everywhere and soon the theater resonated with the mantra. On their elevated wrists, the Children displayed the woven metal bracelets that King Jorash had given them. The wristbands had become part of their daily dress since they had left Atlantis. Then Billius shouted something that interrupted the chant.

"We need to get rid of all of these wristbands!" Billius wrenched the tri-colored metal bracelet off his arm and threw it to the ground. The Children, one by one, repeated the ceremony. Some even stomped the wristbands into the dirt with fervor. All the Children did this except for Aria . . . and Savot out of respect for his princess.

The young king kept his eyes fastened on the princess as the rest of their peers disavowed her father. Although no one else seemed to care at the moment how their actions affected Aria, Savot waited for a reaction from her.

Aria stood very still drenched unmistakably in grief. Huge tears rushed down her cheeks. Because she happened to be standing on the outskirts of the crowd, Aria slipped away from the theater as the Children began cheering in solidarity. The chant continued. No one but Savot even noticed Aria leaving.

***

Entering her house alone, Aria began picking up every item she laid eyes on and throwing it—at walls, at furniture, to the floor, everwhere. No one could hear her loud, angry shouts as she wept and raged on and on. Had anyone heard her, they'd have thought that she had gone mad. After hurling as many objects as she could easily seize, her heated glare rested on the specially made cabinet that held her crystal figurine.

Aria settled herself down and mopped her cheeks. Then slowly and deliberately, she strode toward the cabinet. Opening its door, she took the figurine out. She held the statue up to the window so that it sparkled brightly in the sunlight. Then the princess spoke to it as if it was King Jorash.

"Father. You have betrayed me. You've betrayed all of us." Her lip curled in a trembling sneer. Still she spoke in a controlled tone. "You've betrayed Mother and she's dead because of you." The princess sauntered around her disheveled house, addressing the figurine.

Then she stood still, straight, and tall. Raising the crystal figure to her eye level, Aria spoke these words resolutely:

"I hereby reject you as my father." In one swift and decisive motion, the princess flung the costly figurine to the tile floor. It shattered into innumerable slivers.

Aria's ceremony wasn't over. Next she removed the gold, silver, and orichalcum bracelet from her right arm and cast it into the flames of her fireplace.

"And I hereby reject you as my king." She took a deep, cleansing breath as she neared the end of her ritual.

"Melt!" she whispered with revulsion. "As you have melted Atlantis with your wickedness, I now melt you out of my memory." She stared at the gleaming flames and then finished her pronouncement. "*I am no longer your daughter.*"

***

Savot had wanted to follow Aria when she had left the assembly, but he was, of course, in the middle of a most important national meeting. After the New Atlantean chant had died down, Savot addressed his subjects again.

"You have made me very happy today. Had you not agreed to follow my leadership, the military would have had to force your obedience. But now, life will be easier for all of us."

Before the king dismissed the meeting, he announced his decision to hold a public assembly once a week on the evenings of Rest Days. Shouts of elation rose from the Children, not out of national interest though. This would mean the boys and girls would get to see each other more often. It also meant more work for the eunuchs, though, who moaned loudly at the announcement.

"Aww . . . Your Majesty, please, no!" Win complained.

Eton chimed in, "If we have to do that, then could we at least have a feast every week too?" Eton was a eunuch who was renowned for his gluttony.

Savot realized he had to define this event more clearly. He promised the eunuchs a formal obstaball game after every weekly meeting, but no feast. The non-boys seemed satisfied enough with the compromise.

Savot adjourned the meeting instructing the Children to resume their regular work schedules the next day. The first weekly convention would take place in six more days; on the next Rest Day.

Although morale was now running higher among the Children in general, there were several enemies among the crowd who were assured that Savot's confidence was only temporary. Cain, only two days earlier, had decided it was time to include Shay, Marcum, and Dolius in the plan to dethrone Savot. They had attended his last midnight meeting with Aria and Toren. That made six who were now in on the plan to depose Savot.

***

Savot went directly to Aria's house after the meeting in the theater. Accompanied by Nat and Win, he ordered the eunuchs to follow his plan for a private conversation with Aria.

It took the princess a while to answer the door after Savot's knock. When she finally opened her door, her face looked like gray stone. There were no signs of her earlier tears on her freckled cheeks. When she saw Savot standing at her door, Aria's icy eyes softened and she dropped her head.

"Come in, Savot," she said in a feeble voice. But Savot stood still at her threshold.

"Let's take a walk, Aria," Savot half-invited, half-ordered. The princess mindlessly walked through the doorway of her house and out into the frosty air. Savot stopped her, realizing that she wore only her split dress and thin pants underneath.

"Let me get your coat," the king offered. Without waiting for her response, he hurried back to the house and grabbed the long fox coat that hung on her wall.

Savot couldn't help noticing as he fetched the coat the damage that Aria had inflicted on her house. Broken pieces of wood and pottery littered the furniture, and bits of crystal crunched under his shoes as he walked. He surmised correctly what had just occurred.

"Thank you," said Aria as Savot returned and helped her put her arms into the sleeves of the warm garment. Although the air was frigid, the wind was still and the afternoon sun shone warmly.

The silent princess strode along compliantly beside the king. He led her to the beach as they began talking. Nat and Win followed well behind them as Savot had commanded them to. Savot didn't quite know how to start.

"What are you thinking right now?" he asked.

"I'm thinking that I hate my father," Aria stated bluntly.

"I'm sorry, Aria." No words he could think of seemed adequate. "Ever since The Ghost told Amedis and me, I've been feeling . . . well, really sick about the whole thing." A spark of energy finally emerged from Aria.

"You feel sick? *You* feel sick?" Aria questioned him. Her strength had apparently returned in full, and Savot could tell her anger was about to erupt. Eyes widening and lips tightening, Aria set off into a tirade.

"I've lost my mother. And I've doubly lost my father! You can't imagine how sick *I* feel," Aria shouted. The two eunuchs heard her ranting but couldn't make out the words. Savot just listened. He knew Aria. Once she got started he knew he was in for a long listen. She picked up the pace of their walk. Nat and Win hurried to catch up.

"Do you know what it feels like to have your own flesh and blood lie to you? Betray you? Your whole life?" The princess' teeth chattered from both cold and anger as she spoke.

"He betrayed me, Savot. I'm so ashamed to be his daughter! And now, what if people don't trust me anymore . . . *because* I'm his daughter?" Savot could tell that close beneath the surface of Aria's scorching words was a hurt deeper than he had ever felt himself.

The pace of their walking varied now. Nat and Win watched them walk fast for a while, then stop, then turn around and walk even faster in the opposite direction, then stop again. Aria would march around in small circles flailing her arms . . . then walk on beside Savot again.

Finally, the eunuchs stopped where they were—having been ordered to stay a hundred paces behind the couple. Aria stood in one place for some time, ranting on and shouting. Finally her anger faded into sorrow.

"I don't know who I am, Savot," she said at last, starting to cry now. "I don't even want to be a royal anymore." Aria buried her face in her hands and fully released herself to weeping. The monstrous strength she had displayed earlier in her house, and just then on the beach, was spent. She seemed unstable on her feet now.

Savot went to her and enveloped her in his arms, gathering the thick fur of her coat closer around her. She felt as frail as a baby to him as she shivered, not as much from cold now—he could tell—but more from anguish. Savot smoothed her shimmering blond hair and spoke as many words of comfort as he could think to utter.

After her sobs wore her out, the princess nestled herself in Savot's strong embrace. She looked up at him. Fixating intently on his dazzling lavender eyes, Aria asked Savot a most unexpected question.

"Will you marry me?"

Savot was absolutely stunned.

Aria had urged him to sign the contract before, but now it seemed she was truly asking him to marry her. Savot was still reeling from all the events of the last couple of weeks. He blinked hard as if he couldn't focus his eyes clearly on the princess.

"You've already asked me to sign the contract, and I told you . . ." he began.

"Forget the contract. Forget all the rules for a minute. I want to marry *you*, Savot. I've always wanted to marry you . . . my whole life." Here she choked and tears of long-desired relief flooded down her face. "You're the most incredible person I've ever known." Aria gazed solidly and earnestly at Savot as though she was—through her eyes—compensating for years of longing.

Savot felt that surely he was dreaming. Then he felt lightheaded. *What is she saying?* This should have been the most romantic moment of his life; yet he had to ask the question that was about to burst his mind open.

"What about Cain?"

Then Savot watched as coldness returned to Aria's face. Still, she remained in his arms.

"I despise him," she spoke the words slowly and separately. "I hate Cain as much as I hate my father," she declared. "He was my father's choice for king . . . not you. That's why I had to pretend to love him."

Savot's arms went limp and fell from Aria's waist. *How could I have been so stupid?* he scolded himself in his thoughts. Aria took Savot's hand and led him to a nearby boulder to sit down. Win and Nat stood where they were, watching from a distance but not hearing any of the conversation. They made bets with each other about what was going on.

For the next hour Aria told Savot the whole story. The heavily clothed eunuchs drew pictures in the wet sand, realizing there would be no more walking. The princess told Savot all the slanderous reports her father had spoken about him. She told him how he had convinced her that Cain was the only candidate fit to be king.

"I didn't want to believe what he said about you, Savot. But he was my father," she started. Then, sneering, she added most sarcastically, ". . . who had never lied to me.

"At one point I decided I was just going to tell you all about it while we were still on Atlantis. Remember, I said I had something important to tell you?"

"Of course I remember," Savot replied, recalling how warmly she had behaved toward him that night.

"But then, before I could tell you, Antony came to me saying he had overheard Cain and Toren talking about abducting you . . . and *killing you!*" She went on to relate everything Antony had reported to her. She now knew it had been true. It had to have been her father or Cain who had murdered Antony.

"So then, I was just so afraid! I kind of froze up, I guess. And Father was still depending on me . . . I didn't know what to do but go on with the charade. If they found out I had told you, they would have made sure we both 'accidentally' died . . . just like Antony," the princess explained feverishly.

She then went on for a long time about how hard it had been for her to pretend she'd hated Savot. And how it had been even harder to feign love for Cain.

She told Savot every detail of the insurrection plot.

"I've been trying all these months since we left Atlantis to figure out a way to foil the plan . . . all by myself," Aria told Savot. He heard the loneliness and desperation in her voice and then a sigh of immense relief. "But now I don't have to do it by myself."

"Couldn't you have just told me once we got here?" Savot said, not reprovingly, but so wishing she had.

"No. The ships. I thought they were my father's."

Savot was confused. "I thought you said you knew it was Cain and Toren."

"Oh, but there are other ships out there!" Aria explained. "But . . . oh, I see. Of course you wouldn't have known the difference. 'Pirates' were all they were reporting to you." Even after she'd had a week to make sense of all the new information, Savot could tell there were still elements Aria was just now putting into place.

"But, Savot, I really believe Cain has been planning to kill you all along like Antony said; not just take you to

Athens like he was going to tell everyone. And also, like Antony heard him say, he'd kill me too if I didn't cooperate fully with him." Now the princess confessed, "Savot, I was just so scared." Savot again took her in his arms and spoke consoling words.

After more talk Savot decided Aria should go in. She had been shivering most of the time they had sat on the boulder.

He stood up and offered Aria his hand. Only now, as she gazed lovingly into his eyes, did the reality of her feelings toward him begin to sink in. He felt warm all over. *She loves me! She actually does love me after all!* He gently placed his warm hands on her cold cheeks and moved his face slowly toward hers. Then came the kiss Savot had dreamed of for so very long. The kiss lasted a long time, and the couple wrapped their arms around each other as it continued. When it was over they kept holding each other, gazing at each other, engulfed in the wonder of their mutual love.

"Yes, of course I will marry you," Savot whispered with great joy in his voice and a huge smile on his face. "I would marry you a thousand times." Aria jumped up and down and squealed,

"Oh, YES! Thank you, Savot! I love you, I love you, I LOVE YOU! . . . Oh! I can finally say it! And I promise I will be the best wife to you the world has ever known."

Savot felt his heart would burst and he kissed Aria again. Both the young lovers wanted to keep reveling in the great happiness they were experiencing over their new, true engagement, but Savot insisted on getting Aria out of the cold weather. Having seen all the kissing and hugging, Nat and Win now watched the couple like hawks, hardly believing this change in Aria's behavior toward Savot.

As they started back, the happiest fiancés on New Atlantis had to make themselves break away, for the time being, from their splendid thoughts of becoming husband and wife. They agreed it was urgent to devise a plan against the imminent insurrection. By the time they returned to Aria's house, a reverse-deception plot between Savot and Aria had taken rough form.

Unfortunately Aria was not aware of one crucial part of the mutiny team's plan. Cain had kept it from her.

"When we meet next week, we'll work out more of the details," Savot assured Aria well out of the eunuchs' earshot. "Don't worry. Cain will never be king of New Atlantis."

Aria almost spat her next words. "Just let me be the one who gets to kill him."

Chapter 18

New Atlantis' First Native

"Just let me be the one who gets to kill him!" Aria snarled. All five of her fellow conspirators seemed taken aback at her vicious tone.

"Kill him? The plan was never to kill him," Cain lied. Only Toren knew he was pretending.

"No! I want him dead now. It's *my* right. He smeared my father's name into the mud in front of all the Children!" Aria stomped back and forth across the dirt floor of the smokehouse where the six mutineers secretly met.

"Whatever it was that destroyed Atlantis," she continued, "I'm sure it was just an act of nature. Savot had no right to slander my father and tell everyone it was his fault . . ." In a fury she picked up a knife and started assaulting a nearby bale of hay relentlessly. Toren, Shay, Dolius, and Marcum, all on the border of alarm, looked to Cain to control her. Cain carefully moved toward Aria and caught her right hand in mid-air, stilling the knife.

"Sweetheart, please try to settle down. I understand how you're feeling. Savot is more evil and more devious than we ever suspected." Cain took the knife from Aria's hand and sat down with her on another hay bale. He rubbed her back to calm her down.

Toren, obviously wanting to move the conversation past Aria's outburst, took the discussion back to the kidnapping plan.

"Cain, we can't wait any longer," Toren insisted.

"Yeah," Shay agreed. "The people's loyalty to Savot is growing stronger every day since the earthquake," he argued.

Dolius grunted in agreement with each of the other boys' statements. Cain just listened.

"And that phony speech of his," Shay growled, shaking his head. "I can't believe people fell for that!"

"Aria and I had discussed having him kidnapped after this last feast. But with the earthquake and all, I've decided we *will* wait till after the Month Ten Feast," Cain stated his ruling. "Things need to get a little more back to normal before the Children have another trauma to face. But the night of the new moon after the feast I'll have his eunuchs occupied with some 'urgent' military task. Savot and his roommates will be asleep. Shay, Marcum, and Dolius, you are to gag him, tie his hands and feet, and carry him to the ship."

"Where I'll be waiting with this knife!" yelled Aria. She quickly grabbed the knife from Cain's side where he had laid it. She flew across the room to where Shay was leaning against a post. Quick as a flash of lightning, Aria grabbed the back of Shay's red head of hair, yanked it backwards, and put the gleaming knife to his throat. Shay froze as did the other four boys.

"Aria," Cain said with forced serenity. "Aria, I've never seen you like this before. Now listen to me, put the knife down."

"I wish you were Savot right now, Shay," the princess hissed. "I'd slit his throat so fast . . ."

"But don't practice on me, Your Highness, please," Shay carefully begged. Aria lowered her weapon and burst out laughing so loudly that the boys had to hush her. Shay moved far away from her.

"We're not really going to kill him, are we?" Dolius asked, looking to his leader. Cain didn't have a chance to answer.

"Yes!" Aria insisted. "I was all for just exiling him until he slandered my father! But now he's got to die!" All five boys' eyes turned to Cain as he pretended to consider whether or not to kill Savot.

Marcum had an idea. "She's right, Cain. If we let him live, there's an outside chance he could make it back here and spoil our new government. If we just kill him and tell everyone the pirates did it, then it's all over." Cain had only let Toren in on the full plot at this point. But he was pleased at Marcum's statement and at Aria's insistence that they murder Savot. The team would think killing Savot was their idea now.

Aria paced impatiently as Cain pondered the proposal.

"Let's do it," he finally concluded. All of the group seemed enthusiastic except for Dolius. But even he agreed in the end that Savot should die. The new moon after the Month Ten Feast was set as the night for the kidnapping.

***

Aria stayed in her quarters for long periods of time that next week. Her only outings were to eat meals and to visit Lalera.

After the cold walk on the beach, Win and Nat pestered Savot relentlessly, trying to find out what he and Aria had talked about that had ending in all the hugging and kissing. Immediately after their walk on the beach, Savot had sworn Nat and Win to secrecy—on pain of death—about what they had seen happen between himself and Aria. But the twins were still dying to know for their own satisfaction what had transpired between the princess and Savot.

"It's none of your business," was all Savot would say. Then, since they persisted, he finally threatened the two eunuchs. "How would you two like to guard the prison for a while?"

That shut Nat and Win up about the couple's private conversation. But they raised another issue.

"Savot . . . oh, I mean, Your Majesty, we can't get anybody to work like they're supposed to," Nat complained.

"Yeah, they're all being so lazy! What's with them?" added Win.

I guess they're all as drained as I am, Savot concluded to himself. He told the eunuchs to be patient with their charges and explained that it was probably exhaustion from the recent cataclysm and that they were still mourning.

The king was right. The Children were working lethargically. Some even had to take breaks in their work because they still needed to cry about their families and Mentors. Savot watched his subjects panoramically from the top of the nearly finished palace wall that day.

What should I do? What can I do? They need a morale boost so badly, Savot pondered. Then the Atlantean flag flying over the palace caught his attention.

The next day he summoned Meli, the girls' Area Head for millers.

"How about designing a new flag for us?" Savot asked her. If ever there was a true artist on New Atlantis, it was Meli. Her face lit up with instant excitement.

"Really? Can we do that?" she asked, squirming in the seat Savot had assigned her to.

"Sure we can do it. And I think we should," Savot stated enthusiastically. "Atlantis was our motherland, but we're a separate nation now. I think our flag should be different too. At least a little." Meli's zeal for the project was ignited; Savot could tell.

And so she and the other miller girls—Lexia, Maura, and Aubri—set out to design a flag for New Atlantis. What resulted, within only a few days, was a flag that uniquely belonged to the Children. They took the prototype New Atlantean flag to show the king.

"Your Majesty," Meli announced formally, "we are pleased to present you with the first flag of New Atlantis." Savot took the flag, made an initial examination of it, and then smiled a commending smile.

"You see, Your Highness," she continued, even more excited now, "we felt that the New Atlantean flag should pay tribute to the honorable parts of our heritage so we left the colors and the circles the same. On the other hand, we felt it should declare our new kingdom separate and different from its mother country." Savot could tell Meli had worded this part carefully.

All who heard Meli's philosophy agreed that the New Atlantean flag should somehow be different from the flag that had flown over King Jorash's palace.

Savot studied the new flag in greater detail. As Meli had described, it was same basic design as the Atlantean flag—a blue circle with a green circle inside of it, and a yellow circle inside the green—but the colors had a crumpled appearance instead of a solid one. And it was all one piece of fabric instead of three separate pieces sewn together as Atlantean flags had been.

"I like it!" Savot announced with true gusto. This declaration brought bright beams to the millers' faces. "But how did you get it to look all crinkly like this?"

Meli, a fast talker, spoke even more rapidly because of her excitement. "Well, you see, Sir, it's in the way we dyed the fabric. What we did was . . ."

Lexia cut in. "We scrunched up the middle circle and painted it with a clear pitch. Then we dyed the exposed fabric blue."

Meli took over again. "Yeah, and when that dried we covered up the outside circle area with pitch—you know, the one's that we'd already dyed blue . . ." Savot nodded.

Maura butt in now. "Then we peeled off the pitch in the center and dyed the exposed parts yellow . . ."

"Blue and yellow makes green!" Aubri continued the thought. "That's how the middle circle got green and the inner circle turned out yellow!" All four girls beamed when they had finished their collaborative description.

"I am very impressed!" declared King Savot. The girls impulsively, even if a bit disrespectfully, squealed and clapped their hands at the king's compliment.

Savot laughed. *This is a positive way to get things moving ahead again,* he thought. Dismissing the miller girls, he sent Teran to the Council with an official recommendation to approve the new flag.

Even after the encouraging meeting, when Savot was left alone in his throne room, he felt his insides constricting. He couldn't escape thoughts of the trap Cain and his troup were preparing for him. But at least he now knew when to expect it.

The Council readily approved the miller girls' design and the New Atlantean flags soon replaced the old

Atlantean flags that had flown over each building. The Children's spirits seemed lifted for the following week or so. But then something dampened them again.

***

Three days after the new flags were raised, Risa sent word from the prison that Lalera was in labor.

"Only Aria, Jamin, and the doctors are allowed to go," Savot had to declare when he heard that most of the girls wanted to leave work to be with Lalera.

After Jamin had seen Lalera briefly, the doctors asked him to wait outside of the prison. Aria insisted on holding Lalera's hand throughout the five hours she endured the painful contractions. The laboring mother was weak. Her face, feet, and hands had been swelling for several days, and she'd had a terrible headache.

"This is too early, isn't it?" Aria asked Calum, the doctors' Area Head.

Calum looked grim. "It's pretty early," was all he would say.

Risa, who had cared for Lalera throughout her pregnancy, supervised the delivery. The other nine doctors assisted in one way or another. Risa called for cold rags to keep the swelling from getting worse. Water was kept boiling to sterilize each instrument and cloth.

With each contraction Lalera shrieked in pain. Risa could tell she had developed a high fever as well. Lalera clutched the toy cat Jamin had made for her as though her very life was tied to it.

After three hours, Phaedra, the head girl doctor, seemed on the brink of hysteria. She dragged Calum outside, far enough so she thought no one would hear them talk.

"I told you I've never had experience with this, Calum," Phaedra reminded him. Emery, one of the other doctors, had followed them out of the prison and heard Phaedra say this. Emery responded.

"Well, I had plenty of it helping my father deliver babies. And this doesn't look normal to me at all. She shouldn't be swelling like this. And she shouldn't have a fever."

Inside where Lalera labored, the hardest contraction yet came upon her and she tried to scream but it came out more as a whisper.

"Somebody go quickly and get Jamin," Aria ordered. Denit retrieved Jamin from the front entrance of the prison. He warned Jamin before he went in that Lalera was not doing well. Jamin ran in and stationed himself by her side. The contractions were still coming at irregular intervals.

"Lalera, marry me," he said. "Now." He had caught her in between contractions.

"What?" Lalera questioned weakly. "Jamin, what are you thinking? I'm dying. Why would you want to marry me now?" She had a hard time getting her next breath. "I probably won't even live till tomorrow."

"Go," Jamin commanded Denit, the least experienced doctor. "Go immediately and bring Amedis to marry us. And tell him to bring the ring in my trunk." Denit did not hesitate.

Jamin tried his hardest to encourage Lalera before her next contraction. "You're not going to die. Giving birth is always painful," he told her, even though he knew he was being overly optimistic. The doctors exchanged doubtful glances. "And your baby needs a father." Then hesitantly he added, "Especially if you . . ." He couldn't finish but kept himself from tearing up.

Lalera grabbed Jamin's hand and was about to speak just as the next contraction started. After the contraction had passed, Lalera—still clutching Jamin's hand—looked up at her admirer.

"You are so very kind, Jamin," Lalera said, tears seeping from the corners of her swollen eyes. "I could never have expected . . ." She ran out of breath but managed to draw his hand to her face and kissed it.

"Yes, I'll marry you," she finally consented in a whisper. "And . . . thank you."

Amedis and Thea arrived within the hour with Denit. By this time Lalera's contractions were regular and close together. Amedis' hands trembled as he read the wedding vows that Jamin and Lalera repeated. Three times they had to stop the hurried service for contractions.

After the third contraction, Amedis pronounced the blessing that finished the wedding ceremony. Jamin bent over and kissed Lalera. He slipped the gold ring onto her right forefinger.

"I HAVE TO PUSH!" screamed Lalera. She pushed for only a few minutes and the baby emerged. It was a miniature boy.

The doctors scrambled, half of them attending to the baby, half to Lalera. After Livia cleared out his mouth and throat, the newborn gave a strong, high-pitched cry.

"That's the healthiest yell I've ever heard for such a tiny one," Emery remarked, seeming relieved.

"She's having trouble breathing," Aldo alerted the doctors attending Lalera.

"Let me . . . see him," Lalera insisted between gasps. As soon as the umbilical cord was tied off and cut, Phaedra laid the undersized infant in his mother's arms.

"Jamin," Lalera whispered, "I want . . . his name to be . . ." She struggled hard to take the breath with which she spoke the baby's name. "Pate."

Jamin's eyes flooded. 'Pate' sounded like the Atlantean word for 'kindness'. Jamin gently stroked Lalera's curly, red hair and then for a moment rested his forehead on hers.

Lalera's breathing problem worsened rapidly. Looking to her husband intently but peacefully, she instructed, "Take him." It was all she could manage to say before she couldn't speak anymore. Within an hour, she was gone.

***

The funeral was even sadder than Antony's had been. Lalera had been well-liked by most of the Children despite her loose reputation. Aria tried very hard to maintain her composure, but still wept throughout the service. So did Risa who had lived with and cared for Lalera so diligently in the prison. Jamin held baby Pate swaddled in his arms with a bottle of goat's milk nearby in case the infant woke up, which he didn't.

As the Children slowly filtered away from Lalera's gravesite, several girls offered to help Jamin take care of the baby. Though he was resolved to fulfill his duties as the captain of the Army, Jamin insisted on keeping Pate with him in the house that would have been his and Lalera's on the residence island. As Jamin and Pate would be the first family to live on the island, Savot also allowed two eunuchs to move there so that when Jamin was absent Pate would always have someone to look after him.

Enough witnesses had been present to verify Lalera's intention to have Jamin raise Pate as his son. So the very day of the funeral Parius had the lawyers draw up papers that made the adoption legal.

The baby, though born a month early, seemed to thrive his first week under Jamin's care. To the doctors' amazement, Pate didn't manifest any of the problems common to premature babies. And the goat's milk seemed to meet all his nutritional needs. Pate was strong from his beginning.

Jamin told Savot he loved being a father. Savot's already high respect for Jamin grew even more as he watched his friend care diligently for the tiny infant. Dayra had volunteered to keep Pate while Jamin was working, and the Navy girls under her command gladly adjusted to accommodate the beloved baby Pate. And so began Jamin's career as a single parent.

**

With the Month Ten Feast only a day away, and the moon four days from its phase of total darkness, Cain met for the last time with his conspiracy team. In the smokehouse where they had been meeting of late, the general began reviewing the details for Savot's kidnapping by lantern-light.

Aria walked fretfully around in circles. Cain addressed the princess' responsibilities first. Aria, between now and then I want you to pretend to show even more interest in Savot. All right?"

"All right," Aria agreed briskly, squeezing her fur coat around her. "I'll ask to meet with him every day. That will distract him some, I'm sure. Just in case he suspects any-thing."

Marcum spoke up, "Yeah, he's acting so confident—making new flags and all. What a fool!"

"Yeah," Shay chortled. "He really thinks *everyone* is on his side. He's even dumber than I thought!"

Toren added, "He thinks he's totally in control. I can't wait to see the look on his face once we get him aboard the ship."

Then Dolius posed a question. "Do we really have to kill him?" The other five glared at him.

"Why are you wavering on this, Dolius?" Cain snapped. "You agreed to it at our last meeting."

"It just seems pretty extreme," Dolius returned. "Couldn't we just sail him to the eastern continent and dump him off there? That'd at least give him a chance to survive."

Aria exploded at this suggestion. "Survive? Why should we give that snake any chance of survival?" Cain told her to quiet her voice. She continued in a lower tone but with just as much vehemence, "He doesn't deserve to live. I told you . . . *I'm going to kill him myself!*" Her eyes flashed at Dolius.

"She's right," Cain affirmed. "Not only does Savot de-serve to die after dishonoring King Jorash the way he did . . ." Cain moved intimidatingly close to Dolius, "we've already talked about this. Letting him live is just too risky."

Dolius didn't press the issue any further.

Cain went on. "So it's all set. Everyone clear on what their part is?"

The other five affirmed they knew their roles. Aria's part was, first of all, to distract Savot by showing him ex-tra attention for the next three days. Secondly, she was to row out to the captors' ship once they had abducted Savot and, as she had requested, slit his throat.

Dolius, Shay, and Marcum were to kidnap Savot from his house. Cain and Toren would have the fastest ship waiting to take Savot out to sea. Then there was one other element of the secret part of the plan that Cain had not wanted Aria to know. Because she was present they didn't discuss it then, but all the boys knew.

Cain had instructed Dolius, Shay, and Marcum to drug Savot and his two remaining roommates at the evening meal the night of the abduction. The roommates would be knocked out and wouldn't be able to stop the kidnappers from binding and taking Savot away in the darkness of the new moon. Cain was not really sure how the drug would affect the three victims so he had decided to keep that information from Aria. For all he knew, and for all he cared, it could kill all three of them. But he could blame that on the 'pirates' who had kidnapped Savot.

***

The Month Ten Feast came and went without any unusual incidents. Aria did as she said she would. She sat with Savot at the feast and then asked to meet with him each day after that. And their meetings went long. Nat and Win were forbidden from entering the house while the two talked. At least once during each meeting, though, the eunuchs made up excuses to interrupt the couple and more often than not found them embracing or even kissing.

"Wow! I can't believe this," said Win. "All of a sudden, since the beach, they're kissing and hugging every time they're together." Win looked pensive. "And what about Cain?" Win continued. "I thought he was the one she was in love with."

"Yuck! Just shut up about all of it, would ya?" spluttered Nat. "All that mush makes me nauseous! And especially after the way she's treated Savot for so long . . . man! If I were him, there's no way I'd let her wrap me around her royal little pinkie like that!"

***

The night before the new moon—the night before the planned kidnapping—Savot and his two roommates spent the evening practicing their music. Billius played his lute better than usual. And Savot contributed a melody line on a woodwind. Lian, however, was obviously in one of his worst moods ever. He only half-heartedly thumped his drum every few measures, not adding much at all to the concert. They all missed Jamin though they understood and supported his reason for not living with them anymore.

Inside his gilded cage, Memphis perched half-asleep. Usually when the boys played music the bird was alert and tried to contribute some sort of noise to the recital. But tonight the music seemed to lull Memphis. He had again found a way to let himself out of his cage the night before and had been missing most of the day. And, once again, Savot had worried that a wild animal had killed his bird.

"BOO!" Lian tried to scare Memphis awake in the middle of the song. This startled Memphis and he fluttered and grumbled. Then, wide-awake, he spoke a new phrase.

"Put it in Savot's drink first. Put it in Savot's drink first," Memphis squawked.

"Put what in my drink?" Savot asked.

Billius startled and looked up at the bird. "Where did you hear that, Memphis?" he asked, almost as if he thought the bird could answer the question.

"Well, does it really matter?" Lian barked, alarmed at the bird's statement. "Someone's planning to *poison* Savot or something! Memphis can't just make up phrases like that out of his own head."

Aria had let Savot know the exact date her conspirators were planning to kidnap him, but now he understood how they had devised doing it. But he didn't want to let Lian and Billius know all that he knew yet.

Then Billius reminded Lian and Savot, "Memphis said, 'first'—'put it in Savot's drink first'. Someone's planning to poison all three of us!"

"Let's keep a close eye on our cups at each meal, okay?" Savot instructed his friends. "It's always a possibility there's someone plotting to overthrow me."

Lian and Billius took turns guessing who the conspirators might be. But Savot kept quiet for the time being.

Any premature accusations of fellow-New Atlanteans could complicate what was about to happen.

***

The next day the three roommates agreed to eat all their meals together. It was apparent after breakfast and lunch that the conspirators had not yet tried to poison Savot, Billius, and Lian. They had kept a close watch on their food and drink. The roommates decided that this was the meal at which they were to be poisoned.

Savot had, by then, told Lian and Billius all that he knew about the coup.

Though it had now been over a month since the earthquake, the mood among the New Atlanteans at all four shifts of supper was still sullen in both the girls' and the boys' mess halls.

Lalera's death had set them back, Savot reasoned. Still it saddened him to see the gloom that lingered on most of the Children's faces each time he studied them.

Shay, Marcum, Dolius, and Cain found out when Savot and his roommates were planning to dine and were already present at the last shift of supper. Shay had the vial of potent tranquilizer in his pocket.

Savot and Billius came into the mess hall later than the conspirators. They picked up plates, loaded them with food, and sat in their usual places. Shay had been mingling around the dining hall, but when he saw Savot enter he quickly grabbed a plate and seated himself beside the king.

"Where's Lian? He's supposed to be sticking close to us," Billius, seated on Savot's other side, whispered to the king.

"He told me he'd be right behind us. He'll be here in a minute," Savot assured.

The reality was that Lian had staged his entrance for when he knew the maximum number of boys would be present. He hadn't greeted the boys with his signature salutation since before the earthquake. But now, being one of the more resilient of the boys, Lian was ready to lighten things up . . . and to distract whoever might be planning to poison him and his roommates that evening.

Lian finally appeared at the door, pulling back the entrance curtain and stepping inside with a dramatic flair. He scanned the room to make sure no girls were present. Then he cleared his throat loudly to make sure everyone noticed him. The jester then stepped up on a bench and turned around. All the boys knew what was coming. Lian swiftly yanked down the back of his pants and flashed his bare rear-end toward the other boys with a silly wiggle.

The boys roared with laughter as they always had in the past. Savot rolled his eyes at Billius but realized Lian was providing some needed comic relief for the boys. And it gave him a chance to keep an eye on his food and drink more closely for at least a few moments. The more Lian wiggled his bottom, the more the boys cackled. Some began throwing pieces of leftover food at the performer. Lian pulled up his pants, picked up the food and flung the scraps back at the boys. This began an all-out food fight. The conspirators made sure food was flung into Savot's and Billius' eyes—an unexpected advantage for the mutineers.

The chaos of now-flying food presented Shay the perfect opportunity for his sinister assignment. While Savot and Billius wiped food off their faces, Shay swiftly emptied the contents of his vial into a nearby pitcher of wine.

While the amusement continued, Shay offered to fill Savot's cup. Savot accepted. Shay repeated the operation with Billius. Lian finally made his way to where Savot and Billius sat. As Lian approached, Shay poured a fresh cupful of wine and handed it to him. He set it down and continued in the banter. He grabbed a piece of roast pheasant from Billius' plate and stuffed it into his mouth, still throwing items of food with the other hand.

Shay, Dolius, Marcum, and Cain only minimally joined in the carnival. Their priority was to keep their eyes on Savot and his roommates. They watched to make sure the three victims all took sips from their goblets. The roomful of boys eventually resumed their meals and Savot could tell their collective melancholy had temporarily lifted. Savot and his friends occasionally raised the wine to their lips as the others poked fun at Lian about his stunt.

After a few minutes, Amedis burst into the mess hall shouting, "Fire! Fire in the Temple! We need everyone to help."

The whole mass of boys responded at once. They quickly scuttled out of the tent, trampling the food that littered the ground. Before he left, Cain eyed Savot's wine cup as well as those of the other two. All were nearly empty.

Chapter 19

The King Is Kidnapped

The girls had also been summoned to the Temple to help put out the fire. They worked with the boys, assembly line style, transferring buckets of water to douse the flames. Sparks from a burnt offering had apparently set nearby curtains ablaze. That was the conclusion of the Army personnel after the flames had been extinguished. Cain ordered Sensia to supervise the clean-up. Grumbling under her breath about Cain's condescending attitude toward women, the girls' general set her troops to the task.

Shay, Marcum, Toren, and Dolius watched Savot and his roommates closely as the crowd around the Temple dispersed. Yawning and rubbing their eyes, the three intended victims did appear to be feeling the effects of the drugged wine. As soon they had helped all they could with putting the fire out, Savot, Billius, and Lian retired to their quarters.

The ship Cain planned to use waited for him and Toren so they went directly to it and prepared it for a fast start once they had Savot on board. The other three saboteurs stationed themselves in the nearby woods until lanterns went out inside Savot's house and all had been quiet for a while.

Moving stealthily toward the house in the now pitch-black night, Dolius, Marcum, and Shay prepared their ropes and gags. They sneaked into the house cautiously, taking extra time opening the door so it wouldn't creak. Memphis' cage was covered so he didn't make any noise. After observing the three motionless roommates for a few minutes, Dolius motioned to the other two to proceed with the kidnapping.

First they tested to make sure Savot was unconscious. They nudged him. Then they tickled his feet. Finally, they brushed his nose with a feather. The king didn't move

at all. If he had, they had planned to knock him unconscious with a club that they carried.

Marcum and Dolius then gagged Savot's mouth. Shay
bound his feet with sturdy ropes while Dolius did the
same to his hands. Then, hoisting Savot over his shoulder, Marcum carefully bore the king out of the house. The
other two kidnappers followed Marcum and soundlessly
closed the door behind them.

After they had stolen back through the woods, they finally got Savot to the ship and plopped him down on the
deck. Marcum grinned and nodded at Cain who stood at
the helm, ready to launch. Surveying Savot's limp form
by Toren's lamplight, Cain smirked. Shay and Dolius hurried off the ship and onto the dock.

"Shove off," the general shouted in a whisper. Shay
and Dolius gave the ship a huge heave and then quickly
jumped into the vessel. Marcum and Toren raised the
sails as noiselessly as possible and the other two started
rowing.

The boys could hardly see one another in the black-
ness. Marcum then took guard of the captive king while
the others maneuvered the sails and oars. It took a half
hour for the ship to travel far enough beyond the horizon
to be unseen from New Atlantis. There the insurgents anchored and waited for Princess Aria who was traveling in
another vessel to join them. The five conspirators had a
moment to revel in their victory. The boys, not afraid now
of being seen or heard, lit ship's lanterns.

"Congratulations, Cain!" Dolius gave a loud whoop and
slapped Cain on the back. "Or, I should say, 'King Cain'."

"Yes! We did it. Everything went exactly according to
plan!" added Toren. He prodded Savot in the side with
his boot. Savot was still unresponsive.

"What post did you promise Toren again, Cain?" Shay
wondered.

"He takes my place as general of all the military," replied a buoyant Cain. Toren, having been the third person to join the mutiny plot, had gotten his first choice
of post under Cain's new rule. And he had, predictably,
chosen the highest position possible.

Shay sulked. "And what about me?"

"You can stay captain of the Navy or you can take Jamin's place as captain of the Army. Whichever you want."

The others knew that Cain had planned all along to demote Jamin because he was one of Savot's closest allies.

"And what about us again?" Marcum and Dolius asked almost at the same time, seeming to need assurance.

"I told you guys! One of you gets the other captain's station. And the other gets to be my personal bodyguard."

This sparked the revisiting of an earlier dispute between Dolius and Marcum. Both preferred the bodyguard position so that they could be in on everything that Cain did.

"Decide later!" Cain ordered. "We've got to focus on getting rid of Savot right now." But the two kept up their argument, migrating to the stern of the boat and keeping their voices lower.

After an hour had passed, Aria still hadn't joined them. She had assured Cain that her plan to get there was completely safe and would remain secret. Narsis, probably the most capable of the Navy girls, was to sail the princess out to meet Cain on his ship for what she had been told was a 'romantic encounter' and then leave.

Narsis owed Aria many favors. Before the Marriage Rules were changed, Aria had protected her numerous times when she unlawfully met Shay in the middle of the night.

When the princess didn't arrive on schedule, the five traitors got nervous.

"Let's just kill him ourselves," Marcum proposed.

"Yeah, we can tell her he tried to escape and we had to," Toren urged.

"No!" barked Cain. "I want to *see* her kill him. That part is important to me."

Finally a sail broke the horizon. The conspirators were relieved.

"Whew! There she is, finally. Much longer and the drug would have worn off," said Marcum, surveying Savot's still-motionless body.

They watched the sail as it approached. Yes, it was the smaller boat Narsis had planned to bring Aria in. As the vessel neared the boys, Aria shouted a greeting to Cain. He hailed her back.

Boarding the ship by a connecting gangplank, Aria waved goodbye to Narsis. Now all six mutineers were together and poised to execute their long-planned over-throw of King Savot. They watched as Narsis' ship vanished over the horizon back toward New Atlantis. Aria fixed her eyes on Cain in the lantern light.

"After all this time. After all our planning. Here we are, Cain. My father would be pleased," Aria mused.

"Woo-hoo!" Cain yelped loudly. He seized Aria around her waist and swung her in a circle, causing her feet to fly out from under her. Cain's elated gesture took Aria off guard.

"Put me down!" she commanded. Irritation rang in her tone. "You might wake Savot up."

"I hope I do. Then he'll find out how much you really hate him. You brought your dagger, right?"

Aria pulled aside both sides of her cloak to reveal a sheathed dagger belted to her right side and a sword attached to her left.

"I'm ready. It's time to put an end to New Atlantis' greatest menace," she said with a rough tone. Cain looked toward Savot as she spoke, but the princess' eyes remained on Cain.

"Do you really want him awake? I can manage that," laughed Toren fiendishly, grabbing a bucket tied to a rope. "I'll get some water and splash him awake." Cain waited for Aria's response.

"Yes," she decided. "Let's do that. Then I can tell him what I really think of him before I kill him."

As Toren lowered the bucket down over the side of the ship, a sudden howl from Dolius startled all the boys.

"Look! Narsis is coming back!"

Sure enough, the small ship that had just sailed away from them was now moving back toward them. The five boys widened their suspicious eyes to watch the approaching vessel. And what they saw next set them into a panic.

More sails appeared. Many more.

"Pull up the anchors!" shouted Cain. "Sail south! Fast!"

"Somebody found out! What did you tell Narsis?" Marcum barked at Aria.

"Guard Savot, Aria," commanded Cain. Aria stationed herself by Savot, pulling out her dagger and resting it on Savot's shoulder.

"I told her I was meeting Cain. That's all!" Aria snapped back at Marcum.

The kidnappers scrambled wildly, drawing up the anchors and setting the sails tightly to blow the ship southward. But the brisk north wind that caught their sails had already given the ten approaching ships the speed that quickly doomed Cain and his crew. The twelve ships were rapidly gaining on the kidnappers' boat. The armada's lead ship drew close enough for Cain to both see and hear them.

"Surrender, Cain!" It was Jamin. At the helm with him stood Lian and Billius—Savot's roommates—as awake and alert as ever.

"What?" demanded Marcum. "We all saw them drink it."

Cain glared at his comrades in rebuke. "They should all still be out cold!" he shouted.

The villains now realized something had gone wrong with the tranquilizers. Their eyes turned simultaneously toward Savot. The king opened his eyes and sat up.

But Aria put her dagger to his throat.

"Kill him! Kill him quick, Aria!" Cain commanded her.

The princess hesitated. Cain's eyes searched for the sword that had hung at her side. It was gone from its sheath and Savot held it tightly in his right hand.

Aria, with one swift motion, slashed the gag from Savot's mouth with her dagger.

"Don't worry, Cain. I *will* see that justice is done," Aria answered him loudly and smoothly.

Savot sprang to his feet that had—along with his hands—already been freed from the ropes. He brandished Aria's sword and postured himself for a duel.

"Come on, Cain, let's have one final contest," Savot challenged.

Cain drew his sword, but his wide eyes and drooping mouth revealed his shock. As soon as the other four conspirators realized what was happening they rushed to tackle Savot.

"Stop!" Cain commanded them. "I can do this myself. Stand back."

Circled around Savot now, Shay, Toren, Marcum, and Dolius quickly consulted one another through glimpses and nods. Reluctantly they agreed to obey Cain's order and backed away. Savot and Cain stationed themselves to fight, and Aria seemed to have disappeared.

CRASH–RING! Two flashing swords met harshly in mid-air. Swinging their weapons with brilliant skill, the well-matched opponents moved as swiftly and as gracefully as New Atlantis' dancers. With each move both Savot and Cain barely dodged the other's sword.

As the two enemies fought, Cain's allies watched tensely. But then they realized they needed to tend the sails and row hard to outrun the pursuing ships. All four soon abandoned the duel and took up their posts.

The ships came nearer swiftly despite the traitors' best efforts to make headway. Straining his eyes to see who he could recognize on the other vessels, Shay caught a glimpse of someone whose sight made him bellow.

"*Narsis?!*" His fiancé's drawn sword flickered in the torchlight that also illumined her face. Her defiant stare let Shay know he had lost Narsis' allegiance. The lead ship was upon them now.

Distracted by Shay's outburst, Cain had missed a split-second move by Savot. *Slash!* Savot's sword sliced the air close to Cain's left ear. Cain ducked and made a quick turn. He jumped onto a nearby barrel and then sprang off it as if it were a trampoline. Plunging toward Savot, Cain's sword caught Savot's shirt, pinning it to the cabin door.

The king, mindless of his shirt ripping off his back, pulled away and distanced himself before his foe could remove his blade from the wood. When Cain turned to face Savot, he met sharp silver floating in front of his nose.

"Drop your weapon," Savot commanded.

Cain caught a glimpse of Aria, hiding behind a crate. A motion of his eyes to Toren sent his accomplice toward her. Then Cain's sword fell to the deck with a loud clunk.

"Go ahead, finish me, 'Your Majesty'," Cain said sarcastically.

"Yeah, Savot. You finish him . . . and I'll finish her," Toren warned. Savot didn't have to turn around to see what had happened. Toren had Aria in a tight clutch, his knife gleaming at her throat.

"No. I won't kill you, Cain," Savot answered, still not turning around, "though you would have killed me without a thought. You'll face your justice back on New Atlantis."

By this time Jamin, Lian, Billius, and a score of other military boys had boarded the ship and seized Marcum, Dolius, and Shay. In a flash, Jamin rushed to Cain and tackled him, pinning him to the deck. Lian was there instantly as well, rabid with anger. He whipped his sword out of its sheath and placed its point directly under Cain's chin.

"Kill her!" Cain ordered Toren. Just as he yelled the command, Aria somehow managed to slide through Toren's arms, twirl rapidly, kick her leg up and slam Toren in the jaw with her heel. Toren fell to the deck unconscious. The livid princess then whisked her dagger out of its sheath and charged at Cain.

The petite royal leapt on Cain as though she was Sensia at her meanest. The sight shocked everyone so much that they could do nothing but watch with their mouths drooped open. Cain, still pinned to the deck by Jamin, tried to plead with Aria. But her rage was set. She raised her sharp weapon and—with all her might—thrust it toward Cain's chest.

Savot caught her by the wrist.

By now Toren was barreling toward Savot. Still holding Aria's wrist, the king slashed his sword through the air with his other hand toward Toren, warning him to stay back. Just then two Navy boys grabbed Toren and restrained him.

"Aria, do you really want his blood on your hands?" Savot asked.

The princess' arm struggled against Savot's grip as her mind apparently struggled with his question. At last her taut muscles relaxed and she rose to stand beside Savot. After carefully removing the dagger from her hand, Savot pulled the princess to his side. Aria accepted the position nobly but still glared at Cain through hot tears.

With Lian's sword still at his throat, Cain begged, "Don't, Lian . . . please."

At this cowardly groveling, Aria abandoned her momentary dignity and exploded in fury. The princess fell on Cain, pounding his chest with her fists, slapping and clawing at his face. Feverish partial phrases mingled with her sobs.

"You *demon*! How could you? I hate you, I HATE YOU!"

Savot honored Aria's need to vent her anger. He motioned to his friends to hold Cain down and let her continue. When she finally finished her explosion, Aria had left Cain's face bloody and bruised. He groaned from her sharp blows to his torso. Aria stood up again and, as a final gesture of personal vengeance, spat on Cain—right in his eyes.

"Take him, Jamin," Savot instructed.

Jamin, Billius, and Lian, tied Cain's limbs with the ropes that had held Savot. They gagged him as well to silence the profanities issuing from his bloody lips.

"You're right," Aria told Savot. "He deserves worse than a quick death."

***

Early the next morning all of the Children were called to a meeting in the theater. Together they learned about the events of the previous night. The five conspirators had been detained overnight in the prison where Lalera had stayed. But this morning, they stood bound, gagged, and lined up across the stage for all to see.

By the time Savot finished describing the attempted coup, his subjects could no longer contain their wrath. Many of them rushed the stage, trying to attack the militants. Sensia, along with Jamin—the new head of all the military—kept the mob from executing justice right then and there on Cain, Marcum, Shay, Dolius, and Toren. After a while, the military Children were able to settle the audience down to some degree of civility.

Aria then took center stage. When the Children beheld their princess' resolute posture, their lingering protests silenced. All Savot had told them so far about Aria's role in overthrowing Cain was that she had played a vital part in thwarting the mutiny.

Most of the Children had concluded long before that Aria loved Cain and didn't care at all for Savot. Some had even speculated that she would have preferred Cain as king instead of Savot. So they were all eager to hear what the princess would say now.

And what Aria said surprised them all, even her closest friends.

"You haven't known me for the past two years," Aria began. "You've thought I was someone else, and I led you to think that. But now I can explain why I behaved the way I did." Caris and Stacia exchanged curious looks. They, more than anyone else, had known Aria hadn't been herself for a long time.

"I love Savot," Aria stated plainly. "I can't remember a day in my life when I didn't love him." Many of the Children blinked in belief. They all looked totally stunned. Murmurs rippled throughout the theater as Aria continued.

"But I loved my father too." The princess then spent a long while explaining the excruciating dilemma she had suffered over the previous two years. Most of the girls shed tears of sympathy for their beloved, tormented friend as Aria recounted each thorny point of decision she had faced. The boys listened intently, seeming to understand her deep loyalty to her father.

"When the earthquake happened and we saw the glow in the sky and the smoke . . . then Amedis told us what

The Ghost had said, it was only then that I knew who my father really was. I didn't want to accept it at first." A reverent stillness blanketed her audience now.

"But then I had to admit it to myself. My father was a criminal. And all his plans were criminal." It seemed no one in her wide-eyed audience dared even to breathe.

"After that I privately disowned him. So I now declare in the presence of all of you, my countrymen, that King Jorash of Atlantis is no longer my father," Aria announced, looking more regal than she ever had before. The New Atlanteans listened respectfully.

"I regret his life. I regret having been his daughter. I regret having gone along—so naively—with his plan to make a king out of such a monster as Cain." She practically hissed Cain's name and sent him a reviling glare. Cain bristled.

"But most of all, I regret having hurt Savot. He is the most valiant of us all." At this the princess walked to where Savot stood and slipped her left arm through the crook in his right arm. "He's the most noble, wonderful man I've ever known."

Savot felt a tingle rush through his body. *She called me a man*, he mused in wonder. *She considers me a man now!* Among all the complimentary words she'd just spoken about him—'valiant', 'noble', 'wonderful'—the word 'man' meant the most to him.

"I don't feel worthy now to become this man's wife." *She had said it again! 'this man'!* "Or to be your queen. But if you will still have me . . ." she addressed her people. Then she turned to Savot, "If *you* will still have me . . . the position would be the greatest privilege of my life."

The Chosen Children hardly let a second pass before exploding into a rousing cheer of acceptance for Aria. Savot pulled the princess to himself and held her as though she was the most treasured object in the world. And, to him, she was.

"YES! Yes, yes, yes," was all he could say. Only Aria heard his answer, but the Children assumed it from the tight embrace he gave her. *Man, I want to kiss her!* Savot thought. But he wouldn't dare do that in front of everybody. Instead, with both arms still wrapped around Aria, Savot announced,

"Sorry, you couples at the front of the wedding calendar. But we're going first!" He gave the whole congregation a wink and no one objected, not even Billius and Caris.

Shouts of celebration and unbridled applause filled the theater. Cain had never looked so downcast. And Shay, Toren, Dolius, and Marcum looked terrified.

Chapter 20

The Year of Merger Begins

The Court met the first week of Month Eleven. It didn't take the ten lawyers even an hour to decide the fate of Cain, Toren, Shay, Marcum, and Dolius: life in prison, accompanied by heavily guarded hard labor on the nearby farmland. Some had argued strongly for the death penalty and all agreed the traitors deserved it. But Savot, in his benevolence, had requested the Court to give the prison sentence instead.

The verdict was announced at the Month Eleven Feast. Most of the Children thought the judgment was too lenient for the crime of high treason. But they knew that it was King Savot's wish, and they admired him for his mercy.

Without the convicts attending, of course, the Month Eleven Feast was the best ever. For old time's sake the obstaball players decided it would be a second national game of boys against eunuchs. The two teams enjoyed a long, vigorous match. The score stayed tantalizingly close the entire game, and every contestant seemed supercharged with energy. Even Savot played in this game. The boys won in triple overtime. And everyone was in such a good mood that the eunuchs didn't even mind losing . . . just this once.

Next the thespians presented a brand new musical play. Small talking animals indigenous to the New Atlantis islands acted as the main characters. The play was quirky and hilarious. It had nothing to do with reality so the Children laughed themselves silly watching.

The only sore encounter of the entire evening occurred between Lian and Stacia. Stacia hadn't heard from Lian at all since the last feast when she had broken off their engagement. The lack of initiation on Lian's part since then had upset Stacia greatly because, as she had told

219

Caris and Aria, she still had feelings for him—for some reason—despite his immaturity.

All day at the feast Lian hardly acknowledged Stacia's presence. So toward the end of the evening, Stacia decided to approach her ex-fiancé. She asked him to join her in the garden outside of the theater before the production started.

"Lian, are you all right?" Stacia asked.

"Sure. I'm fine," Lian answered indifferently.

"Are you mad at me?"

"No."

"No?" Stacia had to drag information out of the boy.

"I wasn't ever *mad* at you."

"Well, why have you been ignoring me?" she asked outright.

"I just don't feel the same way I used to about you," Lian stated flatly. He wouldn't look at Stacia. She couldn't speak for a moment after that answer, nor could she breathe very well. Her eyes filled with tears and she turned away.

Always before when he'd said something that hurt her, Lian had made some attempt to repair the situation. But now he stood still and quiet, uncharacteristically distant and unfeeling. He didn't offer Stacia any kind of comfort.

At last Stacia turned back to face him.

"Lian, you know how I feel about you. It's just, I can't stand the self-centered way you act sometimes. That's why I broke off our engagement."

"I know. But the way I act is who I am," Lian said dispassionately. "If you can't stand that, then you can't stand me." Stacia started to say something in reply but Lian continued, "And since I've had some time to let that sink in . . . well, I just don't feel anything toward you anymore."

"Nothing?" Stacia probed.

"Nothing at all," Lian answered her bluntly. Stacia tried to speak but she couldn't. Instead she turned and dashed away, running toward her house. Lian watched her go.

***

Billius, Lian, and Savot talked later that evening in their temporary quarters.

"You know who was signed up to get married fuwst, Savot?" Billius asked, teasing his friend. Of course Savot knew.

"Let me see. I think it was . . . umm . . . you and Caris?" Savot played along.

"Yep. Just 'cause you'we the king, you got to bump me," Billius said, faking indignation.

"Oh, good grief, Bill! Don't give me that pouting stuff. My wedding only puts yours off by a day. Surely you can wait twenty-four hours!" Savot bantered.

"Oh, okay. I guess I'll *let* you go ahead of us," Billius taunted his friend. Savot knew he was teasing.

Savot chuckled and then sighed reflectively. "I still can't believe she *loves* me." He folded his hands behind his head and lay back on his pillow.

"Savot, I'm happy for you. I really am," said Lian. "You too, Bill."

Savot felt suddenly selfish. *Lian may never be this happy*, he thought. He knew how much Lian really did care for Stacia, though he'd lied to her about it. Carefully he broached the subject.

"Has Stacia given you any hint of changing her mind?" Savot asked him.

Lian's head dropped. "No. She's not going to change her mind."

"Do you want me to go talk to her?" Billius offered. "I could get Cawis to go with me."

"No. I got letters from both Caris and Aria telling me to 'grow up'!"

Neither Savot nor Billius could argue with that suggestion.

***

After the Month Eleven Feast Savot and Aria spent every day together. No one minded the exception the lawyers had made for them regarding the Separation Rules. With their wedding only three weeks away now, Savot was sure that no two people had ever been so fully content.

The royal fiancés went together every day to see what progress the construction Children had made on their living quarters within the palace. Aria had definite opinions about the colors, fabrics, and furnishings that would decorate their home. Savot didn't care about all those details.

"Whatever you like is fine with me. You have such good taste," he complimented his bride-to-be. "All that matters to me is that we're going to be living here—together."

Aria then ventured to ask, "Do we really have to have *that bird* live with us?" Savot knew she had never cared much for the loud creature.

"Oh, Memphis? Yeah, I know he can be kind of obnoxious sometimes. But remember he was the one who cued me in to the guys putting the tranquilizers in our drinks," Savot reasoned. Aria raised an eyebrow at him, not looking persuaded.

"Yeah, but that doesn't qualify him to live with us. Maybe Jamin would keep him," Aria suggested. "Pate would enjoy having a pet."

"We'll see," Savot said. Then he changed the subject. There was no way he was going to get into an argument over a bird right now.

"You know, for the longest time I really thought you hated me," Savot said, shaking his head. They walked arm in arm out of the palace.

"I had to make you think that. You understand now, don't you?" Aria asked.

"Yeah, but . . . man! You're a really good actress! We've got to cast you in the next play," Savot joked.

They talked for an hour in the palace's outdoor gazebo this warm, winter day. They told each other more of what they really had been thinking and feeling over the past two years. They agreed that, of necessity, their relationship had been very weird.

The more Savot heard about Aria's side of things, the more he realized her strength of character. He found himself loving her even more, though he had thought that impossible. Her sense of loyalty and duty toward New Atlantis amazed him.

And so their conversations went. Sometimes their talks even deeper but most were lighter. All of the conversations served to bond the two of them together even more. No weighty matters of state—not for now anyway. And finally no more of the awful tension that had existed between them for so long. Aria laughed more than Savot had seen her laugh since they were little children. Like an eagle set free from a caged captivity, the playful princess seemed totally herself again . . . at last.

It seemed like heaven to Savot that Aria fit him so well. He thought about the last letter he'd written her. It was so true. She made him complete. And he would have remained unfinished had she not chosen to be his wife. He felt stronger and more vigorous than ever. Yet strangely, at the same time, he sensed a fragileness in himself that he had never noticed before. So much depended on Aria now that it scared him.

***

The last days of Month Twelve were passing so quickly that no one could believe it. The Year of Merger was upon The Chosen Children. Jamin and his infant son flourished in one of the first completed homes on the residence island.

Finishing the rest of the homes on the western island was now of highest priority. Once the Year of Merger began, a newlywed couple would be moving into one of the houses each day. The girls worked to put finishing touches on the homes after each was built. Savot and Aria, along with the Court, had decided that within five months after the Year of Merger began all 113 girls would move into the new houses, with or without husbands.

This would leave most of the boys in their temporary quarters until they got married. This put unwanted pressure on some of them who really just wanted to stay single for a while. It gave needed incentive to others who were just dragging their feet for no reason. So, as a result of this decision, many of the boys got more serious about pursuing the girls they had been interested in, or even those who'd been interested in them. After all, they didn't want to live in short-term quarters for years and have to cook for themselves.

***

The Month Eleven Feast had been the last of the kind the Children were accustomed to. The Month Twelve Feast was to be Savot and Aria's wedding. Savot also wanted it to be their official Coronation Day.

On Atlantis this had never happened—a wedding and coronation combined into one ceremony. But then many things about New Atlantis made it different from its motherland. The Month Twelve Feast promised to be a huge blowout of a celebration.

The miners and engineers had invented a new form of fireworks to be used at the Month Twelve Feast. Three days before the big event, the inventors gave the Children a preview of the light show to come. The fireworks astonished and delighted the spectators.

The boys also decided that they should have equally balanced teams for obstaball, which usually had not been the case. Most of the time the boys and eunuchs just randomly divided themselves into teams at the last minute. But they wanted this game to be a real contest. Given that the eunuchs were generally smaller—though more agile—than the majority of the boys, the players all agreed that it was only fair for the eight teams to be composed of a combination of boys and eunuchs. So eight permanent teams were formed.

Each team picked a name, and the boys decided that the Month Twelve Feast would begin a tournament. There were the Warlords, the Hawks, the Tigers, the Sharks, the Shooting Stars, the Tide, and the Conquerors.

As one of the team captains, Lian insisted on his team being called the Gorillas. No matter how much they argued his teammates couldn't talk him out of it. This gave Lian the opportunity to function as the team's mascot as well. His primate imitation, complete with grunts and swaggers, sent everyone into side-splitting guffaws. But

Savot knew this was just one of Lian's many tactics to camouflage his heartbreak over Stacia.

The two teams chosen to play against each other for the big feast were the Hawks and the Conquerors.

The architects and engineers had agreed that the theater would serve best for most of the official ceremonies, including the weddings. Since the seats were set into a sloped floor, everyone would have the best view possible. The construction workers had built an elaborate altar for the stage during this, the last month of the Year of Construction.

Work was completed in all areas on New Atlantis just in time for the Month Twelve Feast. The warmer weather of early spring and the daylight hours lengthening contributed to the speed of progress. But so did the Children's enthusiasm over completing their elaborate project.

"Our Mentors would be so proud of us," Medo, the chief architect, told Savot as the two surveyed the work.

"Our Mentors," Savot said in almost a whisper. "May the God of Heaven grant rest to their souls," the young king stated somberly.

Savot was proud of all the Children's accomplishments, and he made sure he wasted no opportunity to tell them so. But, more importantly, Savot was relieved that a tremendous burden now had been lifted from his kingdom and from his own shoulders.

The covert rebellion that Galen had sensed early on had been discovered and quelled. He was now firmly accepted as king; the only finishing act was his coronation. And Aria was at last positive about being his wife—very positive! New Atlantis now felt like a totally different place to Savot.

Two nights before his wedding, Galen's diary brought tears to Savot's eyes as he read a special portion of it again:

I do believe she favors you, Savot. I studied her today as she watched you play obstaball. She smiled when you scored and grimaced at your injury. Despite her odd behavior right now, she's the very best of Atlantis. And you deserve only the best. I pray for you daily, and I always include a request that someday you and Aria will be a happy husband and wife to each other.

"That day's almost here, Galen," Savot whispered. "Thank you for praying for me. Thank you for everything you did for me."

***

The day before their wedding Savot took Aria to the highest hill on the main island so that she could survey the completed city. It was truly magnificent with its shining buildings and concentric moats. The drawbridges that connected the circular man-made islands made the city look like an enormous wheel carved into the earth. Or, more appropriately, Savot thought, like the sun with its radiating rays.

Savot and Aria watched from their faraway perch as their countrymen prepared the city for the next day's festivities. The millers decorated the theater with colorful fabrics. The smiths had crafted large pillars covered with orichalcum that now served as stands for dozens of the freshly-made New Atlantean flags.

Farmers brought in wagonloads of spring flowers with which they would dress the stage and the periphery of the theater the next morning. Rain had cleared the air so that, from Savot and Aria's vantage point, the city looked as sparkling and bright as paradise.

***

Early the next morning the festivities began. Dances, singing, and a theater production proceeded as the bride and groom prepared themselves for the evening wedding and coronation. The only event Savot attended that day was the obstaball game. The Conquerers indeed conquered, and the king was glad because that was Jamin's team.

Caris and Stacia spent all day helping Aria prepare for her wedding. They let her sleep late and then helped her take a long, relaxing bath. Early in the afternoon they went to work on the princess' thick hair, pinning it into an elaborate twist of golden curls on top of her head. The miller girls had worked for the previous two months creating her wedding gown, which was bright, multi-colored, and inlaid with gold threads and shimmering jewels.

As Savot put on his all-purple outfit—a velvet robe trimmed with orichalcum braiding, a flowing tunic, and silken pants—he couldn't help admiring how he looked in the mirror, which was something he rarely did. *I look older*, he thought. *I feel older too.*

It was almost time. Both Savot and Aria looked completely royal for the occasion. And completely happy.

The wedding ceremony was to begin just before sunset. The coronation would follow immediately while Savot and Aria were still on the stage. Gazing out of his western window, Savot knew for sure that there had never been a more beautiful sunset in the history of the world.

Amedis and Jamin waited at Savot's temporary quarters as Savot finished dressing. When it was almost time to go to the theater, Savot asked to be alone for a few minutes. There, in his fine wedding clothes, Savot dropped to his knees on the wooden floor and then with his face to the ground he began to pray.

"God of Heaven. How can I thank you? You saved my life. Not only from destruction on Atlantis but also from my enemies here. You've instructed me when I would have otherwise been without clear direction. And now you've given me this most incredible . . . incomparable . . . woman to be my wife."

He didn't know what else to say. The young king, the noble Savot, was completely overwhelmed with gratitude. Finally he vowed, "I can do no less than devote the rest of my life to you. I determine right now that I will always follow your commands in everything I do every day until my very last breath."

Then, struck with the weight of the vow he had just made, Savot second-guessed himself. *What if I can't? I'm human. I fail. Maybe I shouldn't have made such a pledge to him when I'm not sure I can fulfill it.* So he added more.

"If you'll help me, that is. I can't live like you want me to without you giving me the strength and wisdom to do it. Please . . . please help me do it."

Still with his face to the ground, and feeling somehow both dependent and strong now, Savot heard a voice.

"Well done, King Savot." The king recognized the voice of The Ghost. Savot looked up quickly but The Ghost was nowhere to be seen. He jumped to his feet and started toward the door to call Amedis in as his witness.

"It's all right, Savot," the voice said, stopping him before he reached the door. "This is of no national concern. It's just for you." Savot stood bewildered still looking around for The Ghost, but there was only his utterance. And the voice said only one more thing.

"The God of Heaven is pleased with you, king of the Chosen Children. As long as you keep the faith of a child, he will be with you and will bless you as a man." Then there was silence.

Jamin and Amedis, at that moment, opened the door of the house.

"We thought we heard a voice," said Jamin.

"I was just praying," Savot answered, now with tears on his cheeks.

"What are you crying about?" Amedis asked. "Is something the matter?"

Jamin answered for Savot. "He's just happy. Right, Your Majesty?"

Savot laughed. That was the biggest understatement he'd ever heard. "Happy? . . . Yeah. Oh yeah. Definitely!"

***

And so it was that the kingdom of New Atlantis was established in 496 B.C. Many more adventures took place after Savot and Aria's wedding and coronation. Many more couples married. And the mysterious lights that occasionally appeared on the horizon were eventually identified. King Savot's reign was indeed blessed by the Unknown God, or 'the God of Heaven' as Savot later called him. History records little of Atlantis and even less of what happened on its daughter kingdom, New Atlantis. But the fledging nation was one of the most prosperous—and most unique—of all those that have ever existed on earth.

LaVergne, TN USA
26 February 2011
218048LV00005B/8/P

9 781609 114015